ACCLAIM FOR *IN THE SHADOW OF SINAI*

I was there! I felt like I was right there in the palace of ancient Egypt. Carole Towriss brought the Bible to life. Amazing how an author can make me wonder what's going to happen next, even though I know what's going to happen. After all, it's a Bible story. But told from the unique perspective of Bezalel, a Hebrew Egyptian slave, I couldn't help but wonder what was going to happen to him and Ramses' lovely concubine, Meri.

Bezalel's name means "in the shadow of God." He thinks it's a negative place to be, but it's a good place because that's where he's safe. A great spiritual lesson, and something we all need to realize when we don't want to submit to God. His shadow is our protection!

In the Shadow of Sinai is a definite page-turner.

Sandi Rog
Award-winning author of *Walks Alone,*
The Master's Wall, and *Yahshua's Bridge*

I was spellbound as I read her gripping descriptions of the palace, and life back in those days, the slaves, the royalty, and the reactions to the plagues that both sides had. *In the Shadow of Sinai* is absolutely riveting and I couldn't put it down. I had to find out what happened with Bezalel and some of the other characters. I can't wait for more books by this talented author. If you like biblical fiction, you won't want to miss *In the Shadow of Sinai.*

Laura V. Hilton
Award-winning author of *The Amish of Seymour*
series (Whitaker House)

An impressive debut by author Carole Towriss, *In The Shadow Of Sinai* is the riveting story of the Exodus of the Hebrews from the land of Egypt as you have never heard it told before. Seen through the eyes of a Hebrew slave assigned to the Pharaoh's palace, the cast of both Egyptians and Hebrews is mesmerizing. I look forward to the second offering in the Journey to Canaan Trilogy, *By The Waters Of Kadesh.*

A J Hawke
Author of *Cabin On Pinto Creek, Caught Between Two Worlds,* and *Mountain Journey Home.*

Through the eyes of Bezelalel, a Hebrew slave with a gift that makes him invaluable to the Egyptians but despised by his own people, we catch a glimpse of what life may have been like during the Exodus. *In the Shadow of Sinai* is a beautiful novel of hope amidst despair, trust in the face of terror, and a love that binds. Debut author Carole Towriss turned a familiar story of liberation into an unexpected love story that resonates deep in the hearts.

Jennifer Slattery
Novel Reviews

In the Shadow of the Sinai brings the Biblical story of the plagues and the Exodus to life. Carole Towriss remains true to the factual, Biblical account, yet allows readers to experience the Exodus anew through the eyes of the Biblical Bezalel and fictional Meri. While the Exodus is a familiar story for many, the story of Bezalel and Meri is new and brings a fresh perspective to the Biblical account. While set in ancient times, modern readers struggle with similar doubts as Bezalel and Meri: Can they trust in El Shaddai? Bezalel is an artist and slave in Pharaoh's household. Meri is one of Pharaoh's concubines. Readers will be drawn in by Bezalel and Meri's story and will be frantically turning the pages to find out what happens to the characters.

Heidi Glick
Author of *Dog Tags* (Pelican Book Group, 2013)

Everyone knows the story of Moses, but with this story you live and breathe it. Told in an astoundingly vivid way *In the Shadow of Sinai* gives the reader an unique Old Testament experience. I was swept along the dusty march in the desert, held in awe of the parting waters, amazed at the miraculous events. New light was shed on an old, old story. I look forward to future books by Carole!

D.M. Webb
Author of *Mississippi Nights*

I first read a portion of Carole Towriss's *In the Shadow of Sinai* as a judge in a contest. I was impressed then, and I'm even more impressed after reading the entire book! Carole has brought ancient Egypt alive at the time of the Exodus. I felt as if I were right there with Bezalel, viewing the events of his time through his eyes. The opulence of the palace, the warmth of the Israelite village, the mass exodus of God's people from Egypt, their fear when they were backed up against the Red Sea—all word pictures that placed me in the setting. The characters who people this book are real and varied. I love how the author tied Bezalel's name (which means "in the shadow of God") with the theme of resting in God's sovereignty even when things go wrong. *In the Shadow of Sinai* is an excellent example of biblical fiction, and I'm looking to see many more books from this author in the future.

Marjorie Vawter
Freelance editor
Author of Author of *A Shelter from the Storm*
(Barbour Publishing, April 2013)

In the Shadow of Sinai

Carole Towriss

DEWARD
PUBLISHING COMPANY

In the Shadow of Sinai
DeWard Publishing Company, Ltd.
P.O. Box 6259, Chillicothe, Ohio 45601
800.300.9778
www.deward.com

In the Shadow of Sinai is a work of fiction. Names, characters, places, and incidents are either a product of the author's imagination or are used fictitiously. Any resemblance to actual persons, living or dead, events, or locales is entirely coincidental.

Printed in the United States of America.

ISBN: 978-1-936341-48-1

For El Shaddai, my rock, my refuge, my hiding place.

*Whoever dwells in the shelter of the Most High
will rest in the shadow of Shaddai.*

Psalm 91.1

One

Pi-Ramses, Egypt
Late 13th Century BC
First month of Ahket, Season of Inundation

The crash of the drum echoed in Bezalel's ears as he slipped out from behind his pedestal on the portico and hastened to the throne room. He dared not risk the penalty for being late—again. His tunic still stuck to his wounds from the last beating and ripped them open whenever he moved the wrong way.

He dropped to the cold limestone floor on one knee and lowered his head, raising it just enough to watch pair after pair of bare feet shuffle west toward the dais. The heavy scent of perfumed oil stung his nose.

The old king ascended his throne as the bare-chested attendants silently lined the walls on either side of the spacious hall then turned toward their sovereign and bowed low.

This daily routine was absurd, pretending that Ramses was a god. He was no more a god than Bezalel was, although Bezalel couldn't say that El Shaddai was doing him much good at the moment either. In fact, he seemed utterly incompetent. Or callous.

Bezalel rose. From the tiled hall that led beyond the throne room to the private quarters beyond the dais, he heard the jingling of bracelets and anklets. A young girl emerged from the entryway behind a number of women who had no doubt dressed her, perfumed her, painted her face, and adorned her with the excessive jewelry of a concubine.

She was roughly twenty strides away. As she neared he saw she was Egyptian and quite young, several years younger than he—perhaps no more than fourteen. A vague scent of jasmine hung in the air.

She glanced at Bezalel as she passed and his mouth went as dry as the desert surrounding him. She was the most beautiful girl he had ever seen.

Even behind the heavy kohl he grasped the misery in her eyes. His chest constricted in a way he had never felt before and an inexplicable urge to grab her and pull her away from the group overwhelmed him. The king used to take consorts often. Why was she different?

Guards led her to the center of the room. The other girls retreated to the rear. She knelt and bowed low to the king, her head nearly touching the floor.

Bezalel's face grew hot and his breathing became shallow.

The girl—for though she was to be a consort, he could hardly call her a woman—stood.

Ramses stepped off the dais and walked stiffly toward her. He circled her like a vulture, looking her up and down. He lifted her chin with his wrinkled hand and studied her face. Her shoulders tightened beneath his touch.

Bezalel's hands curled into fists. The others had seemed more than willing to become part of his harem. Why take one by force?

"She is acceptable. Take her to my chambers."

A guard grasped the girl's arm and started toward the hallway. She stumbled along behind him.

"N—!" Bezalel rushed toward her, but a harsh yank on the neck of his tunic cut off the word as well as his progress. He spun around, putting his hands to his neck and choking.

An older man came toward him, scowling. "Bezalel!"

Forcing his breathing to slow, Bezalel glanced sideways at him then looked at the floor. He put his hand to his throat again and winced.

"Bezalel, you are under my protection here, but I cannot save you from your own foolishness."

"But Ammon, did you see her? She is but a child!"

"And he is Pharaoh! Her age is irrelevant. He can marry an infant if he wishes." The man's voice softened. "You are lucky I was here to stop you."

Bezalel sighed and turned back toward the private hallway. His stomach revolted as the guards led the girl into the elderly king's private rooms. He closed his eyes and tried to shut out his own imagination.

Ammon put a hand on Bezalel's shoulder and led him away. The man looked older than the last time Bezalel had seen him. His paunch had grown, and almost all of his hair had disappeared. Sunlight bounced off the large jeweled ankh hanging around his neck. "Why don't you show me what you've been working on while I've been gone?"

They strolled toward the long, narrow portico that ran along the back of the throne room. Pillars separated the two areas, and the east side of the portico opened onto a large, airy courtyard that let in the sunlight for most of the day, making the portico an excellent place for the artisans to work. Beyond the courtyard, the Nile rushed toward the sea.

They neared a pedestal that stood on the north end of the long workspace.

"Used to people watching you work yet?" Ammon chuckled as he removed a cover from a sculpture nestled in a sandbag.

"That is why I am here, isn't it?" Bezalel turned up one side of his mouth.

"Ah, finally a smile! Or at least the start of one."

"Do you like it?" Bezalel searched his teacher's face for approval as the man scrutinized the work. He craved the old man's blessing, even after all these years.

Ammon nodded. "It's a lovely beginning. What a stunning piece of alabaster!" He drew his hand over the stone. "You've only roughed out the face, I see."

"I started the eyes yesterday. I love that part—they bring the life out." Bezalel rubbed his thumb over the beginnings of an eye.

"You always did. Come, Bezalel, let us go to your workroom."

Bezalel followed his teacher back across the portico toward a whitewashed hall. Opposite it, on the other side of the throne room, the corridor to the private areas extended west. This hallway ran east and contained workrooms and storerooms. Ammon opened a door and entered Bezalel's room. He pulled a high stool away from a large table and sat down with a sigh. A large, south-facing window set high up on the wall showered sunlight on the table. A bed hugged the wall under the window. Bezalel grabbed two cups from a shelf and filled them with pomegranate juice.

"I didn't know you were back from Memphis already." He handed Ammon a cup.

"I returned last night. I intended to see you this morning, after my visit with the king."

"You already saw him?"

"Yes. Bezalel, I am afraid I have some news you will not like." He looked down at his cup and traced the rim with his finger. "I am leaving here. I will no longer be a craftsman for the king. Ramses has awarded me a plot of land … and I am going to live on it."

Bezalel furrowed his brow. Surely he didn't mean right now. "What about the Colossi?"

Ammon drained his cup. "They are far enough along to be finished without me. And the trips to Memphis are too hard on me anymore."

Bezalel sank to a stool. Air left him as if he'd been punched in the gut. "But why?"

"I am old, Bezalel. You can't see it because you love me. But I am old and tired." He stretched the fingers of one hand wide. "My hands ache all night after I carve for even a short time. My back hurts constantly." He smiled. "But I have accomplished more than I ever dreamed I would. The Colossi are my greatest work, my legacy. There is nothing left for me to do."

Bezalel set his cup on the table, stood, and walked toward the door. He whirled around to face Ammon. "But there is always more to do! Ramses needs you. I need you! You can't leave." He spread out his arms.

"You don't need me."

Bezalel's head spun. How could Ammon do this to him? "I do! You are all I have...almost. I have lived in this palace since my eighth summer. You have always been here for me. I have been with you more than my own parents!"

Ammon put down his cup and twisted in his seat. "Yes, I know. And I have loved you like a son, even though you are a slave and a Hebrew. I have trained many artisans, but I have not loved any of them as I have loved you. None of them lived with me here as you have. But it has been twelve years and now you are grown. You are a man. I haven't even been around much for the last three years, and you have done very well. I heard about you even in Memphis."

"And Ramses is willing to let you go?"

"He has you. He knows of you and your work, which is the only reason you were not severely punished just now."

"But I cannot compare to you!"

Ammon stood and crossed the room. He put his hands on Bezalel's shoulders. "My boy, I have taught you—and you have mastered—everything I know. And before me, you exhausted the knowledge of three other teachers. You have surpassed us all."

Bezalel closed his eyes and sighed deeply. This could not happen. There must be a way to change Ammon's mind.

"I have always felt you had a special ability. There have only been a few who can work with so many materials. None had your creativity. Your work decorates many rooms in this very palace, even the king's own rooms. I believe Ptah has blessed you."

Ptah. Bezalel shifted his weight at the mention of the Egyptian god. Why did Ammon always have to bring him up? Bezalel might be angry with Shaddai, but that didn't mean he worshipped Egypt's false deities.

Ammon sighed. "I know you do not worship our gods. You have your own gods—"

Bezalel frowned.

"No matter." Ammon took a deep breath. "I have to leave you now. I doubt I will see you again. My new home is too far away to come here often."

Bezalel wrapped his arms around his teacher. He closed his eyes tightly against the tears.

After several moments Ammon pulled away gently, his eyes moist as well, and laid his hands on Bezalel's face. "Know that you will always be in my heart. And I look forward to hearing many good things about you." His voice was soft.

He opened the door and left.

Bezalel stared at the empty doorway. Emptiness filled his heart. Just knowing Ammon was there—even if "there" was far away in Memphis—had always been a comfort. Now he was on his own. Alone.

His ability had given him an easier life in the palace, but it had taken him away from home. He knew precious few people in the village other than his family, whom he saw only once a week at most. Almost all of the Israelites thought of him as a traitor—as if he had a choice of where to work. Now his closest, perhaps only, ally was gone. How would the new chief craftsman treat him?

He walked to the table and reached for his cup. He held it for a few moments then sent it sailing. Red juice exploded onto the wall and trickled down in rivulets as it made its way to the shattered cup. Then he did the only thing he knew to do, the only thing that gave him pleasure. He left his room to return to his art.

He caressed the pale alabaster, his fingers hesitating on the spots where the ears, the nose, the mouth would be. To him, the face hid in the stone, waiting for him to find it. It was a game, a challenge to get to the final form concealed within, one that often surprised him as much as it did those who had commissioned it.

He picked up a bronze claw. The soft stone gave way easily to the short curved teeth of the long-handled tool. He drew it along in short, brusque strokes, tugging away at the unwanted parts. Bits of alabaster clinked on the floor as he continued to carve, each chunk bringing him closer to the revelation inside.

Bezalel paid little attention to what happened on the other side of the columns, trying to shut out everything but his craft. He looked up only occasionally, to assure himself he did not miss another summons.

After a while, the noise of a particularly large delegation caught Bezalel's attention as its members stomped in from the entrance hall to the southeast of the courtyard. Their dark skin and closely braided hair identified them as Nubians. That meant gold. Lots of gold.

Ten men, in pairs, carried enormous, open black-and-red pots filled with gold flakes and nuggets, tribute for the season. Bezalel's thoughts ran wild as he envisioned the jewelry he could fashion from it. In its present form it wasn't much good to anyone else.

A parade of women in multi-colored garments followed, carrying trays full of copper and gemstones from the Sinai mines, shut down before summer's fury took hold. Light green turquoise, deep blue lapis lazuli, pale purple amethyst, red carnelian, textured green malachite, and clear green emeralds. To most they looked like worthless rocks at this stage, but to him, even unpolished they held unbelievable beauty and possibility.

Before Bezalel could dream about what he might do with the gems, two young girls bolted in from the hall, screaming. He grimaced as an inhuman growl filled the air. Sailors strutted in, one with a golden cat that stood as high as a man's waist, with a long rope tied around its neck.

The animal looked from side to side, as if searching for its next meal. The handler walked the cat up to the throne and stopped, then knelt. The cat, covered with what appeared to be black paw prints, lay down next to him, swishing its tail.

Ramses leaned forward and pointed at the animal with his scepter. "What is this? Is this the leopard I heard about as a child?"

The sailor stood and gestured grandly toward the cat. "Yes, my king. This is the famous leopard. There has not been one at court since Queen Hatshepsut, almost two hundred years ago. But I, Menes"—he put his hand on his chest—"have brought Ramses the second, the greatest king of all, the finest leopard in all the land of Punt." He bowed deeply.

Ramses raised his eyebrows. "Really? In all the land? You searched it all?"

The sailor stood. "Well, it-it is the finest that I found...."

"If I had wanted one, I would have sent for one." Ramses sat back in his throne. "Did you bring anything...useful?"

"Well, yes, there is a myrrh tree, frankincense, ebony, ivory—"

"Very good. You are dismissed." Ramses struck the floor with the heel of his scepter.

The sailor's shoulders fell, and he shuffled off, pulling the leopard behind him.

Bezalel shook his head. Ramses didn't care about the effort the man must have gone to as he captured, trained, and brought such a magnificent creature to him. If it didn't fill his treasury or his harem, he troubled himself little about it, no matter how much sweat or blood it cost.

Crewmen followed, carrying baskets of the promised white elephant tusks and black wood. This afternoon the rare ivory and ebony would be in the storeroom. Bezalel could hardly wait.

❧

The water clock said the day's work was finished, although the sun would not set for some time. Finally, Bezalel's week was over. He needed his family tonight. He packed up his tools and shut the door of his workroom behind him.

He left the palace and headed northwest along the river and, in less than half an hour, reached his village. A day or so was hardly enough time. Thankfully, he lived close enough to come home midweek sometimes, if his workload permitted. Ammon had given him leave to choose his own time off as long as he accomplished his work. Would his new master do the same?

The evening sun cast long, misshapen shadows east over the river, and the cooler air beckoned people outside. River birds darted above the heads of small children who hid among the papyrus reeds. Older children began arriving from the brickfields along with the adults. Several younger boys shouted as they played a game of chase near the river. Bezalel stopped and watched. Their innocent joy refreshed him after days with the selfish king.

"Hey, palace rat, leave them alone! Stay away from them!"

Bezalel flinched, and looked around for the voice that yelled at him.

A group of mud-stained young men his age stood a short distance away, staring at him. The leader stood in front of the rest, arms crossed. His bushy beard made him look older than the others. "I said, leave! We don't need your kind here."

Not tonight. His feelings were raw already. No matter how often he explained, some still couldn't believe he did not have a choice of whether or not to work in the palace. The lack of mud on his tunic and blisters on his hands provided the only provocation some needed to hate him. He had no energy to argue tonight. Still, if they wanted it… He headed toward them.

"Bezalel!"

A familiar voice caught his attention. He turned to see his grandfather ambling towards him. Bezalel stared a moment at the group then walked away.

"*Sabba.*" Bezalel smiled and hugged his grandfather.

"Welcome home, *habibi.*" His grandfather clapped him on the shoulder. "Problem?"

"Not anymore." They fell in step as they strolled through the narrow streets of houses made with adjoining walls. They passed a couple nuzzling near the door of a mud-brick home. A gaggle of boys kicked a ball. Girls huddled, pointed, and giggled as boys walked by. Everyone had someone. Everyone except him. Sometimes—often—he wished he made bricks like everyone else. It would be so much easier. Why did he have to be different?

They reached their small home, removed their sandals and walked through the large room into the open-air kitchen in the back.

"Bezalel, you're home!" His mother dropped the large spoon she was using into a pot, grabbed Bezalel, and held him close.

"Yes, *Imma*, I'm home." He smiled broadly and hugged her back then pulled away and kissed her on the cheek.

"Oh, a week is too long, habibi. Hungry, I hope? I roasted a duck since you are home for dinner tonight. Now, wash your hands."

The two men washed and dried their hands, stepped into the main room, and sat on the floor in front of the low table already set with plates and cups and a pitcher of juice.

Imma set out fresh dates and bread then disappeared again. She emerged with a platter of duck meat, which she placed on the table.

"Thank you, Rebekah." Sabba grabbed a date while she wasn't looking.

"So, what happened at the palace this week?" Imma sat beside Bezalel.

He watched her as she filled his plate with meat and fruit. She looked so tired lately. Gray now streaked her beautiful brown hair, and her bright eyes always had dark circles under them. She looked far older than her years. "The Nubians brought gold again, and the Sinai miners sent basket loads of gems. I can't wait to work with them. The water master came with the first report of the rise in the Nile. Sailors from Punt brought a leopard—"

"A leopard! I thought that was only a legend." Imma's eyes grew as wide as the dates she had served.

Bezalel swallowed his bread. "I guess not. An enormous cat. Gold with black spots. He was stunning, but he scared the servant girls." He took another bite and thought of the girl in the throne room. Her face filled his mind, and once more he wanted to go find her and take her away. What was her name? What was she doing right now? How frightened was she? He shoved the thoughts aside.

"What aren't you telling me?"

Her question pulled him back to the present. "What?"

"What are you thinking about?"

"Ramses took a new wife again. Well, a concubine, anyway."

Imma's mouth dropped open. "Again? But it's been years."

Bezalel nodded. "She's so young this time ... the youngest one yet. And very pretty."

Imma studied his face. "Is that all? You're still leaving something out, I think." She touched the darkening bruise on his neck.

He pulled away. "Don't worry about it." He tucked a stray strand of hair behind her ear. "I guess if he is a god he can do anything, even marry a child."

"God?" Sabba huffed. "He is no god."

"The people think so. He is as good a god as El Shaddai." Bezalel shoved his food away. "Maybe better. Shaddai cannot stop Ramses from keeping us as slaves. He is not 'the Almighty,' and this proves it. No god would bring his people to a strange land and then leave them there to become slaves under these unbearable Egyptians."

"Oh, habibi." Imma reached over and stroked his cheek. "Such anger in one so young."

After dinner, Bezalel wandered outside. He soon found himself at the river and sat on the wide bank. A gray heron stood on one leg, soundlessly hunting its dinner. The setting sun warmed his back.

He lay on the ground, arms under his head, and listened to the flow of the water. The flooding would reach this part of the river in several weeks and cover the very spot on which he lay. His thoughts went yet again to the girl and this time he did not avoid them. He remembered her eyes, the sorrow and hopelessness in them. Or was it fear?

He put one arm over his eyes. He knew what would happen tonight. And then Ramses would discard her, as he did all the others, like so much trash, and return to his beloved, to Nefertari. And then, like him, the girl would be alone.

Somehow, he had to find her.

Two

Bezalel crept along the side wall of the throne room, wishing he had kicked off his sandals. He slid forward until he could see the faces of both the visitors and the king. Dust hung in the light streaming through the windows placed high in the walls. Silence settled on the room like a blanket, making even the early morning air feel heavy. A drop of sweat dribbled down his neck.

Ramses descended from his throne and now stood a breath away from two Israelites.

It was unusual enough that Hebrews would be allowed a meeting with the pharaoh, but that the king would come down to see them face to face? It was unheard of.

Bezalel held his breath, put his hand on his empty stomach to muffle the grumbling.

Aaron's bare feet were still wet from the ceremonial washing required before a royal audience. His full, white beard and gray hair touched the patched brown cloak he wore over a mud-stained tunic.

Bezalel didn't know the other man. He was shorter than Aaron, and stockier. Like Aaron's, his hair touched his shoulders, but his weathered face was clean shaven, like the Egyptians. Tension crept down Bezalel's body.

Ramses stared silently at the man. Light reflected off the old king's thin hair. At eighty years of age, his hair color had faded but it still identified him with Seth, the god that gave his family the power to rule.

"Moses." An odd smile of recognition crossed Ramses's face. "It has been a long time since we studied together at Thebes."

So was this "Moses" an Israelite or Egyptian? He studied in Thebes, he was barefaced, but he dressed like a slave. It didn't make sense.

"Y-yes. It has been many, many years."

"Indeed. Too many years for you to think our common ground has earned you anything other than an audience. You are now but a slave." Ramses chuckled. "Although I hear you rejected even that identity and ran off to hide in the desert." The king looked Moses over head to toe, gave a snort of contempt, then spun around and returned to his throne.

Bezalel let out his breath and his muscles relaxed. He gazed at the ceiling, gold stars painted on a field of blue. At least Ramses wasn't going to hurt anyone. For now.

Moses took a deep breath as his cheeks colored. "I am here now. Th-that is all that matters."

"So you are. Speak to your king."

"My b-brother will speak for me." Moses stepped back.

"Someone *always* spoke for you." Ramses glanced away.

Moses nodded to Aaron.

Aaron puffed out his chest. "This is what Yahweh, the God of Israel says to you: 'Let My people go, that they may meet with Me in the desert.'" His voice echoed off the tiled walls.

Bezalel watched Moses, although Aaron tried to capture everyone's attention.

Ramses snickered. "Who is this Yahweh? I know many gods. I know Ra, and Amun, and Osiris, and Isis, and many others, but I do not recognize any 'Yahweh.' Why should I obey him? I do not know him, and I will not let Israel go." He lifted his hand in a wave of dismissal, but Aaron either did not see it or ignored it.

Bezalel cringed as Aaron defied the king, raising his staff—and his voice. "Yahweh is the God of Israel, the only true God. He met with us last night, and we must make a three-day journey into the desert to offer sacrifices to Him." He hesitated before continuing. "Or He may strike with plagues or with the sword."

Bezalel leaned his head against the wall. *Oh, no, don't threaten him. That never works.*

Moses glanced at Aaron with widened eyes, giving the distinct impression that Aaron went further than he should have.

Ramses stood.

A shiver crawled down Bezalel's back, even in the delta heat, and he slowly sidestepped away from the dais. Ramses was unpredictable, but even Bezalel could tell when the king would explode.

Aaron retreated several steps, but Moses stood firm.

"Moses, why do you wish to keep my people from their labor?" Ramses's voice began calm but grew louder with every syllable. The heavy kohl rings around his eyes made him appear angry even when he wasn't. Right now, he looked positively menacing.

The king stepped to the edge of the dais. "My city is not yet finished, and until it is, no one will leave this delta. Not even for three days! Your worship is not my concern. They all must remain here and keep working, and you are interfering. Leave them alone, and leave me alone. I have indulged you; now *get out!*" He lunged at the men but stopped short of jumping off the dais.

Moses turned to go. Aaron started to raise his rod again, but Moses touched his arm. Aaron closed his mouth and followed his brother out, head bowed.

Bezalel ran a hand over his face and breathed a heavy sigh as he walked to his room. He had just returned to the palace after spending two nights at home. He kicked off his sandals and plopped on his bed for a moment. *What happened out there? Aaron has a brother? One who knew Ramses in Thebes, and meets with Shaddai?*

Bezalel gathered his tools and walked across the portico. He tried to focus his thoughts somewhere else—anywhere else—as he picked up his chisel. He pulled it gently in semicircles, each one deeper than the last, to form an ear. As he worked, the heavy scent of lotus blossom filled the air around him, and he felt eyes boring into his neck. He shrugged off the feeling, but it persisted. His hands continued to carve the alabaster, but he couldn't hold his tool steady. Finally, he stepped back, as if to study his subject, drawing his arm across his forehead to wipe away the sweat.

The king himself stood only a few strides away.

Ramses sauntered toward Bezalel. He reached out and touched the sculpture. The king walked around the white stone bust, arms crossed over his chest, and studied it from all sides. His double crown reflected the sun's rays.

Although Bezalel was as tall as the king, he felt small in his presence. Bezalel's heart pounded, and he feared Ramses could see it under his tunic.

"I like it. You have done well. You capture the power of Ramses." The pharaoh left without waiting for the customary response. Golden threads glistened in the pleated linen *shenti* wrapped around his waist, and jeweled bracelets on his wrists clinked together as he strode back to his private rooms beyond the dais. Several servants followed.

Bezalel staggered and realized he had barely taken a breath since his ruler approached. He gasped, then stumbled backwards and sank onto a couch along the wall behind him. His heart had slowed to near its normal pace and he had caught his breath by the time a tiny Egyptian offered him a cup of water. Bezalel smiled and took it.

"He can be scary, can't he?"

Drops of cool water ran down Bezalel's chin and he wiped them away. "Maybe." He studied the child's face. His eyes were dark brown and his lashes were long and black. He had a tiny scar on his right cheek, and he had lost a tooth. "What's your name?"

"Ahmose." The boy was almost entirely without clothing except for his flaxen shenti. He wore his thick, black hair tied at the base of his neck.

"I've seen you here before. How old are you?"

"Seven." Ahmose put his hands on his hips. "How old are you?"

"Nineteen." Bezalel laughed at the boy's directness. "Why aren't you in school with the other children?"

Ahmose stared at his bare feet, wiggling his toes. "I am only a servant."

"Oh." Bezalel returned the cup. A servant at seven? That was terribly young for an Egyptian. What could the boy possibly have done to deserve that? Bezalel scrambled for words. "Thank you for the water. I needed it. My mouth was so dry I couldn't speak."

"Is this the first time our master has spoken to you?"

"Yes. I am in his presence almost every day, but he has never addressed me directly. I wasn't sure what to expect."

"So why are you in here instead of out there with all the other Hebrews?"

A twinge of pain pricked at Bezalel's heart. *Good question.* One Shaddai had never answered for him. "I am an artist. I make things for the king. So he keeps me here."

"You can't go home?"

Bezalel clenched his jaw a moment before he answered. "No. I must stay here now."

Ahmose nodded. "I have no home, either." The little slave left with the cup and wandered down the hall.

Bezalel crossed the courtyard and headed toward the river. He didn't like that word "either." Maybe the boy didn't have a home, but he did. He had a home; he just wasn't allowed to live there. He had family; he just couldn't be with them. He even had a people; they just considered him an Egyptian, a traitor. How could El Shaddai let this happen? Was he God Almighty or not?

Bezalel picked up some rocks and tossed them into the river, aiming for a turtle. The small stone hit the reptile's shell and it dove under the water and swam away. Even it had a home that couldn't be taken away. It wasn't fair.

❧❦

When the drum rang the noon meal, Bezalel crossed the portico, grabbing a plum and a loaf of bread from a basket set on a pedestal along the way. He pushed open the door to his workroom then sat down and bit into the deep purple fruit.

He was pouring a glass of goat's milk when a man appeared at his door wearing the fine linen shenti of a court official, with gold threads and a jeweled leather belt.

Bezalel rose, and the man strode toward his table. "The king has commissioned new bracelets for his son for the coronation. He wishes them to look like this." He handed Bezalel a drawing on parchment. "You may use the jewels and gold that Nubia brought the other day."

Bezalel set the plum down and studied the drawing. "Very well. Thank you."

"Shall we go now?" The man stepped toward the door and gestured down the hall.

Bezalel raised his eyebrows. "Go where now?"

"To the storeroom, to get the jewels and gold."

Bezalel sat again. "No, I'll go later. I have not yet eaten today."

"But I am not free later. So you'll have to go now."

"I have a key, so I can go later."

The official pursed his lips. "But you're a slave."

Bezalel took a deep breath. "You're new here, aren't you?"

The man stood a little taller. "Yes. I have replaced Ammon as chief artisan. I came up from Memphis with him."

Bezalel walked toward the official and offered a smile he did not feel. "Congratulations. I am sure you will do well." He folded his arms over his chest. "I have worked in this palace for over twelve years. While I cannot work anywhere in the kingdom for pay, I have earned respect and a measure of freedom in the palace. Freedom to go where I need to go as well as to create."

He held up the rolled parchment. "I am never given drawings like this. Ramses only gave me this one because he wants these bracelets to match exactly the ones I made for him a few years ago. He does not know I can remember those down to the last jewel." He shrugged. "Ammon gave me a key to the storeroom with the king's knowledge and consent. So if you don't like it, I am afraid you'll have to talk to him." Bezalel returned to his seat and picked up his plum.

The official narrowed his eyes and his face turned red. "We'll see about that." He spun on his heel and walked away.

That's what I was afraid of.

After he stuffed the last bite of bread in his mouth, Bezalel took a large oil lamp, and a little wooden key hidden under it, off the shelf. He stepped out of his room then walked down the hall away from the throne to the storeroom. There were no windows, so the only light came from the lamp.

When he reached the storeroom, he inserted the wooden key into the lock and turned it. He smiled as he listened to the tumblers fall one by one. The door popped open just a bit; he pushed it the rest of the way and entered. He placed the oil lamp on a shelf made just for that purpose, and it lit up the sizable room. Gold and jewels glittered in the flickering glow, throwing bits of light over the walls in an ethereal display.

He found the pottery jars of gold nuggets and flakes. He thrust his hand deep inside and brought it up full of the precious metal, his fingers splayed, and let the misshapen rocks sift slowly through his hand and back into the pile. Nothing else on earth felt like gold. The nuggets were heavier than they looked, and the sound of them falling back onto themselves both soothed and stirred him. He closed his eyes and let them fall a few more times before he filled a linen bag about as long as his hand, pulling the drawstring closed when it was full.

The unpolished gemstones sat on platters on a series of shelves. He scooped up a handful and took a deep breath. The scent of the earth still hugged the unrefined stones. Each one needed a vigorous polishing, but he could see the finished prize waiting beneath all the dirt and impurities.

He searched the gems one at a time, holding them to the light, turning them over in his hand. He carefully selected those that matched the bracelets he had crafted for Ramses, finding exactly the right stones for them. Each one had a purpose and meaning, at least to Ramses. Bezalel did not believe mere rocks had any power, but the king did, so Bezalel did his best to select perfect stones.

The Egyptians believed lapis lazuli, blue like the heavens and the Nile, had life-giving powers, symbolizing creation and rebirth. Green turquoise brought joy and delight. The dark red of the carnelian symbolized the blood of life and had healing properties. Malachite's green protected the wearer from epidemics, and Bezalel's favorite, amethyst, represented wealth and royalty. He dropped the chosen stones into another pouch.

He was about to leave when he saw the ivory and ebony. Several elephant tusks stood in a corner. He drew his hand down one as tall as he was—far too big for him to pick up alone. From its tip to the base it was dense, without visible grain, and creamy white. Toward the bottom it cracked, almost like cedar. Constructed of rings set one inside another, its center was hollow.

He dragged a fingernail down the side. This was far denser than the hippo ivory he had worked with. This was magnificent. He reached up to a shelf and grabbed a piece of heavy black wood and set it next to the ivory. The ebony was even harder. The black next to the white was spectacular, and his mind raced with possibilities of what he could create.

So different, and yet so similar at the same time. Both smooth, glistening, hard, solid; they would be difficult to carve. They required thought, planning, and special tools. Better to keep them safely locked up for now.

Closing the storeroom door, he heard a soft noise. He held the lamp high, looking all around. Seeing nothing, he reached back and locked the door. But the sound came again, a whimper, like a kitten. He looked once more, with the lamp lower.

Then he saw her.

Curled up in the corner, back to the wall, was the girl from the throne room. She sat with her legs pulled up and her arms wrapped around them, her face buried in her knees. She cried so softly it was nearly inaudible.

Pain enveloped him, as if a giant hand squeezed his chest, making it hard for his heart to beat and for him to breathe. Never before had he been consumed by so much feeling for anyone else, especially someone he didn't even know.

He knelt next to her. What should he do? Neither servants nor Israelites could touch Egyptians without permission. Dared he risk it?

He remembered the way she looked at him in the throne room, her eyes filled with despair. Was she asking for help then? She was in pain of some kind now, and she needed … something. He reached out and gently touched her arm.

She flinched and pulled herself even farther into the corner, crying out as she looked up.

He jumped away from her, falling back onto his seat, his weight on his hands. "Shh! I'm sorry! I just want to know if you need any help."

She stared at him with red, wet, kohl-smeared eyes. Her hair hung around her shoulders in a mess of knots and misplaced decorative pins. Yet there was still something about her that drew him.... Even at her most miserable, she made him dizzy. A few more tears fell, and she shook her head. "Thank you, though." Her voice was rough.

His breath came in shallow bursts. He didn't want to scare her, so he slowly sat up. "Can I get you anything? Food? Water? Anything?" He paused. "Someone else?"

She shook her head again and smiled weakly before hiding her face once more in her wet and wrinkled dress.

He sat on the floor for a few moments, wondering what else he could do. If she wouldn't let him help, there really was nothing to do. Her exquisite linen tunic was ripped at the neck and at the hem, but there were no obvious bruises. Her bare feet were filthy and cut, and somewhat bloody. He couldn't see her hands.

Was she still crying from two nights ago? Was she just lonely for her family? He longed to dry her tears, to comfort her, to hold her until she stopped crying, but he was sure that was exactly what she didn't need—or want—right now.

He waited a few more moments, wishing he could do something, anything. Then he stood up. He would get no answers sitting here.

The walk back down the hallway seemed much longer than the walk to the storeroom.

When he neared his workroom, he saw the king cross the throne room. He paused in the shadows so Ramses could not see him and reached down to place his bags on the limestone floor. He grimaced when their weight shifted, and they jangled and clinked.

The king marched toward his throne, stabbing the floor with his scepter in time with his long strides. His heavy necklace banged against his chest. Crown prince Amun-her-khepeshef scurried behind. "Father, your command makes no sense!" The prince spread his arms. "You are only slowing down the completion of your own city!"

Ramses whirled about, nearly knocking over his son. "They are slowing down the work, not me! The Egyptian workers will no longer gather and deliver the straw. The slaves will gather their own. I am tired of their laziness and their schemes to get out of work."

Unmistakably Ramses's son, the prince shared the same long nose and high cheekbones. He still enjoyed taut skin and straight posture, and women still wanted to be his consort. He didn't have to take wives or concubines by force or royal order, as did his father. Bezalel balled his fists and clenched his teeth and forced his mind back to the conversation.

"...and then if we do not give them the straw—"

"I no longer wish to discuss this! The matter is closed!" The pharaoh's face immediately brightened. He smiled. "I wish to discuss happier things. How are the preparations coming for your coronation as my co-ruler? Will we be ready at the end of the summer?"

"They are coming along well, my king." The prince bowed his head.

"'My king?' Are you angry with me?" The king reached for his son's face and lifted it. "There is no one else here. Why do you address me so formally, habibi?"

"I am sorry, Father. I did not mean to offend you. It is simply habit to address you more formally in the throne room. I had not realized we were alone."

"Good, then. Let us retire and discuss the ceremonies." Ramses wrapped his arm around his son's waist and the pair disappeared down the hall to their rooms. Ramses chattered away, but the prince looked at his feet.

Bezalel grabbed his bags. *This is bad. Really bad.* When he returned to his workspace, he threw the bags on the floor and kicked at the stool. He loosed the leather string at his collar and ran his hands through his hair then clasped his hands behind his neck. He paced as he fumed.

If Moses had bothered to find out exactly what the situation was before he appeared in Pharaoh's court, he might not have forced the king to such an extreme move. And Aaron and all his posturing.

Shouldn't he have stopped Moses in the first place instead of trying to look so important?

There would be chaos in the villages tonight.

Moses should have stayed in the desert.

Three

Second month of Ahket, Season of Inundation

Mud squished between Bezalel's toes as he stood on the edge of the flooded river a stone's throw east of the courtyard. The water swirled around his feet and tickled his ankles. His tunic and long-sleeved *thawb* remained in his workroom, and he wore only his shenti.

He lifted his face to the east, closed his eyes, and let the morning flood over him. This was always his favorite time of day—the sun barely up, but shedding enough light to allow him to enjoy all that surrounded him. No one else was on the river yet, and his loneliness was not so oppressive this early in the morning. He moved closer to the cool center of the river. A sacred ibis dropped a silvery perch at Bezalel's interruption and rose into the sky, flying over the river back toward the sun. The fish darted upriver.

Ahmose dashed down the bank and nearly ran into Bezalel. "They're back again. They're cleaning themselves in the washroom and will soon stand before the king. I thought you would want to know." He bent forward and rested his hands on his knees, wiggling his toes deep into the mud.

"Who's back again?"

"Those two old men. Hurry!" Ahmose tugged hard at Bezalel's wrist then let go and ran ahead.

Bezalel clambered up the muddy bank, grabbing some papyrus reeds to keep from tumbling down. With his long strides he soon caught up with the child.

They entered the palace through the washroom at the southeast corner, rinsed off their muddy feet and dried them, then tiptoed across the portico. Ahmose crept up close to one of the pillars that separated the portico from the throne room and peered around it, while Bezalel stood behind him.

Ramses presided from his heavily gilded throne with the prince on his right. "Moses, why are you here again? I believe I threw you out of my palace."

"Yahweh, God of Israel says, 'Let my people go.'" Aaron's voice boomed throughout the hall.

Ramses glared at Aaron. "I was not talking to you. Let your brother speak."

Aaron thrust out his jaw. "I am the spokesman. Yahweh has declared it so."

Ramses leaned forward. "I said, 'Let your brother speak.'"

Aaron looked at the floor. Moses stepped forward.

Bezalel pulled Ahmose over to the last pillar so they had a better view and knelt behind him. They were still at the back of the shallow throne room, but at least now they were at the corner and could see everyone from the side.

Moses stood tall, not flinching.

Ramses sat back and stared at Moses for several moments. "When you left—fled—forty years ago, I thought I was rid of you forever. Now you are back, interfering again. I want you to leave, and this time, stay gone."

"I c-cannot do that, Ramses."

"You take liberties that have not been granted."

"I apologize, my k-king. But I still must do what Yahweh s-sent me to do."

"Still can't speak in front of Pharaoh? First my father, now me?" Moses remained silent.

"How do I know," Ramses said, "that you are not making up this Yah—what is his name again?"

"Yahweh." Aaron spoke through clenched teeth.

Ramses glared at Aaron, and Aaron stepped back. "Oh, yes, Yahweh. How do I know you are not making him up? Why should I let you worship a God I do not even know is real?"

"How do you wish us to p-prove He is real?" Moses asked.

Ramses smirked. "Perform a miracle."

The officers at his side laughed.

Aaron threw his shepherd's staff to the floor before Ramses. It clattered on the stone and transformed into a snake, a black cobra with a hood spreading from its neck. It raised its head off the floor and thrust out its slender tongue, but made no move to bite anyone. The serpent swayed and turned toward Bezalel and the boy, and though it was too far away to be a threat, Bezalel recoiled.

Ramses watched without reaction then nodded to his son. Amunher leaned in toward his father, and the king whispered in his ear.

"Jannes! Jambres!" The prince clapped his hands once at the sound of each name. Two men appeared from the shadows. They wore gaudy necklaces with strange symbols around their necks and long linen robes dyed with indigo. In his many years at the palace, Bezalel had never seen them in the open, though he had heard much about them. They seemed to prefer the darkness and secret rooms.

Ahmose reached up and pulled Bezalel's face down near his. "That," he whispered, "is Jannes, Ramses's chief sorcerer, and his helper, Jambres."

Jannes threw down a staff, and it too, became a snake, although not as large as Aaron's. Then several more magicians emerged, each with a staff. Snakes appeared one by one, as rod after rod struck the stone floor. The servants waiting against the wall slowly sidestepped toward the portico, as far away from the magicians and serpents as possible.

The hissing and tongue flicking made Bezalel cringe, and Ahmose snuggled back against his chest. He put an arm around the boy, and Ahmose grabbed it with both hands. They watched as Aaron's cobra slithered toward the other snakes. It wriggled toward one of the smaller serpents and swallowed it whole.

Ahmose gasped.

One by one, the midnight-colored cobra swallowed each of the lesser snakes.

Ahmose's tiny body quivered, and Bezalel held him a little tighter, placing his other arm around him as well.

The cobra grew in size with each snake it swallowed.

Bezalel glanced up at the king. Ramses glowered at Jannes, who seemed to be doing his best to avoid the king's gaze.

The only snake left was Jannes's. The shorter snake flicked its tongue at the cobra, and its dark eyes followed the cobra's movements. Without warning, the cobra struck, and the head of the smaller snake vanished in the cobra's mouth, the rest of its body following it.

Jannes sputtered and stormed off toward the inner rooms behind the throne. Aaron reached down and picked up the bulging cobra by the tail.

Ahmose gasped and turned, throwing his arms around Bezalel's neck. "He will be bitten!"

But the cobra again became a rod, and Moses and Aaron exited through the open courtyard. Ramses and his son strode in the other direction to their rooms. Doors down the hall slammed one by one, and Jannes could be heard screaming at his assistants.

Bezalel pulled Ahmose away from his chest. The child's face was wet with tears, and his body still shivered in fright.

"Why are you crying now? It's over, habibi." Bezalel held Ahmose's face and wiped away the boy's tears with his thumbs. How could he feel such affection for this little servant he had met only days before?

"Weren't you scared?" Ahmose wiped his nose with the back of his hand.

"No. Were you?"

"Of course! All those snakes, and everybody was so mad. It was awful." Ahmose paused. "Why weren't you scared?"

"Because I know the God Moses and Aaron speak of. And He would never hurt me." He wasn't sure he believed that, but he couldn't let this little child know that, could he? Besides, Shaddai may have abandoned Bezalel in the palace, but He wouldn't actually hurt him.

Or would He? He did let his people die in the brickfields year after year.

He wasn't sure what to believe anymore.

✿✦✿

The breeze flowed through the long, narrow portico from the open courtyard, carrying the scent of narcissus flowers. A cat meandered into the room, jumped onto the dais, and curled up under the throne. Servants bustled throughout the palace, delivering messages, following orders, gathering food.

Bezalel removed the linen cover from the bust and set out his tools. He ran his hands over the face as the early morning sun danced on the smooth stone. The shape of the eyes, the curve of the mouth—the tiny things that gave a statue life were almost complete.

He glanced up as Ramses passed him on his way to the river for his morning bath. Servants followed, some with food and drink.

Bezalel drew a fine-pointed chisel across the alabaster to shape a scepter.

A servant appeared at the edge of the courtyard and summoned him. "Ramses commands you to come. He is pleased with this sculpture, and desires that you make one of his beloved wife, Nefertari. He has instructions to give you. Follow me." He whirled about and headed toward the river.

Bezalel caught his breath, and his heart beat faster. His instructions had always come from the chief craftsman.

Servants were standing in the water when Bezalel reached the river. Ramses waited on the edge as they prepared the oils and lotions for his bath. Date palms swayed gently overhead and a turtle circled lazily in the water. Bezalel walked a few paces down the wide slope of the river toward the king and stood on the bank. But before Ramses could address him, Moses and Aaron approached from the Israelite villages to the north.

"I thought I told you to keep them out of my palace!" the king barked at a helpless servant.

Aaron stepped into the water, several strides from the ruler. "You choose to worship Hapi, god of the Nile. You believe the Nile is the life-giving blood of Osiris. But Yahweh, the God of Israel says—"

"Yes, I know what he says!" Ramses strode toward the pair. "But for the last time, I am not going to let you or your people go anywhere! Your little tricks last week prove nothing!"

"'You have refused to listen to Me,' says Yahweh." Aaron continued when Ramses stopped moving. "'Now you will know that only I am God. I will strike the water of this river, and it will become blood. The fish will die, and you will have no water for your animals, or your people.'"

Aaron raised his staff high over his head and brought it crashing down on the water. Bezalel ducked at the crack of the rod. A streak of scarlet rippled out from the tip of the stick and swept across the river. Birds scattered, frogs jumped, the turtle ducked under the water. Blood was everywhere—the river, the mud, the reeds on the banks, on clothing, cups, plates of food.

Servants, covered in crimson, screamed and shoved as they raced for the palace. Some reached for pitchers of drinking water to rinse themselves off, but found that these vessels, too, contained only blood. Men fell to their knees and begged the gods—any gods—for mercy.

At first Bezalel could not take his gaze off the river. No matter which way he looked the color grew, farther and deeper and darker. His mind didn't want to think and his legs refused to move. He had to fight to keep from being knocked over by fleeing servants. His chest heaved as his breath came faster. He had to get out of there.

As he climbed the slope up from the bank of the river, he noticed his feet were dotted with crimson. When he saw his legs, he froze and stared, his mind trying to process the fact that he was not injured and yet covered in blood.

"Be quiet! That's not blood! It's only the red color that happens every year!" Jannes screamed as he raced down from the palace, followed by Jambres and a flock of assistants. Some were spattered with blood, and had obviously raced to tell him what had happened to the Nile.

Jannes stomped over to a servant. "Give me that pitcher!" He grabbed the container of water and poured it out on his hand. The thick liquid was obviously not just red-colored water.

Jannes threw the pottery at Moses's feet, breaking it and splashing even more blood. He turned to face Moses, jabbing a jeweled finger in his face. "Your pranks are commonplace. You are nothing but an imposter! I will do this, too. You will see!" He stormed off, taking Jambres and his magicians with him. Ramses and his attendants trailed behind.

Bezalel finally willed his body to move and slogged to the palace. He cut through the washroom, but it was a crimson-covered mess. Trudging through the hall and into his own room, he pulled his tunic over his head, smearing blood across his face. He picked up a pitcher on his table, but it was full of blood; he couldn't even wash his face.

As he changed his clothes, his mind kept returning to the bloody river. The Nile did turn red sometimes during flood season. The sudden increase in water from the Blue Nile, full of deep red earth from Abyssinia, often made the Nile a deep scarlet for several days. But that occurred at the height of flood season, still weeks away. And it definitely wasn't blood.

Sinking onto his bed, he ran his hands through his hair, realizing too late he had just smeared blood through it. He didn't care.

This was serious. This was life-threatening. What would happen if the river remained blood? Would they all die? The vague fear he felt from the cobras was dwarfed beside this terror caused by the blood of the Nile. He did not worship the Nile, as did the Egyptians, but still, without water, there was no life. Did El Shaddai not care for them at all?

☙❧

Five days had passed since the river turned to blood. The water was clearer, but still not drinkable. Women dug along the banks where there was scant water, though it could hardly be called fresh. It was brackish, and it tasted terrible, but it was enough to sustain life. The land reeked of the decaying fish that blanketed the banks.

Long after the noon meal, Ahmose pushed open the door to Bezalel's room and peeked in.

"Ahmose!" Bezalel beckoned the lad, who padded over.

"What are you making?" Ahmose stood on his toes, straining to see the tabletop.

Bezalel walked around the table and lifted the little slave onto a stool. "You are almost too big for me to lift!" He leaned on his elbows on the table and picked up one of a pair of jeweled wristbands.

"I am making a set of bracelets. See, this blue part is lapis lazuli, a rare and precious stone brought from far away. This is an amethyst—it's my favorite. And this, of course, is gold."

Ahmose sat up on his knees. "Oooh, it's so shiny! Where does it come from?"

"It comes from mines south of here in a land called Nubia. Look." Bezalel untied the drawstring of the bag of gold flakes, dipped his hand into it, and brought some out, letting it sift through his fingers.

"It looks like sparkly sand!" Ahmose took a nugget from Bezalel's palm. "But some of it is still rocks."

"Yes, some. We have to melt it first, in a very hot fire. Then we can turn it into sheets, or wires, or tiny balls, like the ones on these bracelets."

Bezalel returned to the other side of the table and turned his attention back to the jewelry. He held a band wrapped around wood in one hand and a tweezers in the other. He painstakingly positioned each minute ball of gold onto the heated bracelet. Each band contained hundreds of the gold balls, set in perfect rows.

He glanced up at Ahmose, who studied him from the other side of his workbench.

"Why don't you have a beard, like all the other Israelites?" Ahmose stretched toward Bezalel and gently stroked his cheek.

"The Egyptians prefer those who work inside the palace to be clean shaven, as they are. That's why I pull my hair back like yours, too, when I am here."

"Does it hurt?"

"What? Shaving?" Bezalel chuckled. "No, but it irritates my skin sometimes. I put almond lotion on it. It helps."

Bezalel continued working in silence for a moment. Then he glanced at Ahmose. "You look sad. What's the matter?"

"I'm not sad. But I keep thinking about the snakes from the other day." Ahmose picked up a chisel and examined it. "I have seen

Jannes and Jambres and the magicians change their rods to snakes many times, but they can never turn them back. Aaron is the only one I have ever seen do that."

"Why does that bother you so much?"

"Well, I know how Jannes does his trick."

"You do? How?" Bezalel added another gold ball to the bracelet.

Ahmose hesitated. "You must keep it a secret if I tell you."

"I promise." Bezalel glanced up and winked.

Ahmose fingered a bracelet as he spoke. "They use a special kind of cobra. It is called a *naja haje*. When you push on his neck, he gets stiff and falls asleep, sort of, and looks like a stick. When you throw him down, he wakes up and squirms away. But you can't pick him back up, not by the tail anyway, like Aaron did, or he will bite you."

"So you can explain Jannes, but not Aaron, and you don't like that. Is that it?"

"It scares me." Ahmose remained quiet for a while. "Did you know that Jannes made water turn to blood yesterday?"

"He did?" Bezalel looked up. "How do you know that?"

"I saw him. He says he can do anything your God can do." Ahmose put the bracelet down. "Do you remember when you said your God wouldn't hurt you?"

"Yes, I do."

"Then how come he took all the water away? That hurts people."

Bezalel put his tools down and gazed at Ahmose for a moment. "My God is trying to stop the king from hurting us."

"But we are getting hurt, too."

"I'm sorry. I can't explain that. I have no water, either, but I have some cool goat's milk. Want some?" Bezalel handed him a cup of milk.

"Oh, yes!" Ahmose drank deeply, until Bezalel took away the cup.

"Don't drink too much at once, or you will be ill. You can come and get more later."

"Thank you! I will come back later. Remember my secret!" Ahmose scurried off.

"I will," Bezalel promised.

৵৵৵

Bezalel entered his house and was shocked to find Moses and Aaron with Sabba. His grandfather handed him a plate of fruit and gestured to a spot against the wall, placing his finger against his lips.

Bezalel leaned against the wall and gnawed on a plum.

"My brother, please sit down. You are making me tired." Moses bit into a slice of cool watermelon while Aaron paced.

Aaron raised his hands in the air. "But you have no idea what you have done! You have been gone too long. Everyone *here* knows Ramses panics at the thought of a takeover by outsiders. That happened once, and he will never let foreigners take control of Egypt again. And we are most certainly outsiders, no matter that we have lived here for over four hundred years. You can't come here and start making changes when you don't know all the circumstances." He dropped his hands and stopped pacing. "Do you have any idea to what lengths he will go?"

Moses set down the watermelon. Juice ran down his hands and he wiped them on a towel and then looked up at his brother. "Of course I do." His voice was calm and soft.

Aaron sat on a low stool and studied Moses's face for a long moment. "I'm sorry. I was only three years old, but I still remember the look on the princess's face when she pulled you out of that basket."

What is he talking about? A princess? Who is this Moses?

"And now I am the brother you haven't seen in almost eighty years. I am glad—a bit surprised maybe, but very glad—that you welcomed me here. That's a great deal of trust." Moses grinned at his brother.

Aaron smiled back. "Trust in El Shaddai, my brother, not in you. I do not know you."

"Nor I you." Moses reached for more melon and held a slice out to Aaron. "And yet here we are."

Aaron ignored the offer. "Yes. Here we are." He rose and paced again. "In the most difficult situation I can imagine." He paused for several moments then said, "Did you know Ramses would react so badly?"

Moses shrugged. "How did you expect him to react to a request to give up all his free labor for three days?"

"I don't know. When you said El Shaddai had given you signs to show him, I suppose I thought he would respect them. He believes so strongly in magic."

"True enough. He has many magicians."

Aaron crossed his arms. "Did you know about the blood?"

"Not until Yahweh told us that morning. He did say that He would do many wondrous signs, but that Pharaoh would not listen, and then He would punish Egypt, and finally the king would let us go."

Aaron rolled his eyes and spread his hands. "Finally? How long is 'finally'?"

Bezalel leaned forward. *That's what I'd like to know.*

Moses shook his head. "I—"

A group of men shouting outside the house interrupted them.

"Aaron, get out here *now*! And bring your brother!"

Moses took a sharp breath and looked at Aaron. "Do you know who that is?"

Aaron shrugged.

When the brothers did not immediately go out, the man kept yelling. "Get out here and explain yourself, if you can! You can't hide forever!"

Sabba opened the door far enough to stick his head out. "Leave them alone. Your quarrel is not with them."

Aaron opened the door wide and stepped out. "I am not hiding, but it does take a while to get up these days. I am an old man."

Sabba exited next, and Moses followed, favoring his left side and rubbing his hip. Before either could speak, a chubby fist flew out. The punch missed Aaron's face.

Bezalel positioned himself between Sabba and the other villagers. No one was going to touch his family.

"Hebron!" Two other men grabbed the would-be attacker and held his arms.

Hebron scoffed. "First no straw, now no water? Why didn't you stay out of this? Did El Shaddai tell you this would happen, too? Or didn't He know?"

Another man pushed to the front. "Don't pay any attention to Hebron. He's quite drunk." His voice was gentle as he pointed to the wobbly man behind him. He looked at Bezalel. "He will not hurt them. We will not let him." The man's gaze returned to Moses. "But you must understand. You have not lived the life of a slave. Our work has never been easy. It's backbreaking. We wear out long before our time, our bodies too drained to do anything else." He took a deep breath. "But it is the life we have been given. And I never thought it could get worse ... until now."

Moses closed his eyes and sighed deeply. He raised his shoulders, his hands clasped at his chest. "I can only do what Yahweh tells me to do. I am sorry; I did not plan this, and I did not know it would happen this way."

"Sounds like you didn't know much of anything. Why don't you go back to the desert?" Hebron broke free from his companions and laughed as Aaron jumped back. He stomped off, and the others followed.

Bezalel, Sabba, and the two brothers stepped back inside the house, but before they could be seated once more, Hebron appeared in the doorway, his face dark. "May El Shaddai judge you for the trouble you have brought upon us." His words slurred. "You have handed Ramses the sword he will use to annihilate all Israel. Remember that when you are the only ones left."

Four

Bezalel tapped his foot as he waited on the portico to present the bust to Ramses. Silvery moonlight illuminated the room, and the scent of the river wafted through the palace on the cooler evening air.

He took a deep breath and tried to slow his heartbeat. All his work before had gone through Ammon; he had never presented it himself.

A servant appeared. Bezalel picked up the white stone sculpture and followed him into the throne room to a waiting pedestal. He carefully placed the figure on it and removed the linen cloth.

Ramses circled the bust. He touched the alabaster crown, the lips, the eyes. He ran his fingers over the stone necklace and trailed them up the scepter. "I am pleased. You are a gifted artist and you have done much to honor Egypt. Ammon always spoke so highly of you. I see he did not exaggerate.

"I have another project for you. I started to tell you a month ago, but we were … interrupted. And then I was needed in Thebes. But now I wish you to make another sculpture, this time of my most beloved wife, Nefertari. It must match this, but of course be somewhat smaller."

Bezalel bowed. He let out his breath, only then realizing he had been holding it. He could not help smiling, and struggled to keep from shouting. Praise from Ramses's own lips! But he calmed himself and when he lifted his head, his face was again expressionless. "Would pink alabaster be pleasing to my king? We have recently acquired some that would be enough to sculpt her likeness. It would look exceptional next to your white alabaster figure."

"Yes. That would be quite satisfactory. How long will it take?"

Bezalel started to answer, but suddenly, Aaron approached the throne from the open courtyard. His brother followed a few steps behind. Yet again Aaron gave the now-familiar warning: "Yahweh, God of Israel says, 'Let my people go, that they may come and worship Me at My mountain.'"

Ramses ignored them. "How long?" He put his hands on his hips as he repeated the question.

"Well, this one took—"

"'If you do not let My people go, I will fill your land with frogs. They will be in the river, in all your water, in your houses, in your sleeping rooms, in your food, and on your people.'"

Ramses stepped beyond Aaron and halted in front of Moses. "I do not believe you. You were an obnoxious imposter when we were in school, and you are one now. If I wait long enough, you will simply leave, as you did before. As you always do." He stared at his former classmate.

Moses said nothing, but closed his eyes tightly and then looked at the floor.

"You choose Heqet, goddess of fertility, over Yahweh. Very well. Fertility you shall have, at the hand of Yahweh, the only giver of life." Aaron turned and stretched out his rod and pointed it toward the river. "Fill the land, and fill the waters. Let no place be undefiled, let no person be unbothered. Multiply and spread out over Egypt."

The brothers started to leave, but Ramses called to them. "To whom were you talking?"

Moses stopped and looked back. "The fr-frogs, of course."

Bezalel rolled over on his mat on the roof above his workroom and stretched. The sun was just rising over the Nile; the full moon was setting. The morning animals stirred as the night creatures returned to their nests and dens. He stood up then reached down for his thawb and shrugged into it.

He walked to the edge of the roof and climbed down the ladder. At the bottom, his foot came down on something cold and clammy. Yanking back his foot, he looked down. Frogs!

Regretting he had left his sandals downstairs in his room, he found an open spot to place his foot. He rubbed it into the sand to remove the stickiness. Frogs crept all around the palace, crawling more than leaping. Their croaking was sharp and relentless. He stepped between them and made his way through an archway on the side of the building onto the portico. Inside, the cold limestone floor was still clear of frogs. He checked his room and breathed a sigh of relief; there were none in there yet.

He padded down the hall to the kitchen and grabbed a loaf of bread. On his way back, a plopping alerted him to frogs creeping onto the portico from the courtyard. Hurrying into his room, he shut the door. Then he stuffed his thawb in the space between the door and the floor to keep the creatures out. He shivered at the thought of the disgusting animals.

Bezalel reached for the piece of pink alabaster he had picked out for the bust of Nefertari. He turned it over and over, searching for the grain, his fingers caressing every exposed bit. Tenderly, he set it on his table and reached underneath for two large sandbags. Placing them next to each other, he nestled the stone between them and reached for the largest claw, then began stripping away the pieces of rock that hid the face of the queen.

༐ ༐

The croaking outside the window high in the wall was louder now and assaulted Bezalel's ears. The water clock told him it was well past the midday meal and the rumbling in his stomach finally drove him from the sanctuary of his room. He opened his door to a barrage of sticky green frogs. He stumbled backwards but could not find a place to step without squashing one of them. His feet were still bare and he cried out in disgust.

The floor was a moving blanket of frogs crawling, croaking, creeping. He backed up enough to grab his sandals, leaning against the wall with one hand while he slipped them on, but shoes were of little use since the repulsive things crawled on top of his feet as well.

In the kitchen he found no food, nor any servants—only frogs. Frogs everywhere: in the grain, in the ovens, in the vegetables, sitting on bread, swimming in juice, crawling over fruit.

Still hungry, he vainly tried to avoid the creatures on his way down the hall and across the courtyard, and walked toward the Nile. The frogs were dying now, from being stepped on, from suffocating each other, from lack of food. The stench of rotting flesh grew stronger by the moment. The croaking bounced around in his head and threatened to explode his skull.

He stared as thousands of them climbed up the banks and crawled toward the palace. How could there still be more? He looked north toward the villages and south toward Nubia. As far as he could see, frogs left the river and clambered up onto the land.

He headed back to the palace. Maybe he'd just go to bed. They were crawlers, not jumpers, so they probably couldn't get on the roof.

As he approached the courtyard, he saw Jannes and Ramses in the throne room. He tried to stay out of sight but still be in a position to hear the conversation. Pharaoh had three servants whose only job was to keep the frogs away from him. Jannes stewed silently beside him.

Amun-her approached and bowed before the king. "My father, I was told our magicians have succeeded."

"Yes," Ramses said dryly. "Jannes here, to prove his consummate skill, has also caused frogs to 'multiply and fill the land.' They've been multiplying all afternoon. But he can't seem to make them disappear. Any suggestions?"

"What about Jambres?"

"He, too, has tried and failed."

"Then I have no other suggestions, my lord." Amun-her folded his hands in front of his chest and shook his head.

"I have one, I am afraid." Ramses inhaled a long breath. "That Israelite, Moses." He sneered as he said the name.

Jannes crossed his arms and turned away.

"Bring him to me." Ramses went to his rooms.

Bezalel stayed out of sight until the king left and then picked his way through the portico full of croaking frogs and under the archway to the ladder up to the roof. As he thought, it was free of frogs, but his stomach was still empty. He gazed across the sand toward the river. Even the crocodiles and herons had eaten their fill of frogs.

He looked around him at other rooftops. All were full of people trying to escape the vile creatures. Most of the roofs had families, groups of people laughing, talking. Some even had food.

Few lived in the palace itself, as he did. There was the king. And his personal servants, of course. And the harem. The harem was actually just beside the palace, attached by a walkway. The king's wives, concubines, and their children occupied these special chambers.

He studied each rooftop, and could not find a single one other than his own with only one person. He wondered again why Shaddai had given him a "gift" that had taken away everything else in his life—his family, friends, any chance at a home and family of his own. Some gift.

Some God. He didn't seem any better than the Egyptian gods. They abandoned their people, too.

The girl crossed his mind. Where was she? Was she still alone? Was she still crying?

Eventually his thoughts ran in circles and doubled back on themselves and his mind went blank. The croaking became unbearable, and he put his hands over his ears and lay back on his mat.

∂∽⌘

The shadows of the palm trees were growing long and the water lilies were closing for the night when the grumbling in Bezalel's stomach awakened him. He must have drifted off to sleep. He sat up, stretched. He could see Moses approaching from the north under the light of the full moon. Bezalel sprinted for the ladder and jumped to the ground, ignoring the mass of amphibians beneath him.

Moses stood before Pharaoh as ordered.

Bezalel knelt behind a pillar. Torches lit up the throne room, but he remained in the shadows.

"Where is your brother?" Ramses raised an eyebrow.

"You may speak to me now." Moses bowed his head.

"Pray to your God, that he will take away the frogs, and then I will let your people go offer sacrifices."

"We will pray, but you must set the exact time you wish them to go, so then you will know that it was Yahweh, and Yahweh alone, who made the frogs return to the Nile." Moses spoke deliberately and softly, but without faltering.

"Tomorrow. At dawn."

∂∽⌘

Bezalel arose before the sun was fully up. He hadn't slept well. Between wanting to see if the frogs would retreat as Moses promised, and the gnawing in his gut, he had tossed and turned most of the night.

He slid down the ladder, entered the portico, and made his way to the kitchen. A few disgruntled kitchen workers were there this time and he grabbed a fresh loaf of bread. Dead frogs littered the oven floor. On his way out he bumped into Ahmose.

"Habibi! What are you doing up so early?"

"I'm hungry."

"Can't you wait for breakfast?"

"You didn't."

Bezalel chuckled. "That's because I didn't eat all day yesterday."

"Neither did I."

Bezalel knelt to face the boy. "Didn't anyone feed you?"

"No. I usually have to get my own food. And I couldn't find any yesterday."

"But why? Doesn't anyone look after you?"

Ahmose remained silent.

Bezalel pushed some unbrushed hair away from Ahmose's eyes and decided against questioning the child further. "Wait here a moment." He stepped into the kitchen and grabbed another loaf and a little covered pot of honey that had not been ruined. "The frogs are supposed to leave this morning. Want to watch?"

"Where?"

"I know a place by the river where there are some high rocks I don't think they can climb. They can't jump very well. Let's go there and eat while we wait." Bezalel held out his hand and Ahmose slipped his tiny one into it.

When they reached the outcropping, the pair scaled the miniature mount. It was high enough to allow them to see the river and escape the frogs, and they made it just as the sun rose above the water. While they ate the first bites of bread dipped in honey, frogs whirled around and crawled toward the river. Within moments every frog was creeping toward the water.

Ahmose bounced on his heels and squealed with excitement.

Bezalel laughed and grasped the boy's tunic to make sure he didn't topple off the rocks.

"Look!" Ahmose pointed as the creatures hopped toward the Nile. "There they go! Like you said!"

It was fascinating to watch. Like an army of tiny green soldiers, the hordes of frogs marched toward the sea. Once they hit the Nile they were swept north toward the delta, leaving the river running with fresh water once again.

Ahmose and Bezalel climbed down and headed for the palace. Ramses already had slaves sweeping dead frogs into great piles.

Ahmose stopped and stared at the heaps of dried and decaying little bodies, most towering over him. "Oh, that smells awful!" He held his nose. "Will they just leave them all there?"

"No, habibi, they'll probably burn them."

"That sounds like great fun!"

"I don't think so."

"Why not? I don't see how it can't be!" Ahmose laughed as he scampered off.

౷∾ও

Later that night, and for the next several nights, Bezalel watched from the roof as bonfires lit up the sky. An acrid stench filled the air. His eyes watered when the ash stung them. Coughing, his own as well as everyone else's, made it difficult to sleep. His chest burned with every spasm.

Dust covered everything during the day. Fruit had to be washed several times before it could be eaten. Most of the bread left over at night had to be thrown away every morning, so breakfast usually didn't happen for many hours.

The frogs may have disappeared in half a day, but the damage lasted for weeks.

၁~၆

It was late in the evening, long past the time he normally went home, but Bezalel had stayed a little later to finish adding the gold balls to the bracelets. It took so long to get the bands heated to the exact temperature to fuse the gold balls to the base, but not melt them, that he preferred to stay and finish rather than start all over another day.

The frogs and their aftermath had slowed him down for over a week. Now that they were finally gone, he had to catch up. Ramses demanded the bracelets for his son's coronation. But Bezalel didn't really mind staying late; at least while he was creating he could forget—for a time—that he was only a slave. He finished as Ahmose walked in.

"Why are you here so late?" Ahmose whispered.

"I had to finish putting the gold on the bracelets. I'm finally done now. Want to see them?"

"No." Ahmose moaned as he climbed up on the stool.

"Do you want some more milk?"

"No. I'm fine."

"I can't stay. I'm late already." Bezalel cleaned his tools and packed them into a basket. "I want to go home tonight. I haven't eaten and I'm hungry. I'll be lucky if Imma lets me eats so late."

"That's all right."

Bezalel stopped his work and leaned on the table. He studied the boy's face. "Will you come see me tomorrow?"

"I'll try."

Bezalel walked to the front of the table and bent down in front of the child, resting his hands on his knees. "You're awfully quiet tonight. Is something wrong?"

"I'm all right. You better go home."

"Ready to get down?" Bezalel grasped Ahmose under the arms to pick him up. The boy cried out.

"What's wrong? Did I hurt you?" Bezalel let go and looked at him.

Tears streamed down the boy's face.

"I couldn't have hurt you that much. Something else is wrong. What is it?"

Ahmose sobbed. "I'm not s'posed to say."

Bezalel thought for a moment then went to latch the door of his workroom. He gently pulled up the short tunic Ahmose wore and turned the child to see his back. The flesh was ripped apart in several places. The bleeding had stopped for the time being, and dried blood had closed the wounds.

Tears came to Bezalel's eyes.

The boy whimpered.

"Oh, habibi, I'm sorry." Bezalel hugged him, but avoided his injured back. "I am so sorry," he repeated.

"You don't have to be sorry. You didn't do it."

Bezalel could not help but smile through his tears at the boy's innocence. "Come on, hop on my back. You're going home with me. My imma will fix your back. Put your arms around my neck and your legs around my waist, and I'll carry you."

Bezalel considered his choices as he hiked home. He knew severe punishment awaited any slave who ran away, but he could not leave Ahmose behind. A seven-year-old could not have done anything to deserve such a beating. From anyone.

Ahmose was asleep by the time Bezalel stepped inside his house. He hated to wake him up, but he knew his back must be tended to.

Imma came out to the main room from the kitchen beyond it, towel in hand, and her eyes opened wide when she saw the boy on Bezalel's back.

"This is Ahmose, a servant at the palace."

Ahmose awakened as Bezalel lowered him to the dirt floor.

"Why on earth would you bring him here? He's an *Egyptian!*"

"He's a little boy, Imma." Bezalel set him down on the low table and showed her Ahmose's back.

Imma gasped. "Oh, my! Who did that?"

"I don't know. But I intend to find out. In the meantime, I hoped he could stay here."

"Of course he'll stay here." Imma headed to the kitchen. "I'll get some oil."

Bezalel sat on the floor near the table. His mother returned with oil, honey, and cool, wet cloths and knelt across from him. Ahmose curled up on Bezalel's lap, his chest to Bezalel's, his face buried and his arms tight around Bezalel's neck as Imma tended his wounds. The scents of honey and oil melded and soothed Bezalel's frayed nerves as much as Ahmose's back. Occasionally, Imma would hurt him as she removed the dried blood to get to the wound below. He did not cry out, but held more tightly to Bezalel, who marveled at how Imma's motherly instincts seemed to have overtaken her fear.

"Hush, habibi. We are done. Now it's time for you to go to sleep." Bezalel stroked the boy's hair.

"Have you eaten?" Imma asked him in Egyptian.

Ahmose nodded.

"I'll take him upstairs, then." Imma took his hand.

Sabba came down from the roof where he had been resting.

"I am sorry we disturbed you, Hur." Imma gave him a weak smile.

"The cruelty of these Egyptians will never cease to amaze me." He shook his head at the sight of Ahmose's wounds. "They even beat their own."

Bezalel followed Imma up to the roof.

Ahmose winced as he lay face down on the sleeping mat.

Imma left Ahmose's shirt off so that the breezes might cool his back and help ease the pain. She sat next to the exhausted little boy and tenderly rubbed more oil and honey on his back.

She stroked his straight, coal-black hair and gazed at him as he slept.

Bezalel watched his mother's face as she tended to the abandoned child, and knew the old pain flooded her once again. It was not fair that this little boy should be so unloved and unwanted when she had more than enough love for ten children, but only one on which to bestow it. She blinked back a tear.

"El Shaddai has His ways, however difficult they may be for us to understand," she whispered to the child. "I pray He will watch out for you, habibi, because surely no one else is." She stroked his battered back once more, leaned over and kissed his cheek, and left him to the care of El Shaddai for the night.

Five

Fourth month of Akhet, Season of Inundation

Kamose poured water into a basin and immersed a rag into it. He wrung it out and wiped his face with the cooled cloth. He hung it on a hook above the small table and drank deeply from a pitcher.

Sitting on the chair by his bed, he laced up his sandals below his knees, then stood and slipped his dagger into its sheath on his right hip, and gold bands onto his upper arms. As he leaned on the table, he sighed. The king would rise soon. It promised to be a very long day.

Because he was captain of the guard, charged with protecting the life of Ramses, Pharaoh of Egypt, Kamose's modest quarters were across from the king's. Kamose stepped into the hall. Four soldiers stood at attention outside Ramses's door. Normally there were only two, but these days, Ramses was suspicious of everyone. Kamose authorized a shift change, and four new watchmen took over.

The captain returned to his room and sat on a low bed. He closed his eyes and listened to the call of an oriole in the courtyard. A bowl of grapes and loaf of hard bread had been placed on the chair beside his bed by a servant while he stepped out. He picked up a bunch of grapes, but his thoughts ran away with him, and he did not eat.

Ahmose had disappeared.

He had been gone for over three weeks now. Kamose rested his elbows on his knees and held his head in his hands. A thousand possibilities as to what may have happened ran through his mind, none of them good. Jannes could have beaten the boy literally to death, he could have given him to someone else, he could have sent him away, or locked him up....

Kamose had told no one that Ahmose was his nephew. He had promised to keep that secret. Still, he had watched the boy grow for the past seven years, even once declining a transfer to field duty to remain in the palace.

He stood and clasped his hands behind his neck and closed his eyes. Somehow, he must find out what happened to the child. But how could he do that and honor his promise?

☙❧

The sun shone brightly as Bezalel walked to the palace. The cloudless blue sky reflected the lightness of his spirit—no one had come for Ahmose, things were back to normal at the palace, and even in the village the anger over the straw had abated somewhat.

He stayed at home with Imma, Sabba, and Ahmose more often now. His house was close enough to the palace, and as long as he got his work done, no one cared. The new chief craftsman was far more interested in impressing Ramses than keeping an eye on Bezalel.

Flood season was nearing its end and the air was cooler now. Bezalel strolled beneath the sycamore trees, their branches full of leaves spreading out like umbrellas. He quickly reached the edge of the village on his short walk to the palace.

Moses and Aaron stood silently in the sand.

Bezalel halted several paces away and waited.

Moses raised his face to the sky and closed his eyes. After a moment, he turned to his brother. "Yahweh says, 'Stretch out your rod over all the desert, and strike the ground. The dust will rise into the air and become gnats to cover all of Egypt.'"

Aaron lifted his shepherd's staff and extended his arm. "Praise be to the only God, the Living God of Abraham, Isaac, and Jacob, the great I Am." He spun slowly to face the whole of Egypt.

What happened to all his bluster and drama?

After one complete turn, Aaron lowered his staff sharply to the ground and dragged it along in a second circle. As the dust climbed skyward the particles of earth became tiny gnats, growing wings and flying away toward the city.

The brothers started back toward the village.

Bezalel crossed over to them and stood in their path. He folded his arms. "Again? Things just settled down!"

"I must obey Yahweh." Moses spoke quietly.

"Aren't you going to warn Pharaoh?"

"I have warned Ramses three times already. He refuses to listen. Perhaps this will open his ears." Moses stepped around Bezalel and headed for the village.

Bezalel groaned and sprinted for the palace.

The palace buzzed with frantic activity by the time he arrived.

Servants raced across the throne room and courtyard with pitchers, bowls, and other containers. Some were empty; others were full of fresh palm wine. Guards rubbed the wine over their skin to repel the bugs. Almost everyone scratched violently—face, arms, legs, everywhere.

Bezalel smacked a gnat on his forearm and a red welt sprang up. He scratched the bite, slapped a few more bugs. He dreaded another encounter like the one with the frogs. Better to get out of here while he could. Perhaps the insects weren't so bad at home.

Exactly how harassing the Egyptians—and the Israelites at the same time—was supposed to secure their freedom eluded him. Ramses had promised to let them go if Moses sent the frogs back to the river but afterward conveniently forgot any such promise. Ramses seemed even angrier.

Shaddai's plan—if He even has one—is not working so far.

Bezalel grabbed an armful of yellow-flowered wormwood plants that grew beside the path on his way home. The strong smell kept the gnats away.

Noisy clusters of little children also carried fistfuls of the bush as he entered the village.

He set the silvery-gray branches on the table in the front room and took a couple back to Imma in the kitchen.

"They got you, I see." She chuckled and took the feathery branches and spread them around. The bitter odor filled the little house. Then she ripped several leaves from a stalk of basil and crushed them with the back of a spoon.

"There are not nearly as many here as at the palace." Bezalel dug at the bites on his arms.

Imma grabbed his hands to stop him from scratching. "When Moses and Aaron came back this morning they told us to gather wormwood." She continued to smash the basil. "It doesn't smell as good as palm wine, but it works, and there is certainly plenty of it around."

"Guess I must have missed that warning." Bezalel allowed her to rub the excreted basil oil over the bites. The extract soothed the itch and the swelling started to fade.

"What do you intend to do with Ahmose, my son? It has been almost a month."

Bezalel blew out a long breath. "I haven't decided yet. I hate to take him back to the palace. They are quite hard on runaways." He didn't wish to tell her the whole truth yet about what punishment might await Ahmose.

"But he didn't run. You brought him home to tend to his back!"

"They don't know that. Do you think they will care? Besides, I thought I might keep him." Bezalel winked, and a small smile escaped Imma's lips. "Where is he, anyway?"

"He went to the river with some of the boys."

Bezalel grabbed some honey-sweetened bread and dried meat and left. He tried to resist scratching as he wandered the riverbanks looking for Ahmose. He could feel the moisture in the air from the Nile, and the coolness of the breeze felt good on his bites. He finally saw the boy and called to him.

Ahmose skipped over and Bezalel offered him some bread.

Ahmose shook his head. "I ate a long time ago."

"Why do you get up so early?"

"I'm used to it. My master always made me." Ahmose dug his bare toes into the dark, wet earth at the edge of the river.

"Jannes? The magician?"

"Yes."

"So that's how you knew his snake trick."

"Yes. I know lots of his tricks."

Bezalel finished his bread and ripped off a piece of dried meat. "Why are you a servant? You are so young; Egyptian children your age aren't usually servants."

"I know. Jannes hates me. It has something to do with my mother. She died when I was born. That's why I'm his slave."

"Why did he beat you?" Bezalel pulled off his sandals and piled up a mound of soil on Ahmose's foot with his own.

Ahmose giggled and pulled out his foot. "I spilled a pitcher of water on his potions." He tried to cover Bezalel's feet.

"That's all? You spilled some water?"

"He's been very mad lately, because of the blood and snakes. Ramses is angry at him, so he's scared."

"That's no reason to beat you."

Ahmose shrugged. "He doesn't need a reason."

"Had he beaten you before?"

"Yes. Many times," Ahmose answered, matter-of-factly, as if nothing were wrong with that at all.

৵৽

After the evening meal, while Ahmose slept, Bezalel talked to Sabba and Imma about what he had learned from Ahmose that morning.

"What I don't understand is that he lives in the harem with the royal children, but he is a slave to Jannes."

"Many times," Sabba said, "when a concubine dies, her children are made servants. They still live in the harem, if no relatives take them, taken care of, barely, by the other concubines. They can't kick them out, since they are the king's children, but they can ignore them. And they work every day instead of enjoying the leisure and education of the other royal children."

"The harem? You mean his father is Ramses?" Imma set a bowl of figs before them.

"Quite possibly." Sabba reached for a fig. He peeled it and handed half to Bezalel.

Bezalel continued the thought. "I have heard it said Ramses has fathered a hundred children. When you see all his concubines, it is not difficult to imagine."

"I am, however, sure that Ahmose does not know." Sabba took another fig.

"But why should Jannes hate him? And get him as a slave?" Imma asked.

"Perhaps his mother was Jannes's sister, or daughter, and when she died he blamed Ahmose for her death." Sabba shrugged. "It could be any number of things. We may never know. It doesn't matter, anyway, because somehow, Ahmose ended up as his slave, and now he has, for all intents and purposes, run away."

"We can still keep him, can't we?" Imma poured a glass of juice.

"I don't know. Listen when you are at the palace, Bezalel. See if anyone mentions him. Then we shall know how to proceed. Until then, this must remain a secret. A carefully guarded secret."

꙰

The bugs were gone by sunrise. They had come and gone in a day, leaving only welts and the smell of palm wine behind. The king had retreated to his private rooms; Jannes and Jambres were in hiding after the fiascos of the frogs and the blood.

Bezalel stayed in his workroom finishing several small gifts, the kind Ramses liked to have on hand for state visitors. The sun climbed to its zenith and bathed the land in light and heat. It was time to gather some information if possible. As a king's artist, Bezalel knew no guard would stop or question him, though he was only an Israelite. He summoned his nerve and strolled down the hall, trying to look as if he belonged there. Beyond the throne room, he stopped outside what he knew to be Jannes's substantial and opulent quarters, although he had never seen the inside. The room, like its owner, was shrouded in secrecy. He looked down the hall, and behind him, and then, his back to the wall, crept up to the barely open door, hoping to hear something, anything.

Jannes was inside with Ramses, and the king was not happy. "You have tried three times, and failed three times, to alleviate my suffering! The Nile, the frogs, and now these infernal bugs! And that doesn't even count the snakes. Are you a magician or not?"

"I have tried everything, every kind of magic I know," the sorcerer said. "I cannot summon the bugs. I tell you, my king, we are dealing with something more than magic."

Bezalel shifted his weight outside the door. He noticed a shadow down the hall. Someone else was hiding, but he could not tell who it was.

"Maybe this is the work of their God." Jannes paused. "I don't know what it is, but it is not as simple as you say."

"Perhaps Jambres can make it simple. You have until sundown to prove this is not the work of their god."

Knowing the conversation was at an end, Bezalel retreated and backed around a corner. The king's bracelets clinked as he swept out of the room and down the hall. The slight sulfur odor of palm wine followed him.

Bezalel knew well what Pharaoh's simple statement meant. If Jannes did not succeed by dusk, he would be executed. Bezalel peeked around the corner and noticed the other spy leave too. He tried again to see who it was, but could make out only the flash of a red-trimmed thawb.

At least no one had mentioned Ahmose, so Bezalel returned to his room to work a while longer, at least until dusk, so he could see what happened with Jannes. After just a short time, the door to his workroom opened quietly although there had been no knock. Bezalel looked up to see an unusually tall Egyptian. The man reached behind him and quietly closed the door.

Muscular and clean shaven, he was exceptionally well built. He wore only a simple linen shenti around his waist, but the jeweled gold bands around his massive biceps identified him as captain of the guard, the highest-ranking soldier in the palace.

Bezalel knew not only his name, but his reputation, a fact which did not make him feel more comfortable in the guard's presence.

Bezalel dipped his head in a slight bow. "Yes?"

"I am Kamose." His voice was so deep it inspired fear by itself. "I have come to ask you about Ahmose."

Bezalel caught his breath. "Why should I know anything?" He avoided looking at the captain.

"I saw him come in here a few times before he disappeared."

"We are both servants. That is not so unusual."

"It was not easy for me to come here." Kamose took two long steps closer. "The boy is my nephew. I am only trying to find him, to watch out for him, as I promised my sister I would. I do not wish to harm him."

Bezalel took a deep breath and tried to appear unconcerned, though his legs trembled behind his table. "I'm sorry. I cannot help you."

Disappointment covered the officer's face. After a silent moment, he left.

Bezalel gasped and braced himself against the table. The captain of the guard was not someone to have as an enemy.

Shortly after Kamose left, a cry pierced the air. Bezalel rushed outside. The gathering crowd told him the shriek had come from Jannes's quarters. Jambres stood in the doorway, massaging his temples, black kohl smudged around his eyes.

Bezalel pushed his way to the front of the group.

"What happened?" Kamose stood before the magician.

"Jannes wouldn't let me follow him inside, even though I am always with him to help him in his work." Jambres's exaggerated grief nearly made Bezalel burst into laughter. "I waited and waited for him to come out. After a while, I decided to go in. And this"—Jambres caught a ragged breath—"is what I found."

The captain peered inside. "Poison?" His eyes narrowed at Jambres.

Ramses arrived with his entourage and the crowd made way for him.

"Report." The king looked at Jambres.

Jambres turned from Kamose to the pharaoh. "It appears he killed himself rather than face you, my king."

"Coward. I detest cowards. Jambres, you are now my chief magician. Do not disappoint me."

"I shall try my best, my king. Jannes was my mentor. I do not know if I can measure up to him." Jambres bowed low.

"Neither do I." Ramses's voice oozed disdain. "But do try."

Jambres clenched his fist but held his tongue.

The king turned and strode toward his rooms, followed by the captain.

The crowd dispersed.

Bezalel peeked into the room after the others left. He had seen many dead bodies, including a few suicides. Slaves died all the time. He had helped bury many of them. Jannes looked like a poisoning should look. His body was on the floor, face drawn up into a grimace, hands clenched. A bottle of potion lay nearby. Then Bezalel looked at the magician's neck. There were raised red marks around it, welts, like something had squeezed tightly. But Jambres said Jannes poisoned himself. There shouldn't be marks around his neck if he were poisoned....

"May I help you?" Jambres spoke from behind him.

Though Bezalel felt the sorcerer meant to be anything but helpful, he turned to face him. "I'm sorry. I was ... curious."

"We have to clear this room now. Death contaminates it. You must leave."

"Yes. I'm sorry." Bezalel watched as Jambres, his composure suddenly regained, picked up several bottles and his thawb.

"Here, hold this while I lock the door." The magician shoved the luxurious wrap at Bezalel. It was of the finest linen, gold strands woven throughout. Jambres locked the door, grabbed his thawb, and took off toward the courtyard.

Bezalel couldn't help but notice that Jambres's garment had red trim.

On a whim, Bezalel wandered farther down the hall. After the magicians' rooms came the kitchen, and then the walkway to the harem. The king's private quarters, taking up a third of the palace, lay beyond that.

He turned left. He wanted to see where Ahmose had lived. The harem would be empty and unguarded during the day. The children usually studied and played outside this time of year, often relaxing on covered barges on the river. It should be safe for him to look around.

He parted the layers of linen curtains and stepped inside. The narrow entrance belied an enormous room, with a limestone floor comprised of two levels. Stuffed cushions and mats, grouped together in twos and threes, littered the wide outer level. Tunics and combs and boxes of ointments and perfumes lay near each set.

He walked down the steps and into the spacious center filled with trays of fruit, wooden toys, and parchments rolled into scrolls. Mothers and children must sleep on the outer level, and eat and play and spend time together in the center. A lovely arrangement—unless you had no one to share it with.

Bezalel took the two steps back up in one jump and was almost out the door when someone coughed. He turned to his left and spotted the girl sitting on a cushion, her back against the wall near the door. She hid in the shadows, and had she not made herself known, he would have walked right by her again on his way out. She stood and glided toward him.

He took in a sharp breath. She was even more beautiful than he remembered her. Without her heavy kohl makeup, her deep brown eyes seemed to take up her whole face, though they still radiated sadness.

Bezalel's mouth went dry. He started to speak but no words came out. He felt like a fish that had landed on the bank gasping for air, his mouth opening and closing. The closer she got, the more stupid he felt.

Her long, black hair fell straight this time—no fancy pins or flowers. Her new tunic was not torn as before, and made of the silkiest linen, not rough and coarse like his. It skimmed her body perfectly, and when she walked it swayed and made his head spin. Three vertical rows of tiny blue-black dots ran down each arm from just below the shoulder to above the elbow: the mark of a concubine.

"Excuse me." She stepped closer. She was about a head shorter than he was.

That same scent of jasmine. Much as he wanted to, he tried not to close his eyes and drink it in. "Y-yes." He surprised himself by managing to get the word out and then keeping his mouth closed.

"I wanted to thank you for your kindnesses to me … uh … before." She came even closer and reached up to touch his neck but stopped just short. "I see your bruise healed nicely."

His breath came faster. "Yes, it did. And you're welcome." His heart beat wildly, and he could barely hear his own voice over the pounding in his ears. He hoped his cheeks didn't look as red as they felt.

"My name is Meri."

Her voice sounded like honey tasted. "I'm Bezalel." She was so close—he just wanted to touch her. He looked away, over her shoulder to steady his heartbeat, and noticed a ragged mat by itself in the far corner. He glanced around at the numerous opulent cushions and linens and returned his gaze to the mat.

Meri turned to follow his stare. "A little boy slept there for a while when I first came here. He was all alone. I never did figure out why. He was the sweetest child. But he left about a month ago. No one knows where he went."

Bezalel swallowed hard. "Is anyone looking for him?"

She turned back to face him. "I don't think so. No one seemed to pay much attention to him. And when I first came here, I didn't either, I'm afraid. I was just getting to know him. I wish I had tried harder. He seemed so alone." She looked up at him, her dark, sad eyes locked on his, as if she were seeking his forgiveness.

"I think you had your own problems." He smiled, and the smile he received in return sent a wave of warmth pulsing through his body. "Why aren't you with the others?"

She waved her hand toward the river. "They're out teaching their children. I don't have any, obviously. Besides, I hate it here. I don't belong. Everyone else wanted to be his concubine. I didn't. There hasn't been a new girl around in several years and I've upset things. They don't like me, and I'm not too fond of any of them, either." She paused, and let out a deep breath. "That sounds awful, doesn't it?"

A smile spread across his face. "No." He chuckled as he saw her frown. "Not at all."

Six

Bezalel passed a fig tree and plucked several pieces of the sweet, meaty fruit. A desert fox ran across his path.

As he approached his home, Ahmose came running, jumped into his arms, and wrapped his short legs around Bezalel's waist before Bezalel had a chance to bid him good evening. Wearing an Israelite tunic and no makeup, Ahmose looked quite Hebrew. His hair and sharper features could give him away, but only if someone looked closely.

"Hello, habibi! How was your day? Did you miss me?" Bezalel kissed his cheek and squeezed him as he stepped into the main room.

"Yes! But I had fun with Aunt Rebekah. She spoiled me today. I have done no work at all!"

Bezalel put Ahmose down. "As it should be for a boy your age." He shed his thawb and tossed it on the low table. "*Aunt* Rebekah? Really?"

"Well, what should he call me?" Imma shrugged and smiled.

"Can we go to the river?" Ahmose asked.

"No, I have some news to talk to you about. It's better here. Besides, the river is very full and fast right now." Bezalel called his grandfather to the main room.

"Good or bad?"

"I'll let you decide. Jannes died today."

"He did?" A look of disbelief spread across Ahmose's face.

"Yes."

The look melted into one of revelation. "Then he is no longer my master! I can stay here!" He jumped up and down and clapped his hands.

Bezalel chuckled. Imma laughed with Ahmose, but Sabba remained silent.

Bezalel sent Ahmose outside to play with the village children. Although most servants knew Egyptian, and few Egyptians bothered to learn Hebrew, he wanted to take no chances. The three of them discussed the situation in Hebrew.

"So now what happens?" Sabba crossed his arms over his chest.

"Why can't he live with us?" Imma pleaded with her father-in-law.

Bezalel sighed. "I think it may depend on what Jambres wants."

"Who's Jambres?" Imma asked.

"Jannes's assistant, and now the chief magician. He inherited everything else of Jannes's. He may want Ahmose. He may start asking questions, even search for him." Bezalel took a long breath. "There is one more thing."

Sabba closed his eyes a moment. "What else?"

"The captain of the guard came to me today. His name is Kamose. He claims to be Ahmose's uncle, and asked me where he is."

"What did you tell him?"

"Nothing. His interest seemed genuine, but how am I to trust him? For all I know, he's working for Jambres."

"True. Ahmose may stay, but we must continue to be careful." Sabba shrugged. "We shall take it one day at a time."

Under the light of the full moon, Ahmose played with enthusiasm until after dark. Later, on the roof, he fell asleep easily.

But Bezalel watched the stars for many hours before sleep blessed him with its oblivion. He had not told them about seeing Jambres in the hallway, or about the marks on Jannes's neck. After all, what was there to say? He had only questions, and doubts.

రావ్

Bezalel arrived at the palace as the sun rose to find Kamose waiting for him outside his room.

"What did you see when you looked into Jannes's room?" The captain spoke before Bezalel took off his thawb.

"What?"

"What did you see in Jannes's room?"

"Only his body." Bezalel stood behind his worktable, trying to put distance between the soldier and himself.

"Was there anything unusual about it?"

"Are you getting at something in particular?" Bezalel tilted his head.

"I am investigating his death. I need to know if you saw anything suspicious. You were one of the few to see the body before Jambres took it away."

Bezalel turned away for a moment to hide his surprise—and fear. The captain's dark and brooding eyes unnerved him. "You don't believe it was suicide?"

"It doesn't matter what I believe." Kamose took a step closer.

"I saw … I saw nothing that could help you." Bezalel stepped back.

Kamose fixed his glare on Bezalel. "Then follow me."

He marched down the hallway toward the private areas, looking back only once to be sure Bezalel followed. His sandaled footfalls echoed off the tiled walls with each heavy stride. He stopped outside Jannes's old quarters. "Jambres kept all of Jannes's servants as well as his own. And he wants more."

Jambres was elsewhere, but the room still bustled. Although most of Jannes's furnishings remained, servants carried a few pieces out and brought many more in. Workmen cut a huge arch in an inner wall that had divided Jannes's rooms from Jambres's. His accommodations would now be much larger than Jannes's had ever been.

Kamose strode to the center and swept his hand across the growing space. "Jambres claims all this area—more than anyone except Ramses himself—though he has accomplished nothing on his own. Jannes duplicated the blood and frogs, but not the gnats. Jambres has tried to summon them, but failed. And he now demands land and an exemption from taxation."

Bezalel raised an eyebrow. "He is setting himself up as equal to a priest?"

"Apparently." Kamose walked farther into the sorcerer's room and turned to face Bezalel. "I do not wish to see him with privileges he did not earn and does not deserve. It is my duty to protect my king at the cost of my life, and I will do whatever that requires." He crossed back to Bezalel and stopped, folding his massive arms on his chest. "Now, what can you tell me?"

Bezalel rubbed his hand over the back of his neck and shook his head. Jambres might be a threat to Pharaoh and the natural order of the palace. Maybe he did kill Jannes, maybe he didn't. Maybe he had grander ambitions than Chief Sorcerer. But Bezalel could not afford to worry about that, and he would not risk upsetting someone who could hurt Ahmose.

Kamose would have to do this on his own.

First month of Peret, Season of Growing

A cooler wind brushed over the desert sands, and the sun's heat was less cruel. The Nile had called the waters back to within its banks, and farmers planted barley, wheat, and flax. Oxen dragged rustic plows, and farmers trailed behind them dropping seed. Pigs trod the seed into the rich black earth. Growing season had arrived.

Bezalel ambled toward the river as sunlight danced over the water. The king strolled toward the Nile with his entourage. He watched as Ramses reached the water's edge, servants fulfilling his every wish before he even spoke them aloud.

Moses appeared from the north and stopped an arm's length from the king. He drew closer than normally allowed. Guards moved to pull Moses away, but Ramses held up his hand to call them off.

"I assume you are here again to ask me to let 'your people' go."

"I am." Moses lifted his face, eyes blinking in the eastern light. "You promised you would release us once Yahweh called the frogs back to the Nile."

"The frogs returned of their own accord. The Nile called them back, not your God." The king chose a plum from a platter of ripe fruit a young—and barely clothed—girl held out for him.

"And the gnats?"

"You gave me no warning of the gnats. Why should I believe they came from your God?" Ramses's gaze wandered toward the river. He was apparently tiring of the conversation.

"Do you expect El Shaddai, the Almighty God, to tell you all His plans?" Moses smiled. "But so you know, the gnats came from the earth. And your god of the earth, Geb, was not mighty enough to stop them."

"I still have no proof they were sent from your God." Ramses bit into the plum. Juice ran down his chin. The girl wiped it off.

"Very well. Perhaps this will prove it. If you do not promise to let us go right now, before the sun disappears from the sky there will be swarms of biting flies in all of Egypt."

Ramses scoffed. "Yes, but remember that anything I suffer, you will suffer as well."

"Ah, but this time the Lord will deal differently with Goshen." Moses pointed his thumb over his shoulder toward the Israelite villages. "Not a single fly will touch my people in Goshen. As for

Egypt, they will be on you, on your officials, on all your people, in your houses, on the ground, and even on your food."

Ramses snorted. "That's impossible! How can they be here and not a short walk away? Will you build a wall to the sky?"

Moses shrugged. "El Shaddai is the Lord God. Everything is possible."

Ramses raised a finger and guards moved in toward Moses. One put a hand to his dagger.

Moses left quietly.

Here and not in Goshen? This, Bezalel would have to see to believe.

࿇

Until Bezalel could determine whether Jambres was after Ahmose, the magician was still a danger. Bezalel left his workroom to find out what he could about Jambres.

Turtledoves on a perch hanging between two pillars cooed softly as he entered the throne room. He crossed the wide expanse and strode down the hall toward Jambres's living quarters. As he neared the door, it swung open wide and two young girls exited, grabbing on to the doorposts and to each other. They stumbled toward the harem.

He crept toward the door, careful to watch out for anyone else who might come out of the room, then peeked around the doorpost. Jambres lay face down on a rug in the middle of the room, naked, hair wild, his fingers through the handle of a depleted wine jar. Empty beer pots were strewn on every flat surface. Half-eaten fruit and loaves of bread were scattered on the floor. Another of Ramses's concubines lay passed out on the bed, half-dressed.

Bezalel retreated a few steps and leaned against the wall. He ran his hands through his hair. On the one hand, this probably meant Jambres was far more interested in abusing his newfound power than retrieving a tiny slave who could hardly be of much service to him. On the other, it meant he was devious beyond belief. Sleeping with the king's concubines? There weren't too many crimes considered more serious.

Bezalel rubbed his hand down his face, and when he looked up, Kamose rounded the corner down the hall. Bezalel froze.

The captain stopped a moment then disappeared into Jambres's room for a few moments. When he emerged, he carried the sleeping girl in his arms, now with a tunic draped over her, and headed toward the harem.

This would be a good time to leave.

Back in his room Bezalel grabbed a handful of raisins. He had barely sat on his stool when Kamose walked in.

"You know more than you are telling me." The captain stepped across the room to within arm's reach of him. "We should talk."

"Talk about what?"

"What you saw in the room the day Jannes died." Kamose planted his feet, crossed his arms over his chest, and stared down. He obviously planned to stay until he got the information he wanted.

Bezalel poured the raisins from one hand to the other and back again. It couldn't hurt to tell Kamose now. It might even help keep Jambres from Ahmose. "I saw welts around Jannes's neck."

"Welts?"

"Red welts. Like someone had—" He hesitated. Should he make such an accusation?

"Like what?"

"Like someone had choked him." Bezalel let out a long breath. There. He had said it.

"I see. And what did you see in the room before I went in just now?"

"I saw two girls leave and head for the harem. Both drunk."

Kamose shook his head and paced for a moment. "I don't suppose you have anything to tell me about Ahmose?"

Bezalel looked at his feet and said nothing. Could he trust this man yet?

"I thought as much."

When the captain left, Bezalel threw the raisins at the table. Could things get any more complicated?

∽∾

The sun slid behind the horizon and the blue lotus blossoms began to close. A full moon was rising. Bezalel was strolling the palace gardens watching the flowers when an army of flies appeared from the east over the Nile. The bugs fanned out in all directions—into the palace, toward the homes of farmers and officials, and into the fields. The buzzing filled the air and Bezalel's ears.

Bezalel ducked and covered his face with his arms as they flew over him. None touched him. He stepped back inside, and within moments the palace was in chaos. He stood frozen as servants screamed. These bugs gnawed skin wherever they could find it, often so violently they drew blood. Children ran screeching, searching for their mothers. Adults scrambled to find mesh or fine netting. Next to him a small boy gave up, sat down, and simply howled. Unlike the gnats, which were merely annoying, the bite of these flies was excruciating, especially to the youngest.

Bezalel picked up the boy and scurried to the harem. The guards had abandoned their posts. He pushed aside the curtains and set the screaming child down on an empty cushion. He attempted to wrap some nearby netting around him, but the child's hysteria would not allow him to wind it tightly enough to provide any protection.

He wasn't even supposed to be inside the harem, but no one cared enough to send him away.

Bezalel sprinted to his room.

Not a single fly was inside.

Breathing hard, he knelt by his bed and reached under it. He dug through bags, opening some and tossing them aside, until he found what he searched for: a large supply of fine netting and light linen. He grabbed one large piece and stuffed it down the front of his tunic. He gathered the rest in his arms, carried it back to the harem, and passed it among the mothers and older children.

Helping tuck the mesh around tiny squirming bodies was like trying to push the Nile back into its banks during flood season. As soon as one child was covered, another was loose. Their cries pierced his ears and made his heart ache.

And the flies just kept coming.

Bezalel dropped to his knees and groaned loudly. He looked to his left at some of the older children. Their eyes were swollen red masses. He looked more closely. Bugs had latched onto their eyelids. He reached under the netting and tried to pull them off one of the boys. The child screamed and kicked and grabbed at his hands. Bezalel let go, but the bugs continued to suck blood. He grabbed the child's hands with one of his, and the flies with the other, and finally pried them loose.

After tending to what felt like hundreds of swollen eyes, he stood and looked around the cavernous room for Meri. Finally he saw her, crouching in a corner, her arms covering her head, trying to hold a child's tunic over her face to keep the bugs away. He rushed to her.

Flies and angry red spots covered her arms and hands.

He knelt beside her. "Meri?"

He was sure the frantic noise around them made it impossible for her to hear him. He gently touched her arm and leaned closer. "Meri? It's me, Bezalel."

A guttural noise emerged from behind the cloth.

He pulled the softer linen from inside his tunic and wrapped it around her shoulders and arms. "Meri? I'm going to pick you up. Don't be frightened."

He put one arm under her knees, slipped one behind her back, and lifted her off the floor. There was enough chaos in the room that no one noticed he stole a girl right out of the harem.

He took her into his room and laid her gently on his bed then lit a lamp. He sat beside her and lifted the linen and the tunic. He brushed away the wet, matted hair from her face. His chest constricted and he almost cried when he saw the chewed and raw skin on her face, arms, and feet. Her eyes were bulging scarlet spheres. A fly still clung to her left eye, and he pulled it off.

She whimpered and a tear escaped.

"I'm going to the kitchen to get you some basil. I'll be right back," he whispered.

She only moaned.

He ran to the kitchen. His chest ached to think of her in so much pain. Why? *Why, why, why?* This plan was not working! Was El Shaddai paying any attention at all? Just what exactly was He trying to accomplish?

The kitchen was deserted. He found the long shelf in a corner with the herbs and spices but saw no basil. He growled and slammed his fist into the mud brick wall. He leaned his hands and head against the wall and calmed himself then turned and took another look. Eventually, he discovered some basil in a basket under a worktable and ripped off all the leaves he could. He dropped them onto a plate and crushed several with the back of a spoon. When he had a good amount of juice, he picked up the plate and went back to his room, shaking his smashed hand as he jogged.

He knocked lightly before entering. "Meri?" He sat next to her and rolled her toward him. He dipped his fingers in the basil juice and smeared it on her arms. After covering her arms and feet, he used one finger and brushed it across her eyelids. He took off his thawb and placed it over her.

Her breathing seemed to ease.

He brushed her hair away from her face. "I'm going to let you sleep here tonight. I'll go somewhere else. I'll find you tomorrow."

He slipped out as quietly as he could and headed for the river, toward the rocks from which he and Ahmose had watched the frogs retreat. In the moonlight he looked toward the palace. The swarm enveloped the building like honey poured over a wheat cake.

⋙⋘

The warm sunrise breeze in his face awakened Bezalel early. He found himself reclining against the flat side of a rock facing the river, his muscles stiff and sore. He stood, stretched, and looked west. The swarm had withdrawn.

He sprinted for the palace. The courtyard and throne room were silent and empty.

Kamose emerged from the hallway as Bezalel entered from the courtyard. Crimson spots covered every bit of the soldier's exposed skin, and his eyes were swollen.

Kamose strode toward Bezalel, grasped his arms, turned them over. "You are not bitten. Why?"

"El Shaddai promised his people would not be bitten." Bezalel winced and extricated his arms from Kamose's grasp.

Kamose furrowed his brow. "El Shaddai? He is your God?"

"El Shaddai is the creator of all." Bezalel wasn't completely sure that was true, but he wasn't about to admit anything different to an Egyptian. It was true that among the palace residents he, and he alone, was not bitten. And yesterday his room had remained completely free of flies. That was worth some consideration, at least.

Kamose shook his head. "That's what Ptah says he is."

Bezalel took a deep breath. "I have some basil. It will take the pain from the bites." He headed toward his room. They crossed the length of the portico and Bezalel slowly opened the door to his workroom and peeked in. He didn't want Kamose to see he had a girl—an Egyptian girl, at that—in his room.

Meri was gone.

The plate of basil sat on the table.

Bezalel opened the door wide and beckoned the soldier inside. He took a leaf and crushed it between his fingers. He rubbed the crushed leaf on a couple of bites on the soldier's arm. Kamose's continued stare made him uneasy.

"We use this for embalming." Kamose took the leaf from Bezalel and continued rubbing. "I am sure we can get more."

"I thought for now… especially for the children…."

"Thank you. I'll see it gets to them." Kamose took the herb and left.

Bezalel went to the door and watched as the captain walked down the hall and disappeared into the walkway to the harem then returned without the basil, save a few leaves for himself.

Bezalel collapsed on his bed, the bed she had slept on all night. His thawb lay nearby, neatly folded. He picked it up and held it to his face—the fabric smelled of jasmine mingled with the healing herb. He closed his eyes and his head spun. He had not slept much last night. The hard rock, the sight of her swollen eyes, remembering how she felt in his arms… it all kept rattling around and around in his mind and sleep had eluded him.

None of this makes any sense. And none of it is bringing us any closer to what Shaddai has promised.

He had far too many questions and not nearly enough answers. Not the least of which was when he would see Meri again. He put his arm over his eyes and allowed himself to drift off to sleep.

Seven

Second month of Peret, Season of Growing

Bezalel pulled his thawb closer around him as he entered the small house. The coolest part of the year had finally arrived. "Sabba? Imma?"

"Come in, habibi. You must join me for dinner." Even in his old age, Sabba was tall and solidly built, like Bezalel, and like his father had been. What he remembered of his father, anyway. Sabba's dark eyes twinkled when he smiled, which was often. His long hair and beard were completely white, and had been so ever since Bezalel could remember. He still stood straight, even after his many years in the brickfields. His strong hands placed several bowls of food onto the table. "Your mother has gone to help Sarah down the street, who just had a baby. She won't return for a while, maybe not until tomorrow. Ahmose is with her. Hungry?"

"No, thank you, I have already eaten." Bezalel slumped to the floor on the other side of the small table from his grandfather. He absently picked up a handful of fat, ripe dates, dropping several.

"Tired?" Sabba offered Bezalel some water.

"No."

"Unhappy?"

"No."

Sabba laughed. "What is wrong, Bezalel?"

"Why do you ask?" Bezalel peeked under the table for the dropped dates.

"Because you say you aren't hungry but you eat; you say you aren't tired but you stumble; you say you aren't sad but you do not smile."

"What do you think of Moses?" Bezalel frowned.

"Ah. Right to the point. As always. Well, what do you think?"

"I think he is only making things worse. Ramses is only becoming more determined to keep us here."

"Perhaps." Sabba pulled apart a date and removed the large seed. "But let us dig deeper. What do you think of Shaddai?"

Bezalel groaned. "Must we?"

"Must we what?"

"Must we talk about that?"

"Isn't that really the point here? Moses is not the issue. Moses is not doing anything. It is either the work of El Shaddai, or it isn't. It is either the Lord God Almighty, who will in fact free us at the end of these signs, or just a terrible string of calamities. You need to decide soon what you believe."

Sabba leaned on his forearms. "He gave us the name *El Shaddai* for a reason. He is powerful, mighty, strong. You can cling to that, or you can be blown about like a leaf in the winds of a *khamsin*."

Bezalel sat silently and chewed on his dates.

Sabba disappeared into the kitchen. When he returned he carried two cups and some juice. "It has been a long, long time since we talked about anything important." He filled both glasses.

"I've been busy at the palace."

"Oh."

They ate in silence for a while.

"Is that all?"

Bezalel slammed down his cup and sighed deeply.

Sabba placed his hand over Bezalel's. "Why are you so angry, habibi?"

"Why? I'll tell you why. Because I am trapped in that palace. Everyone *there* thinks I am unworthy. Everyone *here* thinks I am a traitor. I don't get to see my family. All because, as you have always told me, El Shaddai gave me a gift. A gift that has isolated me since I was seven years old!"

"Shaddai's ways are not always clear to us. They do not always make sense to us. But I will always believe that He had a reason for placing you there. Someday you will see it, I am sure. I am only sorry that every day is so miserable for you now."

Bezalel could feel a smile come to his lips. He tried to hide it, but it was no use.

"What is this smile?" Sabba bent his head to try to see Bezalel's face. "You have met a girl?"

"She is so beautiful. Her eyes are so...amazing. I hardly know her but..."

Sabba chuckled. "See, your life is not so bad. You can have a home, a family like anyone else."

"She's Egyptian."

"Oh." Sabba raised his eyebrows. He was silent for a few moments as he finished his bread. "We do not always choose whom we love."

"How is that supposed to help me?" Bezalel shoved his food away and put his elbows on the table. "Even if anything were to happen with her, I couldn't bring her here. And we couldn't live there. Besides, she..."

Sabba raised his eyebrows again. "She what?"

"She's part of the harem." Bezalel dropped his head onto his arms.

"Oh, my." Sabba rubbed Bezalel's shoulder and blew out a long breath. "Well, that does complicate things a bit, doesn't it?"

∾ ∿

Bezalel stood in the courtyard in the brightest part of the day. The sun shone over his back onto the rose alabaster, highlighting the striations running through it. The head and shoulders had emerged from the stone, and he drew a fine claw in gentle waves to shape the queen's tunic. He brushed off the dust.

Ramses strode by, flicking a whip. "What do you mean, I have no horses? I have a stable full of horses!"

"They are all dead, Father." Prince Amun-her followed closely behind.

"All dead?" Ramses stopped in the middle of the yard and spun about.

"Yes, my king," an officer added.

"I have hundreds of horses! How are they all dead? Why did the goddess Hathor not protect them?"

"I cannot say. Every head of cattle and every horse in Egypt has died. The oxen and donkeys, too."

"Well, get me some more!"

"From where, Father?" His son spread his hands.

"There are men on patrol on our borders; surely their horses are not dead." Ramses paced.

"Perhaps not, but they are many days' ride away. It will be a while before we can call them back."

"Then I suggest you waste no time standing here! Call them back!" Ramses's eyes were wide and the veins on his neck stood out.

The officer withdrew.

Ramses placed his hand on his son's elbow. "You leave too, habibi. And send Jambres to me." He pointed his whip at a servant. "Bring me some food!"

Bezalel remained still and prayed he attracted no attention.

The servant obeyed, and within moments Jambres appeared.

"Yes, my king." He bowed at the king's nod.

"What can you do to get me back my horses? And whatever else died?"

What doesn't he understand about the word 'dead'?

Jambres stood tall. "It is an enormous request you make of your servant. I shall need time."

"How much time?" The king leaned forward until his face was a hand's width from the much shorter magician's, causing him to stumble back several paces.

"Several…several days. Even then, I may not be able to do anything. Osiris does not give up his dead easily."

The pharaoh reared back. "What kind of magician are you? You are no better than Jannes! What a pair you made!" The king's dry laugh harbored no amusement.

The magician held up a finger. "Wait! The Israelite caused the livestock to die, yes?"

"So he claims."

"Perhaps we should make him pay for his crimes against mighty Egypt."

"How so?" Ramses stepped forward, apparently gaining interest.

Jambres looked around the courtyard and met Bezalel's wary gaze. He lifted a hand toward the throne. "Shall we? There are ears here.…"

The king nodded and walked toward the dais. Jambres followed, and Bezalel was left standing alone.

Pay for his crimes? What was that supposed to mean? Perhaps he should warn Moses. But warn him of what? He had no idea what Jambres meant.

⥼ ⥽

Leaning in the doorway to his home in Goshen, Bezalel pondered Jambres's threat as he braided some linen ribbons. Ramses did not pout as usual, although it had been many days since the livestock died. He seemed to be waiting for something, but what that something was, Bezalel had not been able to discover.

He was still trying to figure it out when a noise from the direction of the palace caught his attention. In just a few moments, the sound grew deafening. Figures appeared at the edge of the village.

Egyptian horsemen rode hard. He stared, unable to move, as they descended upon the village and spread out. Most headed north of the houses to the animal pens; the rest spilled onto the tiny streets of the village. The three on his lane dismounted and kicked in the door of the first house they came upon. After a few moments they reappeared and burst into the next house.

Bezalel finally pulled himself away from the doorpost. He stumbled backwards into his home, still transfixed by the soldiers. Obviously they had retrieved their horses from the border. "Sabba, come quickly! Soldiers! They're searching every house!"

Sabba grabbed his arm. "Fast! Onto the roof! It's the safest place. Maybe they won't bother to climb up. Let them search down here all they want."

Bezalel scrambled up the ladder behind Sabba. Imma already waited, almost in tears.

"Where's Ahmose?" Bezalel glanced around and peered down the ladder.

"He's playing down the street at Sarah's house. He'll be safe." Imma pulled him away from the ladder.

Bezalel paced frantically on the roof, running his hands through his hair. His heart beat wildly and he could barely catch his breath. What did they want? Could they be after Ahmose? Could they be after *him* for taking the child?

"Bezalel, where are you?" A trembling voice called from below.

"Ahmose!" Bezalel jumped down the ladder and landed hard.

The soldiers slammed into the house next door. Through the shared mud brick wall, every noise the men made resounded. Tables crashed, pottery shattered, children shrieked, commands echoed.

Bezalel fell to his knees in front of Ahmose and grabbed him by both shoulders. "You must not say *anything*, no matter what happens. Do you understand me?"

Ahmose's eyes were the size of spring plums. He quivered in Bezalel's grip.

Bezalel squeezed tighter and pulled the boy closer until they were almost nose to nose. "Do you understand?" Though he was learning Hebrew quickly, the child's accent would give him away in a heart-beat. Bezalel had to keep him from talking.

Ahmose gave a feeble nod.

Blood flowed through Bezalel's body faster and hotter, and his heart pounded in his ears. The men left the house next door. Theirs was next.

Imma and Sabba were safe on the roof, but there remained no time to climb back up and join them.

Sweat beaded on Bezalel's forehead and ran down his cheek. He sank to the ground and crawled into a corner, pulling Ahmose into his lap. Tears flowed from Ahmose's eyes. Bezalel put one hand across the boy's mouth and wrapped his other arm around his small body. A crying child would only make things worse.

What could they want? The last time soldiers came into their vil-lage, they killed every male baby without warning. Of course, that was eighty years ago. Sabba had told him about it. Weeping went on for days as women mourned their sons. The soldiers even grabbed nursing babies and threw them into the river. The blood in the Nile that day must have been as much as it was a few months ago.

The door slamming open and the sound of shod feet storming through his house brought him back to the present. Israelites wore no shoes in the house, and neither did Egyptians. Soldiers always wore them.

"Where are your animals?" The soldier pointed a dagger at Bezalel.

"In the sheep pen with the others." Why won't they take what they want and leave?

"You have only sheep?"

"Nothing else."

The officer reached for Ahmose, picked him up by the arm and tossed him to the other side of the room. Ahmose cried out but did not speak.

Everything else in the room faded and Bezalel lunged at the soldier. Rage coursed through his body. But before he could land any punches, another grabbed him from behind, holding his wrists and twisting them up behind his shoulders. Fire shot through his arms and he groaned as he tried to find a position that didn't pull on his joints. He glanced at the frightened child lying still, his back against the wall. Was he dead? Or just terrified?

"What are you hiding?" The first soldier kneed him in the stomach as he gestured to the corner where he had tried to hide Ahmose.

He crumpled but was held fast by the iron grip of the man behind him. His shoulders burned again. "Nothing! Let me go!" He tried to free his arms but could not.

"What is going on here?" A third officer entered the room. Bezalel recognized the voice and stopped struggling.

"Captain!" The soldier holding Bezalel dropped his arms, and Bezalel collapsed. "We thought he was hiding something."

"A horse? Behind his back?" Kamose seized the soldier and shoved him out the door. "We are here to collect livestock, not injure the slaves. Get out of here before I report this to your squad leader. Or worse, discipline you myself."

"Yes, Captain."

Bezalel crawled to Ahmose, his upper arms and shoulders in agony with every movement.

Kamose strode over to the tiny figure slumped against the wall and pointed to Ahmose's quaking body. "My men did this?" He knelt beside him and lifted Ahmose's face.

Bezalel looked at the boy, grateful to see movement. Relief

washed over him and he let out a deep breath. "Yes." *Please, Shaddai, please don't let him recognize Ahmose.*

Kamose's eyes widened as he studied the child's features. He looked over at Bezalel for what felt like an eternity. He opened his mouth and shook his head. Then he simply rose and walked out.

Bezalel pulled the boy close. "Ahmose, they're gone! Open your eyes. It's me!"

Ahmose slowly opened his eyes and searched the room. Then he threw his arms around Bezalel and wept, his little body shuddering with giant sobs.

ॐॐ

Back at work the next day, Bezalel knew Kamose would demand an explanation, and if the captain did not like what he had to say, he could easily have him thrown in any one of Ramses's many prisons. He busied his mind with the coronation bracelets, polishing and shaping the gemstones destined for the bands.

The sun had nearly set before Kamose arrived. Bezalel's empty stomach was a painful bundle of knots.

"Why did you deceive me?" Kamose's voice was low, almost wounded.

Bezalel had never heard the man speak in a manner that was not forceful and sure of himself. It was almost frightening.

"I feared for Ahmose."

"I told you I meant him no harm."

Bezalel let out a long breath. "He was covered in welts and dried blood when he came to me. Would you have believed your story in my position?"

"I suppose not." Kamose pulled up a stool near him. "Tell me, why is he at your house?"

"I took him home after Jannes beat him the last time. According to him, it was not the first beating."

"So you thought you should take him home with you?"

"Yes. Uh, no. Well, first I only wanted to take care of his back. It was a reckless move, I know, but then Jannes died, and I was afraid Jambres would come looking for Ahmose. He hasn't—not yet, anyway. But then I worried Ahmose would be punished for running away. So we ended up ... letting him stay."

Kamose nodded.

"So, are you really his uncle?" Bezalel poured some fruit juice into two cups and offered one to Kamose.

"Yes. Jannes persuaded my sister, Tia, to become part of Ramses's harem. The lifestyle, the riches, they intrigued her. But it destroyed her. When she discovered she was to have a child, she could not bear it. She died the night she bore Ahmose."

Kamose drained his cup. "I told no one she was my sister; she begged me not to. When she knew she was dying, and she realized her child would be treated as a slave instead of a royal child like the others, she called for me. She asked me to watch out for him as best I could, keeping the secret. I agreed.

"She didn't even give the boy a name before she died. My parents named me after King Kamose, a pharaoh hundreds of years ago. His younger brother, Ahmose, established Egypt as the greatest land in the world. I named the baby Ahmose, so the power of that name would rest on him." He stared at his cup for several moments. "I hoped it would protect him.

"I have watched him for seven years, but he doesn't know who I am. I knew Jannes beat him, but I didn't know how badly."

Bezalel took the cup from Kamose. "Ahmose told me Jannes hated him because his mother died. Do you know what he meant?"

Kamose nodded. "To gain favors, Jannes always tried to find pretty young women for the king. And Tia was beyond beautiful. Ramses liked her, and Jannes gained the title of Chief Magician for finding such a beautiful woman for him. Tia was a favorite of

Ramses—for a few months. Then, as with all the others, he grew bored and returned to Nefertari."

Kamose stood and walked to the window. After a few moments, he continued. "She was by this time pregnant, and devastated. She could not face a life of neglect and shame. She knew Ramses would never love her, knew he never really had. Yet she was not free to leave or wed anyone else.

"She would rarely eat. She stayed in the harem's quarters. She would not even let me see her. Childbirth was simply too much for her."

Kamose turned to face Bezalel. "When my sister died, Ramses held Jannes responsible. Ramses made Jambres Jannes's 'Chief Assistant,' but he was more like a watchdog. The two never got along. They fought to be the best constantly. Jannes took Ahmose to be his personal slave to get some sense of revenge, and he took it out on Ahmose every day. Jambres sometimes did, too. I don't trust that man."

"So do you want Ahmose back now?" *Please say no. Please.*

Kamose thought for a long moment. "I don't think that would be best for him. Who am I to care for a small boy? I am a soldier. And they would punish him severely if he returned." He stepped up to the table. "You seem to be an honorable man. It was obvious at your house yesterday that you care a great deal for Ahmose. I think it best he stay with you. If you want him, that is."

"I think you would have a hard time convincing my mother to give him up." Bezalel laughed.

"Then that is where he belongs. Tia would be happy."

As Bezalel lay down to sleep that night, the cool breeze caressed his face. He loved watching the stars. Soon it would be too cool at night to sleep outside. He looked over at Ahmose. The child's face radiated peace. He knew Jannes was dead and he could stay, and that was all he needed to know.

But there was far more that Bezalel needed to know. What was Jambres planning? Was he still a threat to Ahmose? If Shaddai sent Moses, why was there so much trouble? And what was next? Would Ramses ever release them?

He did know a few things now. He knew that no matter what Ahmose thought, this was not the end. He knew there would be more trouble, chaos, and pain to come. And above all, he knew nothing would ever be simple again.

Bezalel bent over the table and inspected the carnelian pebble. The midday sun streamed through the high window and bounced off the ruddy rock and its white streaks. The necklace needed only one more rounded stone. He rolled the small rock back and forth in a groove cut in a long piece of sandstone, spinning the red carnelian around and around to make a perfect sphere.

He stood and dragged the back of his hand across his damp forehead. He looked up.

She stood in the doorway, leaning against the frame, watching him, smiling. Her long hair fell forward over one shoulder, and the gold strands in her tunic reflected the sunlight.

How long has she been there?

She walked in without asking and set a loaf of bread and two plums on the table. "I wanted to thank you for the other night. I know it was a few weeks ago, but I looked pretty bad for a while."

"I doubt that." He smiled when her cheeks colored. He took a plum and sat, and motioned to the other stool.

She sat across from him. "Anyway, I thought I would bring you something to eat to say thank you."

"You're welcome." He bit into the plum, never taking his eyes off her. "How did you get out of the harem?"

"They're on the river again. No one cares what I do, anyway."

"I do." He winked at her.

Again her cheeks turned pink.

Bezalel grinned. He finished his plum and tossed the seed into a basket. "Would you like to take a walk by the river?"

"That'd be very nice. I haven't been outside the palace much."

He grabbed his thawb and led her across the portico and courtyard, and they strolled toward the Nile. When they reached his favorite rocks, he climbed up, spread his thawb out, then turned around and reached for her hand.

She hesitated. "I don't like climbing. It frightens me."

"It's safe. I won't let you fall."

She waited a moment longer and grabbed his hand. She placed her feet carefully and clambered up with his help. When she sat and looked over the river, she let out a long breath. "It's so beautiful."

"Haven't you been down here before?"

"No, I told you. I haven't been off the palace grounds."

"What about before? Where did you live before?"

"We lived way off the river, on a small farm. It was too far to walk here. And we never had a reason."

"I don't know what I'd do if I couldn't see the river every day. I love watching it. I love the animals and birds, all the life on it. It's just amazing."

"Well, I know what crocodiles and hippos are, but that's about it." She giggled. "What's that?" She pointed to a leggy bird in front of them.

"That's a heron. He eats fish. He is magnificent when he flies. His wingspan is wider than a man is tall." He spread his arms wide. "And the white one, with the black ends on his feathers is a sacred ibis." He continued pointing out birds and animals for a while.

She grew quiet. "Bezalel?"

"Hmm?"

"I wanted to tell you about the time you found me. At the end of the hall?"

His thoughts went back to the day she was sobbing outside the storeroom, her tunic torn, her feet bloody.

"You don't have to—"

"I want to. I want you to be my friend—I don't have any friends. I don't have anybody now. So I want you—I need you to know…everything."

He closed his eyes, swallowed hard. Did he really want to know? She apparently thought he did. She trusted him. He had to be worthy of that trust. "All right."

Meri stared at the river as she spoke. "After you attacked the guard, or tried to…" She giggled, but it trailed off. "The guards led me to the king's chamber. He didn't come in for several hours. I had been bathed, perfumed, made up, and dressed…not to mention coached on what to say and do in every possible situation for weeks. I was exhausted. I just wanted to sleep, but of course I was terrified. Even after all that preparation, I had no idea what to expect."

She reached for his hand and held it. A shock went through his body, and he had to work to concentrate on her words.

"He finally came in, but he had drunk so much wine he fell asleep right away. I was so tired that I drifted off for a while, but I was afraid he'd wake up, so I didn't sleep well. The next day, they ordered me to stay and wait in his room. So I did. All day. I didn't eat, or sleep, I just waited." She took a ragged breath. "And that night when he came in, he told me to undress and get in bed."

Meri stopped for a moment. She pulled Bezalel's hand close to her chest and clutched it with both of hers. She closed her eyes and rocked back and forth.

He moved closer to her and leaned near, his mouth next to her ear. "You don't have to," he whispered.

She shook her head.

He ached for her and wanted to do something—anything—to make her pain stop. His chest compressed like a giant hand had squeezed all the air out of him just listening to her, and he could only imagine what telling the story—let alone living it—must feel like for her. But it was clear she needed to finish, so he braced himself for the worst.

She continued. "He took off his clothes and got in next to me. He smelled like wine. I thought I would vomit. He started kissing me, pawing at me." Her voice broke.

She paused again, and tears streamed down her face. She kept rocking.

Bezalel removed his hand from hers and wrapped it around her waist, giving her his other hand to hold.

"He kept that up for a while, but in the end, nothing more happened. I think he's too old. Or he was still too drunk, I don't know. The next day he was angry and sent me back to the harem, like it was my fault!" She stopped to catch her breath. "So I tried to run away. My feet were bare and the rocks bruised and cut them, and they caught me, not too far from the palace. They whipped me. That's when you found me."

He'd only been able to see her bloody feet that night, not her striped back.

He drew her to him and wrapped his arms around her. "I'm so sorry. I'm so sorry." He held her for a long time and let her cry. He pushed her hair away from her face and stroked her back. She felt so small in his arms. If only he could take away all her pain. He just wanted to hold her forever and never let anyone hurt her again.

When she pulled away, she brushed at his shoulder. "Oh, I got your tunic all wet. I'm sorry."

"Don't worry about it. The sun will dry it in no time." He put his hands on her face and wiped away her tears.

She smiled at him and put a hand over his. "You're the only one who's been nice to me. I'm so glad you're here." She pressed her cheek into his hand.

"Me, too."

It took everything he had not to kiss her.

Eight

Third month of Peret, Season of Growing

A soft, gray light slithered into the room from the window near the roof. Bezalel tucked a blanket around Ahmose, kissed his head, and rose. He dressed silently, grabbed a handful of grapes, and slipped out the door, careful to let in as little of the cool dawn air as possible.

The morning dawned crisp and cold. A full moon slid below the mountains as the sun peered above the Nile, as if it, too, preferred to stay in bed. A pair of antelope bounced through the brush across the sands, scattering a flock of pigeons. An owl called as it made its last flight of the night before heading to its nest. So far, it looked to be a beautiful winter day. Bezalel hugged himself against the chill and hastened toward the warm, bright palace.

Up ahead he spied Moses and Aaron walking. He sighed. *No, not again.* The mood in the palace had just returned to normal after the death of the livestock. Must these old men really stir things up again?

Bezalel quickened his pace and caught up to them. He passed them then whirled around. He took a deep breath and blew it out.

Moses stopped and tilted his head, looking at him. "What?" The elder's voice was gentle.

"Do you really have to do this again?" Bezalel raised his hands in the air. "Every time the moon is full?"

"I am only doing what Yahweh tells me to do."

"It's not doing any good, you know." Lowering his arms, Bezalel looked from Moses to Aaron and back again.

"No, I don't know that at all. And neither do you." Moses took his arm and turned him around. "Walk with me." Aaron followed silently several steps behind.

"I am in the throne room every day," Bezalel said. "Ramses does not care about El Shaddai or anything He says. After each incident everything goes back to the way it was before."

"But you do not know what is in his head or in his heart, do you?"

Bezalel stopped and removed his arm from Moses's grasp. "No, I suppose I don't." He stepped toward the Nile. As he rubbed the back of his neck and stared across the water, he contemplated what to say next.

Finally he turned to face the older man and walked back. "But I still don't see how any of this helps."

Moses shrugged. "All I know is that Yahweh said He would do mighty signs and miraculous works in Egypt, and that Pharaoh would at first not listen, but in the end would let us go. What it will take to get him to that point, I am not sure. We can only obey what Yahweh reveals, one step at a time."

"One step at a time." Bezalel scoffed.

They finished the walk to the palace in silence.

Bezalel felt the warmer air on the portico as it drifted from the throne room. He split off from the brothers without a parting word and hurried toward his room, not wishing to be seen entering with them. He ducked behind a pillar to see what happened next.

Ramses sneered in disgust as he caught sight of the brothers approaching.

Aaron strode about halfway into the room and halted, while Moses continued on but stopped short of the dais. He tucked his staff into his cloth belt and bent over the dying fire that lay in a large open brazier at Ramses's feet.

The king leaned forward on his elbows and watched intently.

Moses scooped up two handfuls of cooler ashes from the edges. Then he straightened, backed up into the center of the room, and threw the gray dust high into the air. Some of the powder caught the slight breeze and blew away; most floated gently back down upon the officers and polished limestone floor.

Bezalel let out a soft gasp at Moses's audacity in front of the pharaoh. As much as he didn't agree with the approach Moses was taking, he didn't want the brothers harmed.

Moses returned to his brother, nodded his head and, without a word to Bezalel, the pair crossed the courtyard and left the palace.

Bezalel chased after them. He grabbed Moses's arm and spun him around. "What is it this time?"

"Why?" Moses waited patiently.

"There are people here I care about! These 'signs' are hurting them, and not getting us any closer to our release!"

Moses looked at him with sad eyes. "Did you forget what we just talked about?"

Bezalel put his hands on his hips. "I only know someone—some people—I care about very much are about to be hurt. Please tell me what is going to happen!"

Moses took a deep breath. "They will have dreadful, horribly painful, oozing sores on their bodies. They will hardly be able to move."

"All over? Like the fly bites?"

"Not so many. But even one will be too many."

"But not in Goshen."

"Not in Goshen."

Bezalel closed his eyes and paused a moment. "When?"

"Very soon."

"How long will it last?"

"That's up to Ramses. My guess is he'll call for us before dusk.

They'll call on their healer god Imhotep first, but he will not be able to heal them."

Bezalel huffed. "I hate this."

Moses shook his head. "You're not meant to like it. And I'm afraid I can't do anything about that."

Bezalel glared a moment at Moses then sprinted off toward the harem.

At the walkway's end, two men stood sentry. Each boasted a long blade on his hip, and a spear stood in each corner within arm's reach. He approached one. "I am the king's artisan. He sent me to see Meri."

The guard, not much older than Bezalel, narrowed his eyes and looked him over. "For?"

"He sent me to consult with his newest consort about a royal gift for her, but if you doubt me, have it your way. You can explain to her why her jewelry has not been designed." He started to walk away, struggling to control his fear.

He suppressed a groan. *I just lied to one of Ramses's guards.*

"Wait."

The guard's voice stopped him, and Bezalel took a deep breath before turning around. "Change your mind?"

"Wait here. I'll bring her out." The guard entered the chamber.

Bezalel tapped his foot and stared at the curtains, willing them to part.

The soldier returned and held the fabric back for Meri.

She stepped out and her face lit up, but Bezalel shook his head slightly. She frowned.

"The king wishes for you to consult with me on your gift. Please follow me." He bowed his head.

Meri put a hand over her mouth—to hide a giggle, he guessed.

He started down the walkway and around the corner. When they were out of sight of the guards, he paused and faced her. "You have to come to Goshen with me. Now." He took her hand in his and pulled her toward the portico. "It's the only way you'll be safe."

"Safe from what? You're scaring me." She pulled the other way.

"Another outbreak is about to start. Like the flies, but worse. It will be painful and ugly. Please come with me, I'm begging you."

She jerked her hands away. "No, I don't want to leave Egypt. I don't know that place."

He pounded the wall beside him with his open hand. "Meri, please!" He kept his voice low, knowing they must not be overheard.

As he spoke, a mark on her arm the size of a seed appeared. It blossomed into an open sore bigger than a fig.

Her eyes widened and filled with tears. She gasped and her knees buckled.

He lunged forward and caught her before she collapsed. He tried to help her stand but her legs were no stronger than papyrus reeds, so instead he picked her up and carried her down the hall toward his room as wails and screams echoed off the limestone walls. *Again. Just like the flies. And the gnats.* Officers, servants, women, and children scurried through the throne room. Open, oozing sores dotted everyone's skin.

He opened the door to the workroom and placed Meri on his bed. Another spot grew on her shoulder. He brushed the hair from her face and leaned in close. "I'll be right back."

Bezalel raced back down the hall toward the kitchen. He grabbed all the honey he could find, careful to include the sticky propolis from the comb. He dumped the honey into the biggest pottery bowl on the shelves, and added a bit of sesame oil to thin it out. He rifled through the herbs looking for thyme and chamomile, knocking containers to the floor. Thank Shaddai he listened when his mother talked about plants and herbs.

He poured some of the honey mixture into a smaller bowl and looked for a spoon. He put it and the bowls of honey on a large tray.

Servants had heated a tub of water and left it on a fire for the morning meal before they abandoned the kitchen, and he filled two large cups with the hot water. He threw a handful of fresh thyme leaves in each cup, added chamomile flowers to one, then set both cups on the tray.

He went to Kamose's quarters before he made his way back to his own room. The captain looked helpless as he lay in pain, unable to move without causing even more agony by rubbing against the rough linen of his bed.

"I brought some honey, and some thyme tea for pain." He helped Kamose sit up. He gave him the smaller bowl and then handed him the spoon. He set the tea on the table.

"Why, Bezalel?" Kamose's voice sounded ragged. "Why the attacks from your God?"

"Ramses has been warned—"

"Ramses is supposed to protect us. He is a god." Kamose grimaced in pain as he applied the honey mixture.

"How can he be a god and yet sacrifice to a god at the same time?"

Kamose stared at his bare feet but did not answer.

Bezalel picked up the tray. "I've got to go now. I'll be back later." He left, closing the door behind him.

He rushed back to his room, where Meri lay weeping on his bed. He pulled a stool next to it and set the tray down, then shrugged his long-sleeved thawb and tunic onto the floor. As he kicked off his sandals, he sat down next to her, and then helped her sit up.

She crumpled against his chest. Her whimpers and groans told him she suffered greatly. He dipped his fingers into the honey blend and gently rubbed it onto the raw, red skin on her arm, trying not to cause more pain as he did so.

He did the same to another boil on each leg. He moved her hair out of the way then carefully repositioned one strap of her tunic to attend to the lesion on her shoulder. The scars from the beating she suffered when she tried to run away had faded until they were almost invisible. She must have been well tended—the pharaoh wouldn't like his consort too damaged.

She relaxed against him as the amber liquid soothed the wounds. Finally he finished with the honey and set it on the stool. He reached for the tea and fished out the green leaves and yellow flowers. He blew on it and tasted it to make sure it wouldn't burn her.

"Meri, sit up a moment. I have some tea for you. I need you to drink it." He shifted his shoulder to nudge her up and reached his arm around her head to lift her chin. He helped her to sip most of the chamomile tea, and her eyes began to droop.

He set the cup aside, scooted back, and settled against the wall. He helped her lean her weight against him so none of her boils were touching him.

Her side rested against his chest. She held on to his left arm with both of hers, his hand on her waist. She laid her head on his shoulder, the back of her head nestled into his cheek, and he ran his fingers through her hair. It felt delightfully soft and fell onto his bare chest.

Despite the circumstances, he relished being so close to her. He leaned his head against hers and closed his eyes. The scent of her perfume, mixed with honey, enveloped him. The warmth of her body snuggled into his and the sound of her slow and steady breathing brought a calmness to his world he had not felt in a long time.

As she slept, the mystery and chaos of all that was happening spun around in his head.

It was not lost on him that he was the only one in the palace unharmed, that every other person right now agonized. All because he was one of El Shaddai's "people." Even though he wasn't sure he believed in Shaddai right now.

Well, actually, he had always believed in Him. He was just very angry with Him. Angry with Shaddai for giving him this great talent that could bring him so much joy, and then having that very same skill cut him off from everyone who mattered to him.

He trailed his fingers slowly down the tattoo on Meri's arm, each dot barely raised. Her skin felt so soft. Her hair was soft. She spoke softly. Everything about her was soft and delicate—a rarity in his rough and hard world of stone and metal and harsh reprimands.

The most elusive dream in his life had now become at least a possibility, though he could see no real future for him and Meri. They could never live together here or in Goshen. But he finally had someone he could call a friend, maybe even love. Someone he thought was special. Better yet, someone who thought *he* was special.

Did El Shaddai do that? Did He finally answer that prayer? And if He had, could He work out a way for them to have a future? What had Moses said? One step at a time?

Soon, in the next few hours or even moments, Ramses would call for Moses, the boils would disappear, and by tomorrow Ramses would pretend nothing had ever happened and would not let the Israelites go. And on the next full moon something new and even more terrible would be unloosed upon Egypt. How long could this go on? How many more times would he have to watch Meri suffer? He pulled her closer and kissed her head.

A future. The future seemed so far away. For the moment, all he could do was sit and think. And wait.

❧◦◦❧

Bezalel wrapped the necklace carefully in fine linen and placed it aside. He picked up the matching earrings and was reaching for more linen when his door opened.

"Meri!" He bolted to the door and peered past her down the hall. "What are you doing out of the harem?" He laid his hand on the small of her back, led her inside, and quickly shut the door.

"I wanted to thank you for last week. The sores all healed. See? They're just tiny dots now." She came closer. Jasmine filled the air around him as she moved.

He put his hand on her face and brushed her cheek with his fingertips. "Oh, *habibti*, you are going to get me in so much trouble."

She blushed at his use of the endearment.

He went to the door again, opened it, and looked both ways.

She came up behind him. "There's no one out there. The women are all on the barge with their children and their teachers again. They'll be gone for hours. And Ramses and the court officers just left for Thebes. The palace is empty."

He grinned at her. "Let's go to the garden." They slipped out the side door.

They meandered through rows of sycamore, acacia, and pomegranate trees. Willows leaned over a long, narrow pond full of colorful fish and lotus lilies. Bezalel reached for a lily. "Want a flower?" He winked as he handed it to her.

She took it and giggled, then knelt and gaped at the fish swimming lazily in the pool. "I've never seen fish like these."

"Ramses has them brought from all over the world."

She straightened and faced him. "Why are you working here in the palace, Bezalel? Isn't that a bit odd, since you are a Hebrew?"

"Yes, it is, now anyway. I started out in the brickfields when I was about six, like all the other children. We gathered up unused straw, washed the brick forms, lined them up to be used again, things like that. But I kept playing with the mud, making animals out of it and leaving them out to dry. One of the guards took some home and showed his brother, who was a palace artisan."

He gestured toward the other side of the garden, and they started walking again, up and down the rows of trees. "At that time Israelites worked in the palace often as personal servants, so it wasn't too unusual for many of us to be around. The artisans found I had a great natural skill and trained me, and I've been here ever since. As Ramses has grown older and more suspicious of all those who are not Egyptian, the others have been sent away, but I have been forced to stay." He paused. "And now my own people don't trust me."

Meri put her hand on his arm. "That's terrible! I'm so sorry."

He shrugged. "I am used to it." They reached a pergola covered with climbing ivy and jasmine. He stepped under it and leaned back against the trellis. A large jasmine flower poked through the lattice. He fingered the petals, ripping one off and bringing it to his nose. "This smells like you."

She smiled. "That's what we make the perfume from."

"You make it?"

"There are several of us who do. They showed me how when I came here. We use jasmine and lilies, lotus, many of the flowers from the garden. It takes a long time; you must be patient to make perfume. But I like it. It gives me something to do when they go to the river."

He tilted his head. "How did you end up here, in the palace?"

She tensed.

"I'm sorry. You don't have to answer that. I had no right to ask."

"No. It's fine. I already told you the worst part. And I said I want-ed you to know everything." She pulled the petals off the lotus flower one by one as she spoke. "We went to Memphis to the temple to pay our annual grain tax. We barely had enough to feed ourselves, let alone pay the tax.

"While we were there, one of the priests heard my father talking about how worried he was. That priest told another priest, who then told us he had a way for us to avoid paying the tax for several years. The three of them went into another room and talked for quite a while. When they came out, they told me I was to go with the priest."

Meri tossed the empty stem aside. "So I came here with him. When I left, the priest told me I would be working in the palace. But when I got here, he brought me to Jambres, who told me my father sold me to him to pay for five years' taxes! I yelled and kicked and screamed but it did no good. He locked me up in a room for weeks—almost two months—with little food until I said I would cooperate. And...well, you know the rest."

Bezalel stepped closer. "Are you sure he really sold you? Maybe the priest lied to you. Or maybe he tricked your father, too."

"No, I believe it. He was always complaining about having too many children to feed. He couldn't handle things after Imma died. It would have been a very easy way to solve two problems at once."

Bezalel tucked a lock of hair behind her ear and left his hand there, softly rubbing his thumb on her cheek. "I'm so sorry. I've been forced to work in the palace and don't see my family much, but I know they love me. I can't imagine how it would feel to be here alone and know they weren't at home waiting for me. I-I don't know what else to say, but I'm sorry."

Meri drew closer to him and laid her hands on his chest. "Ramses doesn't bother me now. And I met you. So I'm not sure I am sorry anymore." She looked up at him. Her cheeks had a pink glow to them. Sunlight filtered through the ivy, shining flecks of light on her face and hair. Her enormous brown eyes showed so much trust his heart skipped a beat.

He cupped her face in his hands and lowered his head. His breath came faster. He wanted desperately to kiss her but he couldn't bear the thought of reminding her of Ramses on that horrible night. He moved slowly and searched her face for any sign of fear or reluctance. But when he felt her hands slip around to his back he abandoned all caution and brought his lips to hers.

The kiss was soft, barely a kiss, really. He raised his head just enough to see her eyes again. He wanted to give her another chance to change her mind, to protest. Instead, she embraced him more tightly, grabbing his tunic in her fists.

Her mouth almost touched his, and her warm, sweet breath caressed his face. Each wisp of air that crossed his lips sent a pulse of heat through every muscle in his body and his heart pounded. He could barely think—the feel of her body next to his eclipsed everything else. He finally surrendered. He slipped one arm around her shoulders and with his other hand cradled her head. He kissed her passionately, again and again, as if her touch could erase the loneliness and isolation of all his years trapped in the palace.

After several moments he reluctantly pulled back and studied her face—every part of it—as if to memorize it. He stroked her hair and ran his finger over her lips. Her dark eyes drew him in and would not let him go.

Finally he took a deep breath and scanned the garden. "We should go back."

But before he could will his feet to move, he kissed her one more time.

Nine

After the morning meal ended, Bezalel stood in the gardens, staring at the blue water lilies that lay open in the pond. The star-shaped jasmine nearby had also opened, filling the air with their fragrance and his mind with thoughts of Meri. He had just picked a few of the flowers when Kamose strode by.

"Kamose, wait. Can I ask you something?"

The captain halted. "What do you need?"

Bezalel shifted his weight and looked at the pool for a moment. "Is there any way to ransom someone from the harem?"

"What do you mean 'ransom'?"

"Free them. Rescue them."

"Do you mean that girl I've seen you talking to?"

Bezalel drew in a quick breath and quickly glanced around. "You've seen us?" His stomach knotted with fear for Meri more than for himself.

Kamose chuckled. "Of course I've seen you. You're not that sly."

"Meri said everyone was gone."

"No one else saw you. Don't worry. Now why do you think she needs to be rescued?"

"She doesn't belong there."

Kamose shrugged. "Then she shouldn't have come." He started to walk away.

"She didn't have a choice." Bezalel raised his voice.

Kamose stopped and looked over his shoulder. "They all have a choice."

"What about Tia?"

"Tia had a choice. She made a bad one." Kamose turned around and crossed his arms. "If she is having second thoughts, there is nothing to be done. Believe me, I wish there were. I've been through this before. She's probably just homesick."

"Why would she want to go home?" Bezalel spread his arms.

"Why wouldn't she?" Kamose scoffed.

"He sold her!" Bezalel threw the flowers he held into the pool.

Kamose closed the distance between them in a few long strides. "What do you mean 'sold her'?"

"I mean her father sold her. For money. A priest in Memphis told her father he could avoid paying five years' grain taxes if she came to the palace. The priest brought her to Jambres."

Kamose clenched his jaw, took several deep breaths. He thought a few moments. "That could be your answer. No one can be forced into the harem. I just have to decide how to do this, because he will, of course, deny it." He paused a moment more. "And where will she go if she leaves? If she can't go home?"

"I'm not sure yet."

"You love her?"

Bezalel raked his hands through his hair. "I think so."

"You'd better be sure. If I get her out and you have no place for her..."

Bezalel studied the jeweled armbands on the captain's biceps. Finally he answered. "Get her out."

"You're sure?"

"I'm sure."

"I make no promises." Kamose nodded and left.

Bezalel left the garden and returned to his room. He tossed his tunic on the bed as he entered, leaving on only his shenti, picked up his chisel, and reached for the alabaster. He tried to carve Nefertari's ear, but after an hour or so of simply staring at the pink stone, gave up. He tossed his tools aside.

He'd told Kamose to try to free Meri from the harem, but he had no idea where she would go if he did. Would she marry him? Even if she did, where would they live? There was no way they could live here, in the palace, even in the city around it. A slave could never marry an Egyptian. And she would be seen as royalty, even if she had been sold into the harem, even if she were released. And if she left the harem, the palace certainly wouldn't want her around.

Would they accept her in the village? *They barely accept me.*

There were many Egyptians who lived in the village. Israelites and Egyptian workers generally got along well. It was the royalty and taskmasters the villagers had a problem with.

But Israelites and Egyptians did not intermarry. At least he didn't know of any.

And no one had ever married a girl from the harem. The gossip…the gossip would never stop. And no matter how many times they tried to explain that nothing had happened with the king, there would be those who wouldn't believe it. She would always be a concubine to some. Like the marks on her arms, the marks on her reputation would always be there.

But now Bezalel was making plans for a future—uncertain as it was—after one kiss. Well, several kisses. She had most certainly kissed him back. But was she willing to commit to a future with him? One as vague as he could offer? One that meant leaving Egypt?

He had to know.

He opened the door and was shocked to find Meri on the other side. "Meri! What—"

"I was just coming to see you."

He pulled her inside and shut the door quickly, leaning against it to prevent anyone from opening it. "Did anyone see you come here?"

"No. I was careful. I'm not foolish."

"I didn't mean that. It's just that … do you know what they could do to me? Or to you?"

She smiled—and any argument melted away. He still had her by the wrist, and he pulled her to him. He slid down the door a bit to bring himself to her height, wrapped his arms around her slim waist, and kissed her.

She slipped her arms around his neck and untied the leather strip holding back his hair. She tossed it over her shoulder and slowly ran her fingers through his locks, sending pulsing waves of heat throughout his body. Then she drew her fingers lightly over his eyes, his cheeks, down his neck, and onto his bare chest. Her perfume swirled around his head and made him woozy.

He moaned softly. His heart thumped and his chest rose and fell quickly as his breath came fast and shallow. His eyes held hers for a long moment and then his gaze traveled from her ebony eyes to her lips, to her slender neck, down the strap and along the edge of her one-shouldered tunic—had she ever worn that one before? Between her fingers dancing on his skin and the gauzy linen draping her perfect form, his thoughts started to wander where he knew they should not go.

Tempted as he was to let those thoughts run wild, he removed his hand from around her waist and grasped her hands in his. "Stop." His voice sounded harsher than he had intended.

"What?"

"You have to stop that."

"Why?" She furrowed her brow.

"Because I am not your husband." His voice was a hoarse whisper.

She laughed. "Of course you're not. I'm a concubine. So what?"

"So you have to stop that."

"Why? You can never be my husband. That doesn't mean I can't love you. Or show you I love you. As long as we don't get caught." She pulled her hands free and slid them down his chest, to his waist and down his hips.

Please don't do this. He grabbed her hands again and held them tightly at her sides. He stared at her, breathing rapidly and clenching his jaw repeatedly. His heart pounded as his body fought with his mind.

She glared back, her dark eyes flashing, almost as if she were daring him, and leaned in to kiss him.

He turned his face aside to deflect her kiss, but nuzzled his cheek to hers. He dropped her hands and embraced her tightly, entangling his hands in her long hair. "Meri, I love you." He whispered into her ear. "I love you more than anything. But I can't love you like that unless I am your husband."

She placed both palms against his chest, pushed back, and broke free, propelling herself several feet away. "But you kissed me. I thought that was what you wanted."

He pushed away from the door and followed her. "To kiss you? I did want to kiss you. And I did. I don't under—"

"And now you've changed your mind?" Her voice broke, but he couldn't tell if she was angry or hurt.

"You're not making any sense."

"You're the one not making sense. I am the king's concubine. I can never be wife to another." She crossed her arms. "Don't tell me you love me and refuse to do anything about it." Tears filled her eyes.

He stepped slowly toward her. "I can do something about it. And I will. Just let me expl—"

"No, you won't. You don't want me either. You're just throwing me away like everyone else does!" Tears spilled onto her cheeks. She shoved past him, flung the door open, and ran out.

I don't want you either? He went to the door and looked down the hall after her, but she was halfway to the harem. No one was watching, but it was too risky to follow her.

His chest still heaving, he leaned against the doorframe and ran his fingers through his hair, leaving his hands clasped at his neck. What just happened? He didn't even have an opportunity to tell her there was a chance he could get her out of the harem, let alone marry her.

But now, she probably didn't want out. At least not to be with him.

What had he done wrong?

Fourth month of Peret, Season of Growing

Long morning shadows fell westward over the polished stone floor of the throne room. Kamose waited silently nearby as the trio of old men stared one another down. It had been a month since the boils had healed, but tempers had not cooled.

"We have been over this … how many times now?" Ramses's voice revealed his growing irritation. "If it were not for our common childhood, you would have been banished long ago. But my father liked you because the princess loved you, and out of respect for him I indulge you. But you tread perilously close to the end of my patience." He twirled his scepter in his hand.

"Yes, Ramses. I understand. But you must understand that I serve One greater than even you."

Kamose caught his breath. Ramses was a god in Egypt. No matter what Moses thought, to voice something like that aloud was foolish.

Ramses rose from his throne, descended the dais, and sauntered toward Moses. His double crown glistened and bounced sunlight off the limestone walls. Guards from all corners of the room were instantly at Pharaoh's side.

Kamose took his place on the king's right, his hand on the dagger that rested on his hip. Although he was no longer sure Ramses was god, his job was still to protect the man from all dangers.

Ramses was taller than either of the brothers. He stood, arms crossed, surrounded by armed guards, glaring down at them. "Did you have a particular reason for appearing before me, or are you here only to anger me?"

Moses, in his simple robe and carrying a shepherd's staff, looked more sure of himself than the king. He held his ground, spoke calmly, and his eyes never wavered from the ruler's. The armed guards appeared to have no impact on him, although Aaron took several steps back.

"If you do not free us, Yahweh will send the full force of His wrath against you and your people, so you will finally know there is no one like Him in all the earth, among all your innumerable gods." Moses spoke softly and calmly. "By now He could have wiped Egypt from the earth, but He has time and again chosen to give you another chance. Yet you continue to defy Him. At this time tomorrow, a storm unlike any other will come upon Egypt—"

"I like rain." Ramses backed off and circled Moses. "Nefertari and I enjoy sitting in our barge on the Nile and listening to the rain on the roof, rare as it is. We find it … pleasant."

"I said storm, not rain. Darkness will cover the sun. The sky will become your enemy, and your sky goddess Nut will not be able to protect you. This tempest will destroy your barge. It will annihilate your animals, and your men. It will demolish your buildings and obliterate your crops. If you are wise, you will order your men to bring all animals and slaves inside to protect them from the storm that is to come, or every living thing left outdoors will be wiped out."

"I will not! That's impossible!" The king bellowed, lifting his scepter high. "I do not believe you! Leave me now!"

Moses shrugged and did as he was told.

❧◦❧

Kamose rushed outside behind the palace to the army's animal enclosures. There was not enough room in the stables to house all the horses at one time, not even just the smaller herd they had stolen from the Israelites and those from the border patrols. There had never been a need to shelter them; on the coldest nights blankets were enough for horses.

He called to the nearest officer. "Build a shelter big enough to cover the horses. It doesn't need to have sides, but must be done before tomorrow morning."

"A shelter? For what?"

Kamose shot the officer a withering look. "Are you questioning me?"

"No, Captain. I will start immediately."

❧❦

As the sun reached its zenith, Kamose crossed the sand west of the palace to check on the new stables. He found instead that half of the soldiers had been summoned inside.

"Who called them away?" He barked at a young man.

"Jambres, Captain."

"For *what*?"

"I do not know. He ordered; we obeyed."

"And what about *my* orders?"

"He said he outranked you, Captain."

Kamose's cheeks grew hot as blood rose to his face.

The soldier visibly shrank before him.

Kamose marched to the palace, straight to Jambres's rooms. There Kamose found his soldiers conscripted as common workmen, moving furniture in the sorcerer's quarters. He raced to Jambres, grabbed his arm, and spun him around.

"Who do you think you are, taking my soldiers and telling my men you *outrank* me?"

Jambres yanked his arm free. "I need workers. And they weren't doing anything important." He turned to two soldiers moving a bed and pointed a bony, ringed finger toward the back of the room. "No, a little farther back. Right there."

"They were obeying my orders. Whether you think my commands are important or not, is immaterial."

"Not if you are making the king look like a fool."

"And how am I doing that?" Kamose put his fists on his hips.

"By bringing in the horses and men on the word of that Israelite." Jambres arranged several bottles of potion on a nearby shelf.

Kamose stepped closer to him. "It is my job to protect the king. So it is my decision. My army. My men. My horses." He put his thumb to his chest.

"But it is *my* job to protect the spiritual image of the king."

Kamose took a deep breath and tried to calm himself. "According to whom?"

"According to me. And if you bring in the horses and men, it makes him look like he believes Moses. I won't let you do that."

The captain neared the magician. "Try—and—stop—me." Kamose punctuated each word by bringing his face closer to Jambres's.

Kamose strode to the center of the room. "Soldiers!" His men rushed to face him and stood in formation. "Move out. Now!" They immediately left the room.

Kamose marched back over to Jambres, and brought his mouth next to the magician's ear.

"If you ever order my men to do anything again, you will regret it. You do not outrank me, and you never will."

∼⚬∽

After a long night, Kamose awoke from a dreamless sleep. He dressed, grabbed his dagger, and sprinted out the door.

He checked once again to see that the guards and slaves had been ushered into the palace and then jogged through the enclosed stables, making sure all the doors were secured. He then ran to the makeshift shelter for the hundred or so horses that did not fit in the stables. Several soldiers had refused to go into the palace, choosing to remain at their posts instead, in the belief there would be no storm, no death.

The isolated raindrops became a slow drizzle. Kamose waited in the safety of the shelter, surveying the terrain. To the east, along the banks of the Nile, stretched the "black land," full of crops that would sustain the people for the coming year. Westward lay the "red land," containing only inhospitable desert. At this moment all of it was void of animal life; the creatures seemed to know something was wrong and had taken cover. Even the birds had flown to safer skies, wherever those were. The only sound was that of the rain.

The soft drizzle turned into a downpour. Kamose stroked the horses, calming them one by one, whispering words meant only for them. He rubbed his hand down their noses, along their necks. The mounts relaxed at his touch. He checked the ropes that tied each horse to a line strung between two of the permanent stables.

The rain pounded the roof and Kamose cautiously put out his hand. The drops were so large and fell so hard they stung.

Rain was rare, but he knew it should not hurt. He pulled his hand back and shook it. He looked at the ground. The "raindrop" was actually ice. A tiny ball of ice. He reached down and picked it up, and was surprised to see it melt in his palm. He had seen ice when he was a young soldier, patrolling the high mountains to the south, but there had never been ice in the deserts of Egypt.

As the hail melted, more fell to the ground around it. Bigger and bigger spheres fell, until some were larger than his closed fist. Black clouds moved between sun and earth and the sky darkened. Thunder exploded and launched noise from one side of the sky to the other. The heavens shuddered. Lightning sliced the sky into pieces like broken pottery.

Kamose backed farther under the roof made of cedar that had been imported for chariots. The noise of the sky at war with earth drummed in his head. Light flashed off and on. Horses stomped and neighed, and the captain again checked that each valuable animal was tied securely.

In the bursts of lightning, Kamose made out one of his men racing for the palace. He slipped in the mud, rose and fell again as hail as big as pomegranates pummeled him. Finally the man tumbled to the ground and did not get up.

Soldier's instincts forced Kamose to try to rescue his comrade, but the hail assaulted him and he had to retreat after only a few steps. Under the shelter again, Kamose rammed his fist into a post then groaned and leaned his forehead against it. He closed his eyes tightly.

How many more were out there? He went to the edge of the shelter, peered into the darkness. Whenever the lightning flared he searched to see if any more of his men were headed for the palace, or worse, down. But most were stationed too far away, and he would have to wait to find out if they had survived.

Why hadn't they listened?

ஆ∞ᢙ

In the aftermath of the storm, Bezalel walked among the fields west of the Nile. He dragged his hands along the few naked stalks still standing; most were flattened. The flax and barley, both ripe for harvest, were destroyed. Not a grain remained. Food would be scarce for Egypt this year. There was wheat and spelt left, but over half the grain supply was gone. Barley was the main crop for bread and beer.

He nearly bumped into Kamose, who stood, preoccupied, looking over the fields. A large purple bruise covered his shoulder.

"Bezalel! Why are you here?"

"I wanted to see what damage the hail had done."

"Is it true your fields were untouched?" Kamose's voice registered his disbelief.

"Yes. Our bar—" Bezalel couldn't bring himself to finish the sentence.

Kamose pulled on an empty stalk of flax. He closed his eyes for a moment. "I lost…so many men." He tore at the flax. His huge hands dwarfed the stripped branch as he stared across the fields. His eyes glazed. "I tried to make them all come inside. I ordered them to. But they knew the king had said they didn't have to, and so they chose to stay at their posts in the field. After the storm passed, I went to gather the bodies…I could hardly recognize them. They looked like they were beaten, covered in bruises…."

"Kamose, I'm sorry."

"I had to identify some of them by their daggers." Kamose's breathing was ragged, but he quickly regained his self-control, his face revealing nothing of his despair. "Why was Goshen spared?"

"El Shaddai wants Pharaoh to release us. Egypt needs the lesson, not Israel." Bezalel knew that wasn't the answer Kamose wanted, but it was the truth.

"After this, I'd let you go."

❧❦

Bezalel ambled through his village after dark and brooded over the events of the last months. The moon's light shone on the narrow, packed-dirt streets, illuminating children playing dice games, mothers cooking behind the houses in the cool night air, and cats crisscrossing the alleys. The certainty that something terrible would happen under the next full moon stayed in the back of his mind like a heron lying in wait for a Nile perch.

Since the gnats, nothing had touched the Israelites. Most of the time, they were completely unaware anything had taken place at all until Moses told them.

But what about Meri?

She had suffered every time. So had Kamose. Ahmose was spared because Bezalel had brought him home. But the only reason he had done that was because Jannes had beaten him so badly. And the only reason he knew the boy was beaten was because he worked in the palace, which until recently had ruined his life.

There was no way to sort it all out.

El Shaddai had promised He would protect His people, and He had. In fact, Bezalel could not think of a single promise Shaddai had made He had not kept. Perhaps He had not done things as fast or in the way Bezalel might have liked, but He kept his word.

Is there any reason to think He will not deliver on all His promises?

There really wasn't. Which meant sooner or later, Ramses would release them from slavery.

Sabba said he needed to choose a side. Not in so many words, but that was what he meant. He could cling to El Shaddai's power no matter what he saw happening around him, or live in confusion and fear.

He wasn't altogether sure about everything yet. He knew only two things. Shaddai was definitely in control, and they would be leaving Egypt soon. He had to find a way to bring Meri with him.

If she still wanted him.

Ten

Fourth month of Peret, Season of Growing

Bezalel put a piece of dried meat on his plate and set the platter back on the table. "Sabba?"

"Yes, habibi."

"Why would Shaddai protect me even if I am angry with Him?"

"Would you let harm come to Ahmose just because he was angry with you?"

"Of course not."

"And so it is with El Shaddai. He created you. He loves you. You are His, whether you accept it or not. And He will do as He says and keep His word. He said His people would be protected, and that is what He does."

"I see."

Sabba took a drink of juice. "So, you are not so angry anymore?"

Bezalel pursed his lips and thought a few moments before he answered. "I am starting to see how things can fit together. I don't understand it all, but I am beginning to accept. Bad things can lead to good things; good things can lead to worse things. It depends on how I look at it, like you said." He sighed. "It is hard."

"And does the girl in the harem have anything to do with this change in 'how you look at it'?"

Bezalel cheeks grew warm. "Maybe some. Maybe a lot. I think I have fallen in love with her. Which is dangerous, I know. But she doesn't belong there."

"Habibi, however did you even meet a concubine?"

Bezalel told Sabba about Meri as they finished their meal. Then he was silent a few moments. "I want to marry her."

Sabba's eyes grew wide. "You want to what?"

"I want to marry her. If she will have me."

Sabba took a deep breath. "She is willing to leave Egypt with you?"

"I don't know. I haven't asked her yet."

"You will have a very difficult time of it if you marry an Egyptian. And I'm not even talking about the fact that she is a concubine. You do realize that, don't you?" Sabba's gentle eyes assured Bezalel that any judgment would not be coming from him.

"I know." Bezalel shoved the table away and stood. "But I've been an outcast my whole life for something that isn't true and that I have no control over. How is this any different?"

"I guess it's not. If she will marry you, you have my blessing. I will always be here for you."

"You always have been, Sabba."

Now if I can only get Meri to talk to me.

≈•≈

Bezalel sorted through his work, separating the finished and unfinished pieces, and tried to decide what to work on first. He picked up a necklace he had started before the hail. The piece was made of several strings of gold alloy, each longer than the one before and attached at the ends, so that it formed a cascade when placed around the neck. Now he needed to make countless amulets to attach to each string.

He selected a hefty piece of turquoise. He gripped his knife and sliced off multiple small chunks, each one just large enough for a single amulet. The pendants were to be in the shape of a cornflower, an abundant and beautiful blossom. The soft stone yielded easily and amulets were soon scattered about his table.

"Moses and Aaron were just with Ramses." Kamose closed the door to Bezalel's workroom behind him.

Bezalel set down his knife, put his palms on the table, and leaned on them.

Now what? "What did they say this time?" He hated to even ask the question.

"If Ramses doesn't let your people go, locusts will come tomorrow and devour everything left by the hail."

"There will be nothing left for you to eat." Bezalel shook his head, sat on a stool, and reached for some grapes. He handed a bunch to Kamose.

"I know. Everyone knows." Kamose paced as he spoke, ignoring the proffered fruit. "Every official—except Jambres—has begged Ramses to let you go. Begged him! He will not hear of it. We told him Egypt will be ruined. We will starve. We cannot possibly survive." Kamose stopped pacing and faced Bezalel. "So the king told them you can go, but only the men, because you are clearly planning evil. Then he ran them out of the palace."

"As usual."

"As usual." Kamose reached for the door but turned back. "I have not seen you with Meri for a long time. And I have seen her crying many times. Can I ask if everything is all right? Do you still want me to get her out?"

"I do. I'm not sure she'll want out, though."

"What does that mean?"

"I'm not really sure. She—I-I hurt her—"

Kamose stepped closer, his eyes narrowed. "You struck her?"

"No! I hurt her feelings. She wanted…it's hard to explain…."

"Ohhh."

"What do you mean 'ohhh'?"

"I think I can guess. She became very…affectionate?"

Bezalel felt the blood rise to his face. "Yes. How did you—?"

"From Tia. When they come into the harem, the girls are taught for weeks that that is what a man wants. That that is *all* he wants. They are told that is a woman's only purpose, and they are given very specific and detailed lessons. When you rejected her advances, you rejected *her*.

"I think—I know—Tia knew differently. She knew my father valued my mother for her wisdom, and caring, and many other things. But Meri is very young, and her father obviously did not show her well what love is. If she believed what they taught her, nothing else you said would have mattered."

Bezalel sighed. "She's avoided me for weeks. She won't come out of the harem. And I can't very well go in there."

"I happen to know she sits in the garden in the evenings when the moon is out."

"I can't go out there with her. I'll be seen."

"Ramses is hiding in his room tonight. He thinks he can avoid the locusts. No one else will care if you are with her. This place is in chaos."

"What do I say?"

"You'll think of something. She loves you. Or she wouldn't be crying."

❧◈❧

The pond reflected an unnatural, scattered version of the moon as Bezalel looked under the date palms and willows, sycamore and pomegranate trees. Damage from the hail was everywhere. No Meri. One more time around the wall.

There she was—hiding in the pergola, which servants had repaired in an aborted effort to restore the gardens to their former state. She sat on the ground, arms wrapped around her knees, eyes closed, her face drinking in the moon's light. He strode over to her.

She leaned back on her hands and looked away. "I don't want to talk to you. You don't want me." Her voice had a hard edge to it, almost worse than before.

He sat on the ground, facing her, his hip next to her raised knees. "That's where you are wrong. So wrong. I do want you. More than anything. But I would not honor you if I did not marry you first." He kept his voice low and calm. *Please look at me.*

"But you can't, so that's just your way of saying you don't want me."

He reached to touch her but she jerked her head away. "Meri, I know what they told you in the harem."

She shifted her shoulders. The moonlight gave her skin a soft glow. A lone strand of ivy dangled above her head.

He touched her tattoo. "It's not true. You know, they only teach that in the harem. The rest of the world doesn't think that way."

She still refused to look at him.

"Meri, love can be shown in so many more ways other than physically. You don't have to do those things to prove you love me."

She looked sideways at him. "So … you don't want me to kiss you?"

He leaned across her and put his hand on the ground on the other side of her. "I love it when you kiss me. I love holding you, kissing you. But that day … there are some things we can't do yet, no matter how much I might want to."

She turned to face him. "You do want to?"

He ran the backs of his fingers slowly down the side of her face. Touching her just that much made his heart race. She obviously had no idea what she did to him, no matter what training she had received. "Believe me, I didn't want to stop you. Any longer, and I might not have been able to." He lifted her face toward his. His face was a finger's breadth from hers. "But you deserve more. I love you. I want to be with you forever, not just one night. I want a wife, not a concubine. I want to take care of you, protect you, make a home with you." He kissed her and tasted a hot, salty tear. He pulled away.

Her slender shoulders shook as she wept.

"Habibti, what's wrong?" He brushed away her tears.

"I can't have you as my husband. So I will take you any way, any time I can. You are the only person who has cared for me. No one has ever wanted me. Not my father. Not Ramses. No one. Until you."

"But I could be."

"Could be what?" She yanked at the ivy above her head and pulled off a leaf.

"Could be your husband."

"Don't be foolish. We've talked about this." She ripped the leaf apart.

"No, it's true. I talked to Kamose. It's illegal to force someone into the harem."

"Who's Kamose?"

"Captain of the guard. He says he might be able to get you out. Then you could marry me."

"You would marry someone from the harem?" She scoffed, tossing the pieces of leaf aside. "But what about your family? What will they say when you bring home a girl from the harem? You can't hide it." She pointed to her tattoo. "And what about the rest of your village? It will ruin your life. You can't do it. I won't let you."

He laughed. "Slow down, slow down. One step at a time." He cupped her face in his hands. "First, my family will be happy if I am happy. Second, there are many Egyptians in our village, though I honestly don't know of any Israelite who has married an Egyptian. So, yes, there will always be some who do not like it.

"Third, there will be those—Israelite and others—who will never believe you did not spend a night with Ramses. But I love you.

That is all that matters. And I will protect you from everyone and everything that threatens you, no matter who, no matter how. Do you believe me?"

She nodded.

"Do you love me?"

She smiled. "Yes."

"And will you marry me?"

"Yes." Her dark eyes danced.

He laughed again. "Then all we have to do now is wait for Kamose."

⁂

Bezalel walked with Ahmose at the river's edge after the midday meal. The water tickled their feet as they wiggled their toes in the mud of the Nile, and he turned his face to the sun and let the warmth flood over him. The smell of the wet earth, capable of producing and sustaining so much life, was comforting.

"Bezalel?"

"Yes?"

"Tell me more about your God. What is His name?"

"Most of us know Him as El Shaddai. This is what we have called Him for generations, what our grandfathers' grandfathers called Him. It means the Almighty God. Or just Shaddai, the Almighty."

A gray heron beat his huge wings and struggled into the sky, his long legs trailing far behind.

"What is He the god of?"

"What do you mean?"

"Well, Ra is the sun god, Hapi is the Nile god, Osiris is god of the dead…"

"Those gods are not gods at all, but only make-believe. There is only one God, and He is Shaddai. There are not many little gods running around, each in charge of one little thing. What if they got into a fight? What if one didn't like what another did? There can only be one God. That's the only way it will work."

"This is a hard thing to understand." Ahmose kicked at the mud.

"Yes, it is. But you will see. Just keep watching and waiting. Shaddai will help you understand."

A low hum from across the river drew their attention. They looked up, their hands shielding their eyes from the morning sun. A black cloud in the distance grew larger as it neared, darkening the sky.

"What is it?" Ahmose moved closer to Bezalel.

The whine grew louder. The mass grew larger as it neared the river.

"Bezalel!" Ahmose yanked on Bezalel's sleeve. "What is that?"

"I'm not sure what it is. But Shaddai has protected us so far, and there is no reason to believe He won't now." Despite his words of assurance, he worried.

The locusts!

Pushed by an easterly wind, the cloud crossed the river and headed for the fields.

Bezalel took off after it, with Ahmose close behind. They crossed the paths by the river. The drone pulsated in Bezalel's ears, drowning out all other sound. The cloud dissolved around them into millions of winged insects and dispersed, flying toward the croplands of Egypt.

Ahmose screamed as a number of the bugs settled on him.

Breathing hard, Bezalel bent over the boy and grasped his shoulders. "Ahmose, calm down! They just want food! They won't bite!" Bezalel removed his thawb and wrapped it around Ahmose's head and arms. He pulled the boy close and kept one hand on his back while he stared at the moving blanket of winged invaders.

Locusts landed on him and then flew away. The insects enveloped every stalk of wheat and spelt, each fruit tree, any green thing not destroyed by the hail. The ground was a writhing floor of black, and the pests devoured even what had fallen from the plants and trees.

"Ahmose, run home! There will be no bugs there. I'm going to the palace." Bezalel shoved Ahmose toward the village and bolted for the palace.

At the edge of the courtyard he watched the cloud swarm, amazed at the sheer number of insects. The locusts invaded houses, storerooms, and kitchens. They found every bit of food until there was not a seed left. They climbed under tunics, buzzed around heads, and drove the people screaming outside. There wasn't a surface left—walls, floors, tables, columns—that was not coated with bugs.

After only moments the wind changed direction and sent the locusts back across the river.

Bezalel rushed through the palace. He peeked into the kitchen, only weeks ago overflowing with food when he searched for honey and thyme. Now every pot, every shelf, every platter was empty.

He headed back toward the village, the river on one side, vacant cropland on the other. A young mother sat crying outside her house, an infant boy in her lap cooing, unaware of the calamity that had just befallen his world. An old man wandered helplessly in a field that little more than a month ago held the promise of provision for a year. Others prayed to gods Bezalel knew could never help them.

Bezalel stopped, knelt on one knee, took a scoop of dusty, barren earth in his hand. He sifted it through his fingers. He could not believe that less than an hour ago, spelt and wheat stalks stood tall in this very spot. All the other trials Shaddai had sent—until the hail—had taken at least half a day. This one happened so fast he could hardly comprehend it.

In the cloud's wake was utter destruction. Desolation. For the Egyptians, there was simply nothing left. No food. No answers. No hope.

⟡⟡

Bezalel walked down the hall toward the walkway. He peeked around the corner. As he had hoped, no guards stood outside the harem today.

He pulled apart the curtains and slipped inside. The vast room was empty.

He stepped back outside, crossed the throne room and portico, and entered the gardens. Spring was near and the air was warming. The trees and flowers should have been radiant, but the garden was naked.

He found Meri sitting under a tree.

She leaned against it, holding a stripped branch. She stared at the devastation around her, as if she were trying to make sense of it.

He sat next to her. "Meri? I brought you something to eat." He unwrapped a loaf of bread and two plums. "Look familiar?" He chuckled.

She turned and stared at him. "There is no food."

"I know. I brought you some." He pushed the package toward her. "It's what you brought to me the first time you came to my room."

She looked back at the denuded yard. "It's gone, it's all gone."

"Meri, you have to eat." He broke off a piece of bread and held it to her mouth. "Here, eat."

She took the bread, and nibbled at it.

"Meri, we'll be leaving Egypt soon."

She turned to him with blank, almost lifeless eyes. "What do you mean you'll be leaving?"

"My God has said He will free us. He is responsible for these … signs. He is trying to force Pharaoh to let us go, and soon he will have to. Then we'll leave for the land God promised us four hundred years ago. I want you to come with us. With me."

"Your God did this? Took away the food? Brought the flies? The ice? Those … horrible … sores?"

"Yes, but—"

"And you worship Him? The God who did this to me?" Her voice rose in anger, and she stood and flung the bread to the ground.

Bezalel stood to face her. "Well, yes, but, in the end it will be better for us—"

"In the end? When is that supposed to be?" She waved her arms, and her eyes filled with tears.

He held her by the shoulders. "Meri, please, trust me. I know this looks bad, and it's taken me a long time to understand it, too, but please, just trust me. I have never lied to you, have I?"

"Trust you? Trust you to do what? Let your God send more disaster?" Her sobs shook her body and she wrenched away from him.

"Meri, please." He stretched his hand toward her, but drew it back when she shrank from him. "I am not exactly sure of everything either. I just know that everything Shaddai has said He will do, He has done. I haven't liked all that has happened." He closed his eyes and lowered his voice. "I certainly have not enjoyed watching you suffer. I only know two things for certain. One: We will leave very soon. Two: I want you with me."

She chewed on her nails. "I don't know."

"You said you'd marry me."

"You never said that meant leaving."

He spread his hands and looked around them. "What is here for you? Not your family. Not a home. Why not come with me? I promise I will take care of you. Nothing will hurt you anymore."

"No."

Her answer struck him worse than a fist. "No? But why?"

"Because I can't trust you. Or your God."

"Being with me can't be worse than staying here." He moved closer to her. "I can't be worse than Ramses."

She didn't move away, but she didn't respond. Her ebony eyes held no light for him.

"I love you. Please come with me."

She remained silent.

Eleven

First Month of Shemu, Season of Harvest

Bezalel leaned against a stone column on the edge of the courtyard and gazed northwest toward the voided land. The empty fields were unsettling; farms should be bustling with activity from dusk to dawn. Men, women, even small children should be working under the unforgiving sun until they could no longer stand, trying to get the grain harvested and stored away. Instead, they were trying to figure out where they were going to get enough food to sustain them through the next year.

Kamose joined him at the rim of the palace. Bezalel noticed he always stood like a soldier, never totally relaxed, feet shoulder-width apart, arms crossed, eyes constantly scanning.

"I thought the biting flies were bad enough," Kamose said. "Next the boils ate away at my flesh. Then falling ice killed my men and now, there is no food. I cannot imagine what else there is left to destroy and that man inside"—his hands balled into fists at his sides—"pretends none of it ever happened!" He took a deep breath and calmed himself.

Bezalel lifted his face to the sky. "The moon will be full tonight. Yahweh will send another sign. If the pattern holds."

Several quiet moments hung between them.

Kamose broke the silence. "Can I ask you how Ahmose is doing?"

Bezalel chuckled. "He has grown so much. He loves my Imma. He calls her Aunt Rebekah. Sometimes... it's like he has been there all along, like he's always been my little brother." He paused. "Do you have any siblings?"

"Several." Kamose smiled. "We were a noisy house."

"I've always been alone. My mother wanted more, but I was the only one. She is so happy to have another one. And Ahmose loves having a mother."

"And your father? What does he think about Ahmose?"

Bezalel shifted his stance. "My father died in the brickfields years ago. I have few memories of him. I was already living here and didn't see him much as it was, so there's not much to remember."

Kamose looked at the sand. "I am sorry. I didn't know."

Bezalel shrugged. "Maybe you should come see Ahmose sometime."

Kamose scoffed. "Yes. I should just walk into your village. A soldier. Pharaoh's personal guard, at that."

"You could take off your dagger and armbands. There are many Egyptians there. I certainly can't bring him here."

Kamose breathed deeply. "Perhaps."

❧❦

Later that morning Ramses summoned Bezalel to the throne room.

"I have many guests arriving in three days," the king said. "I need gifts."

"What would you have me make?"

"Indulge yourself. Jewelry, perhaps. There will be two kings, of very small countries, of course, not as important as Egypt, and a queen, as well as several officers. But all you need concern yourself with are the kings and queen."

"Yes, my king. I shall begin immediately." Bezalel bowed deeply.

The pharaoh walked away, anklets tinkling.

Bezalel spent several hours experimenting with his materials and tools to come up with a suitable gift for the visiting queen, and eventually decided on a necklace. He hammered out the soft petals of a bronze flower. Eight blooms would decorate the necklace. He fashioned each one out of a single, tiny piece of bronze, each petal so thin it was almost translucent. They were troublesome to make; he began handfuls before he completed eight. The rest were imperfect, and he destroyed them. When he finished the final flower, he laid it beside the rest of the necklace. He would attach them tomorrow. His shoulders ached from the tedious work of the last several hours, and he was hungry.

He had worked through the noon meal, so he latched the door behind him and started down the hall toward the kitchen. He had taken only three steps when the corridor suddenly became as dark as a moonless night. Several gasps and a few shouts came from somewhere ahead of him. What could have happened? He could think of nothing that could darken the palace like this. He edged his way to the wall on his right, put out his hands, and felt his way toward the portico.

When he turned the corner he should have been able to see some light shining from the courtyard, but there was none. His heart quickened, but he was sure if he could just get out of the building, everything would be all right.

A servant rushed by him, jabbering in a tongue unfamiliar to Bezalel. He walked blindly through the portico, keeping his arms up, one before his face to protect himself and one straight ahead to feel any obstacles. But why was it still so dark?

The chattering servant ran by him again. He crashed into Bezalel, slamming him into one of the stone columns. Bezalel's shoulders hit the solid surface first, then his head smashed into the granite. Searing pain shot from his head through his neck to his upper back. He slumped to the ground against the column. He tried to stand, but waves of pain and dizziness flooded him and he slid down again. He tried once more to rise, but everything was still black. He put his hand to the back of his head, and when he touched it he felt something warm. Then he felt nothing at all.

❧❧

Kamose stood in front of the small mud brick home with his hand raised at the door. The last time he was here was during the raid on the village. Had Ahmose seen him, or had he kept his eyes closed? Kamose had far worse news now, anyway. He rapped on the door.

Bezalel's mother answered.

Ahmose peeked out from behind her.

"Is this where Bezalel the artisan lives?"

She hesitated before answering. "Yes. I'm his mother, Rebekah."

Kamose beckoned two other soldiers, who waited with Bezalel on a stretcher. They carried it into the house.

Rebekah opened the door wide and they gently set the stretcher on the floor. She gasped when she saw her son's still form.

Ahmose rushed to Bezalel and stared at the mess of bloody hair on his head then fell to the floor beside him.

"Is he…?" Ahmose looked up at Kamose and strained to say the word.

"He is not dead." Kamose knelt beside Ahmose and took his hand. "But he is seriously hurt." He stood again and faced Rebekah. "Do you have someone in the village who knows how to treat such injuries?"

"Yes, Samuel knows. Oh, but wait! He's at the canals. He won't be home until dusk!"

"He'll be home any moment. The men have been sent home. It is too dark to work."

An old man entered the house. "What's happening? I saw soldiers—" His gaze fell upon Bezalel on the floor.

"Sabba!" Ahmose ran to him, crying, and threw his arms around the old man's waist.

"Hur, go for Samuel." Rebekah put one hand on the man's arm and pointed to the door.

Hur looked at Bezalel once more and left, while Ahmose returned to Bezalel's side.

Rebekah turned to Kamose, her brow furrowed. "What do you mean, it's too dark?"

"The city of Ramses suddenly went completely dark. There are many who are injured at the palace, not just Bezalel. We lit lamps and torches and searched the palace for any who were hurt, and we found him at the edge of the portico. He appears to have hit his head on one of the columns."

"But the khamsin are not so dark you cannot see!"

He shook his head. "This was no dust storm. I believe this came from your God. We pleaded with Ramses to listen, to free the Israelites. He would have none of it."

Kamose stepped aside as a man rushed into the room, followed by Hur. The newcomer knelt beside the unmoving figure. He carefully parted Bezalel's hair to see the injury. He took Ahmose's tiny hands and used them to hold Bezalel's thick, bloody hair away from the gash.

Kamose's usually strong stomach did a somersault when he saw the fear and pain in Ahmose's eyes. He turned away.

Hur followed him. "May I ask who you are? Do you know my grandson?"

"I am Kamose, captain of the guard." He noticed the flash of recognition in Hur's eyes.

"Then you're—" Hur glanced at Ahmose, still hovering over Bezalel.

"Yes. He doesn't know. I'd like to keep it that way. Please."

"Of course."

They turned back to watch Samuel finish dressing Bezalel's wound.

Ahmose winced as Samuel scrubbed off the blood.

"It doesn't hurt him, habibi. He cannot feel anything." Samuel touched Ahmose's hand. "I promise."

"Why not? It hurt me when Aunt Rebekah cleaned my back."

"Because he is in a very deep sleep. You were not. In fact, he may not awaken for several days."

"For several days? Is it good to sleep so much?"

"No. It's not good. But we cannot wake him up. Only El Shaddai can do that."

Kamose watched Ahmose's face cloud as he realized what Samuel avoided speaking aloud. "What if he doesn't wake up?"

"We shall pray that he does." Samuel stood to face Rebekah. "I will be back tomorrow to change the bandage. Here is something to help the pain." He gave a bag of dried thyme to Rebekah. "Give it to him in a tea—if he wakes."

Her face blanched.

Kamose stepped toward them. "How serious is the injury?"

Samuel gestured toward the door, and the three men moved outside, followed by Rebekah. "It is quite serious, one of the worst I have seen. I have cleaned it and applied copper salts and honey. That is all I can do. The rest is up to Shaddai." Samuel nodded then left.

Hur touched Rebekah's shoulder. "Rebekah, before you go back inside, this is Kamose, Ahmose's uncle."

Rebekah took his hands in hers. "Ah, yes. Bezalel told us about you. Thank you for bringing him home. Would you like to stay a while?"

"I would. Thank you very much."

"I'll get you some food." She hurried toward the house.

He called after her. "No, please don't. I'm fine. Don't bother."

She looked back, her eyes wet. "It's no trouble. I need something to do." She started inside then turned back. "But you might want to remove your dagger. It will put Ahmose more at ease." She disappeared inside.

They entered the house and Hur sat on a low stool.

Kamose removed his armbands and dagger, placed them on a high shelf and sat on a cushion on the floor.

"You have to let her feed you, you know." Hur chuckled lightly. "She needs someone to take care of. She was meant to be a mother, and she never got the chance after Bezalel was taken to the palace. That's why Ahmose is such a blessing."

But right now, that "blessing" was in pain. Kamose could see it all over his face.

⬧

Evening turned into night, and nothing changed. Hur and Rebekah went to the roof to sleep, but Ahmose refused to leave Bezalel's side, waiting for him to wake.

Kamose stretched out on the floor near them.

Late in the night he awoke to a small voice. It took him a moment to realize where he was and who was talking.

Ahmose was talking to Bezalel, repeating the stories he must have learned in his new home. He recited tale after tale. "So Father Abraham brought the knife down, and as he did, he heard a noise. And what do you think the noise was? It was a ram. A great, big ram caught in the bushes. And Father Abraham said, 'Thank you, El Shaddai, for saving my son, Isaac.' And he released Isaac, and they got the ram, and sacrificed him. And then they went down the mountain.

"Would you like to hear another story? How about Joseph and his coat?"

Kamose lay awake as Ahmose continued through the long night, until the child finally lost his battle with sleep. Kamose rose and resettled him next to Bezalel, draping a blanket over his tiny body before lying down again and giving in to sleep himself.

ॐ∽◐

Kamose awoke before anyone else the next morning and started a fire in the kitchen's small clay oven. He had water boiling before Rebekah and Hur came down from the roof, and he shook his head in answer to their unasked question.

"I'll make tea. Go have a seat." He motioned to the main room. He found jasmine and hibiscus and prepared three cups of tea and a small cup of juice for Ahmose. He took cups to Hur and Rebekah and went back for the other two.

When he returned to the main room, he set the juice cup near Hur and stood in the doorframe with his tea.

Within moments, Ahmose awoke and crawled into Hur's lap.

Although Kamose had long ago made the choice to forego family for a life as a soldier, the scene brought a twinge of pain to his heart. Men made for war were not made to be husbands and fathers, in his opinion. He had never seen it work. They were too hard, too unemotional, too reserved, and their wives and children were not cared for properly. He had vowed he would never do that to a woman, and he had never married, or even come close.

Ahmose searched Hur's face. "Bezalel's been asleep almost a whole day."

"I know, habibi." Hur stroked Ahmose's head and pushed the hair from his face.

"Can El Shaddai really help?"

"I believe He can." Hur wrapped his strong arms around the boy, and Ahmose sank into his chest.

Ahmose sniffled. "Our gods cannot ever help. We prayed many times in Egypt, but they never helped."

Kamose knew how that felt.

Hur nodded. "Well, that is because they are not really gods. They are things men have made, of wood, or stone, or they are stars in the sky, or animals, or something else. But Shaddai was not made by anyone. He made the stars and the animals and the wood and stone. He even made you and me. And that is why He can help."

"Does that mean Bezalel will get better if we ask El Shaddai to help him?"

"No, it does not."

That was not the answer Kamose expected. Why wouldn't this God help when asked?

Ahmose bolted upright and turned to face Hur. "But why? Doesn't He want to help him?"

"Yes, but sometimes El Shaddai has something better in mind."

"What could be better than making Bezalel well? I don't understand." Ahmose rubbed his eyes as they became moist.

"Exactly. We don't understand all the time." Hur pulled the boy's hands away from his face and gazed into his eyes. "Do you remember when Jannes beat you?"

"Yes."

"That was not good, was it?"

"No, of course not." Ahmose shook his head.

"But if he hadn't beaten you, Bezalel would not have brought you here to live with us, right?"

"Right."

"And you would not have learned about Shaddai."

"No."

"So, sometimes, good things happen, even when they look very bad. We just have to trust Shaddai, and believe He will always do the best thing for us."

Ahmose sank back onto Hur's chest again. "But I still want Bezalel to get better."

"So do I, habibi, so do I." Hur hugged the boy. "Ahmose, do you remember Kamose? He worked in the palace with you and Bezalel."

"Yes. He brought Bezalel home yesterday." Ahmose hopped off Hur's lap and plodded over to Kamose, who knelt on the floor. "You know, Jannes didn't like you."

"I know. But Jannes didn't like anyone."

"He definitely didn't like me." Ahmose squirmed and absently rubbed his back.

"I heard he hurt you. I'm sorry."

"Does Jambres know I'm here?"

"No, he doesn't. I don't think he has time to look. He's too busy trying to take over everything he can." Kamose touched Ahmose's shoulder. "He's in enough trouble with me already, but I am watching him closely. He won't ever hurt you again."

"Thank you." Ahmose smiled. "You're a soldier?"

Visions of the raid flashed through Kamose's mind, and his heart clenched. Did Ahmose remember? "Yes. How can you tell?"

"Your sandals." Ahmose touched the laced-up shoes. "Only soldiers wear that kind."

Kamose smiled and let out a deep breath. "You're very observant."

"Is that a good thing?"

Kamose laughed. "Why don't we take a walk outside and let your aunt make us some breakfast? I think we could use some fresh air. We could walk down toward the palace and see if it's still dark."

They didn't have to go far to see a cloud hovering over the city. They strolled along the path by the river toward the royal residence. As they neared the palace, Ahmose reached for Kamose's hand. The darkness touched the ground; not a spark of light escaped the layer of shadow that concealed Pi-Ramses. The blackness was palpable; it was hard to breathe. It felt like a wet blanket.

Kamose wished he had grabbed his dagger.

Ahmose began to squirm.

"It's all right, habibi. We'll go back now." Kamose picked him up and placed him on his shoulders and jogged back to the village.

෬෬

Kamose spent another night on the floor by Bezalel and Ahmose. He worried that the child had not cried since he brought Bezalel home—it didn't seem normal. Ahmose stayed awake long into the night repeating stories again, even singing songs. Kamose recognized most of them as lullabies. He grinned at the thought of a small child singing cradlesongs to a grown man.

As the morning light climbed into the room through the high window, Ahmose stopped singing. Kamose listened carefully for the sound of rhythmic breathing to tell him that Ahmose had finally fallen asleep. Instead he heard Ahmose talking. At first he couldn't tell to whom the child was speaking, then he realized Ahmose was praying. To Bezalel's god.

"El Shaddai, my name is Ahmose. Bezalel has taught me about You. He says You are God of everything. And Sabba says You can make Bezalel wake up.

"When I prayed to the gods in Egypt, nothing ever happened. Bezalel says You are not like those other gods. If You are not, please make him wake up. I love him so much, and I want him to get better...."

Tears streamed down Ahmose's cheeks and onto his tunic. Soon exhaustion overcame him, and he dropped onto Bezalel's chest.

Kamose watched him for a few moments as the child slept, sunlight bouncing off his wet face. He had never loved anyone like that; he had never been loved like that, except perhaps by his parents. He was quite jealous, at least for a second. But he was far happier that

Ahmose had found a family to love and care for him. He had abdicated that responsibility. He could say it was because Tia wanted it that way, but he knew it was because he was unable—and unwilling—to provide Ahmose with what he needed. But here Ahmose had a brother, a mother, a grandfather...even a god. Maybe he didn't need an uncle.

When the sun's full force took over the room, Bezalel began to stir.

"Ohh...."

Ahmose sleepily sat up. "What?"

"I'm hungry." Bezalel brought his hand up to his head. "Oh, my head!" Bezalel tried to sit up but collapsed back onto the stretcher.

"Sabba!" Ahmose stood and ran backwards toward the kitchen, never taking his eyes off Bezalel.

Hur came running from the roof, followed quickly by Rebekah.

Kamose moved out of the way.

Hur knelt beside Bezalel and placed a strong arm under his back to help him sit up.

"I feel as if I haven't eaten in days."

"Because you haven't!" Hur laughed.

Ahmose encircled Bezalel from behind and hugged hard.

"Careful!" Hur laughed again and untangled Ahmose's arms from around Bezalel. "He just woke up! You'll squeeze him right back to sleep!"

Ahmose jumped up as Rebekah came to sit by her son. Tears poured from Ahmose's eyes as he laughed and danced around the room. "He did it! He did it!" He kept shouting through his tears. "He really did it!"

"Who did what?" Hur grabbed at Ahmose's wrist.

"Shaddai!" Ahmose squealed. "He made Bezalel wake up, just like I asked Him to! He really is God!" He leaped up into Kamose's arms. "He did it!"

"I see that." Kamose laughed as the boy jumped down and continued to bounce around the room. He noiselessly went to the shelf for his dagger and armbands. He put them on and slipped out the door. He was halfway down the street when he heard Ahmose running after him.

"Kamose, where are you going?"

Kamose stopped and turned around. "I should get back to the palace."

Ahmose looked south. "But it's still dark there. Why won't you stay here?"

"You don't need me here any longer."

Ahmose took his hand. "But I want you to stay."

The remark caught him off guard. "You do? Why?"

"You're my friend. You're Bezalel's friend. We love you."

He said it so simply. So trustingly. For him there were no questions, no complications. Why couldn't life truly be like that? But it wasn't, and a child's naïve view would not make it so. He pulled his hand away. "I think you should just take care of Bezalel for now."

"Please? What will you do in the dark?"

Kamose stared at the little boy with the large, dark eyes. How could he be so trusting after all the evil he had endured?

"Can't you at least come eat with us before you go?"

He had no answer to that. He took the child's outstretched hand and followed him home.

Twelve

Second month of Shemu, Season of Harvest
Israelite month of Abib

Bezalel gingerly lowered himself to the ground outside his house. Ahmose joined him, crossing his legs in exactly the same manner, and handed him a cup. "Aunt Rebekah sent you some thyme tea."

They sat under the waxing moon and watched as women chatted, children squealed and chased one another, and young couples tried to evade prying eyes. The celestial light and warmer nights beckoned many to enjoy the open air after winter's chill. Sounds of hammering filled the air as men built spits on which to roast lamb.

Ahmose rubbed Bezalel's brow gently. "Does your head still hurt? Do you still get lots of headaches?"

"Yes, but they're getting further apart. I should be ready to work soon." He scoffed. "Besides, the palace is in such chaos, no one even notices I am gone." Bezalel sipped the hot tea. "Sabba tells me you told me stories while I was hurt."

"Yes. Did you hear me?"

"Sometimes. Never very clearly. But I knew you were there. I'm glad you stayed by me." Bezalel put his arm around the boy and kissed his head. "See the moon?" He pointed to the sky.

"Yes. It's getting round and bright again."

"Do you know what that means?"

"No. Tell me." Ahmose looked up expectantly.

"That means it's almost time for *pesach* and *mat sot*."

"What are those? I don't know those Hebrew words." Ahmose sat on his heels.

"Well, pesach is celebrated during the first full moon of the spring. This is the month we call *Abib*, when the lambs are born. Each family chooses one lamb, or sometimes a kid, to kill for the meal. The lamb is roasted outdoors over a fire, with bitter herbs for seasoning. The families eat it outside along with mat sot, and the celebration lasts all night. It's my favorite time of the year."

"What's mat sot?"

Bezalel blew on the tea. "This month is also when the grains ripen and are ready for harvest. Mat sot are barley cakes. We make them with barley flour and water, with no fermented dough to make it rise, so they're flat. We don't use the old dough, because we throw it all out so it can't contaminate the new crop. When the new crop of barley flour is ready, we make bread with new dough. That keeps it all fresh and healthy for another year."

"Do they taste good?"

"They're all right. Mat sot are quick to bake and easy to carry, and shepherds ate them during the busy time of lambing. Now, of course, they are only traditional, since we keep only a few sheep. The mat sot festival starts the day after pesach and lasts seven days. They are a celebration of the harvest." Bezalel stretched out his legs and leaned back against the house and drank the cooled tea.

"How's your head?" A deep voice sliced through the chatter.

"Kamose!" Ahmose jumped up and ran to meet him.

The big Egyptian hoisted Ahmose onto his shoulders and strolled toward Bezalel.

Imma brought out some carob pods, baby radishes, and hot bread. She nodded toward the visitor. "It's good to see you, Captain."

Kamose nodded a greeting.

Ahmose hopped down and followed Imma inside.

Kamose's gaze followed the boy.

Bezalel popped a radish into his mouth. "I'm sorry you don't get to see him as much. But you're welcome here any time."

Kamose watched the door for a moment then sat on the ground across from Bezalel, one leg folded in front of him and one knee up. "How are the headaches?"

Bezalel frowned. "How did you know I have headaches?"

"I know how head wounds heal. You were lucky. Trouble remembering things?"

"I can't remember much of that day yet. Bits and pieces come back. I forget things that are told to me just a few minutes later. I have trouble sleeping."

"It should get better eventually." Kamose glanced around at the villagers. "I like it here. At least, I like being around your family."

"Want to play a game?" Ahmose emerged from the house with several dice in his hand.

Kamose chuckled, and the trio played and chatted until Imma poked her head out again. "I hate to break up the game, but it's time for Ahmose to go to bed."

"But I'm winning! I've won five times. I'm better than both of them, and I'm just a boy!"

Bezalel suppressed a laugh behind a cough.

Imma shot him a warning look. "And it's because you're just a boy that you need to sleep."

"All right. I'm coming." Ahmose gathered the dice and obeyed, but not before kissing Bezalel—and Kamose—good night.

Bezalel cleared his throat. "Have you seen Meri?'

"Yes. And as soon as you come back, you can take her away from the harem legally."

"Really? How did you manage that?"

"I threatened Jambres. I told him I'd tell Ramses about his little party with the concubines. Ramses may not be sleeping with them anymore, but I don't think he wants to share them." He rolled a radish between his fingers. "I'd still rather kill that snobby, useless magician."

Bezalel nodded. "Good."

"You don't sound very happy. I expected a better reaction that that."

"I'm sorry. I appreciate all you've done, I do. But I'm not sure she'll marry me now."

"Why not?"

Bezalel leaned his head against the wall. "The last time I saw her, we argued. I told her I wanted her to come with me when we leave Egypt. But when I told her El Shaddai was responsible for all that has happened, she became very angry with me and said she couldn't trust me or my God. I couldn't make her understand that He is doing it all only to make Ramses let us go."

Kamose reached for a fig. "You know she reacts quickly and strongly. She reminds me very much of Tia. Give her time. She's hurt now, but I think she'll understand."

Bezalel smiled weakly. "I hope so."

Kamose was somber as he finished the fruit. "I no longer believe Ramses is a god. I don't know about your God yet, or any gods for that matter, but it's become clear to me in the last months that the king is only a man."

The captain tossed the fig peel onto the platter. "I have to go. I just wanted to check on you and Ahmose. I put myself on night duty for a while. Ramses trusts no one but me right now." The captain chuckled as he stood. "The god needs a bodyguard."

14 Abib

Several days later, when the moon had grown fat and full, Imma set the table for the evening meal. The door banged open. Sabba looked more solemn than Bezalel had ever seen him. His face was ashen.

"What happened?" Imma rushed to his side.

Sabba closed the door behind him and eyed each person. "Moses says it will be tonight. We have much to do to prepare." He spoke quietly, but with a firmness Bezalel had not ever heard from his beloved and gentle Sabba.

"What will be tonight?" Imma's eyes narrowed as she looked from Sabba to Bezalel and back again. "Prepare what?"

"Tonight we will leave Egypt. Pack a bag."

Tonight we will leave Egypt. Sabba said this almost as casually as he might have said, "Tomorrow we will go fish in the river." *Tonight. Right now?* How does an entire people just leave? The concept was too absurd to comprehend.

Sabba put his hand on the door then turned back. "I'm going to get the pesach lamb. I've already packed. While I am gone, Rebekah, you are to ask our Egyptian neighbors for things made of silver and gold. They will gladly give them to you. El Shaddai has commanded this."

Bezalel jammed his clothes into a bag then helped Ahmose fill a sack with the clothes the neighbors had given him.

Sabba returned and peeked inside. "Please come outside with me."

They crowded around their narrow front door. Other families did the same, packing the snaking pathway between houses. The early spring breeze drifted down the street, and the moon shone brightly.

Sabba had a flint knife in his hand, the blade sharper than any metal one Bezalel could have crafted. He knelt behind the lamb he had brought with him from the field. It nuzzled against his leg and softly bleated.

Sabba took the knife in his right hand and the jaw of the lamb in the other. He raised the lamb's head up and swiftly drew the knife across its neck.

Bezalel knew the animal felt no pain, but a faint cry escaped Imma's lips.

Ahmose grabbed Bezalel's hand and squeezed.

Blood flowed down into the trough dug in front of the house to protect it from the yearly flooding of the Nile. Sabba placed a container under the lamb's neck to catch the blood. He reached for a stalk of hyssop lying by the door and dipped it into the pottery now overflowing with the lamb's lifeblood. He brushed it against the top, then the left, and finally the right side of the doorframe. He bent and took the lamb from the ground where he had laid it and gave it to Imma. "As always, for pesach, you are to roast this over a fire, with bitter herbs and mat sot. We will, however, cook and eat indoors this year."

She opened her mouth as if to question the strange instructions but said nothing.

Up and down the street other families butchered their lambs, and most—but not all—painted blood on the doorframes. What would happen now?

❧⚜❧

The soothing aroma of hundreds of roasting lambs saturated the air, punctuated by the tangy smell of horseradish. Sabba had said they could not go out of the house.

Ahmose curled up beside Bezalel.

No one talked, and Bezalel did not want to be the one to break the silence. He was in a dream, afraid he would awaken at any moment to find they were all still slaves, and always would be.

The waiting was agony—then he felt guilty. For four hundred years Israel had waited for El Shaddai to rescue them. Why now? How many of his relatives had died waiting? Why should he live to see it?

Long after dark, Imma told the men the meal was almost done.

Sabba stood. "We must get ready to leave now."

"Leave? But what about the lamb?" Imma was clearly irritated.

"We will eat the lamb, but we will eat it standing, inside, with our cloaks and sandals on."

They gathered their sandals and heaviest thawbs, and as the four of them stood around the table, Sabba cleared his throat. "Tonight, El Shaddai will pass through all Egypt with one final, terrible sign, more terrible than all the others. Tonight, He will strike down the firstborn son in every household, from Pharaoh, to the servants, to the animals."

Bezalel swallowed hard, and Imma gasped.

Sabba took the hand of both as he continued. "*Except* for those who have obeyed His command and put the sacrificial blood on the door. The blood will be a notice to Him, and He will pass over us; He will protect us from death tonight."

"Let us eat quickly," Sabba continued, "for we must be ready to leave at any moment. Whatever we don't eat, we must burn. Eat your fill; we have a long journey ahead of us."

↷∝∽↶

Agonizing cries pierced Bezalel's ears and made him jittery. The coppery smell of blood had displaced the aroma of roast mutton. How many more would suffer?

They had finished the meal, and again they waited. Bezalel sat on the floor with Ahmose in his lap. His stomach was satisfied, but his heart ached. Many Egyptians lived among them in the village, as well as some Israelites who had refused to listen to Moses. Bezalel knew who they were, and knew they now paid a high price for their stubbornness.

Every time she heard the howls, his mother cringed. Ahmose left Bezalel and climbed onto her lap. She clutched him to her breast.

Another scream, followed by heart-breaking sobs. Bezalel pulled his legs up and hugged them, putting his head on his knees. His heart lay like a hunk of stone within his chest. How it must feel to lose a child, especially because you chose to ignore a warning from Shaddai.

His sorrow for those who endured the loss of a son and those who had died waiting warred with the elation of imminent escape. There was also the question of what life would be like beyond the confines of the palace walls. There were innumerable unknowns, but wouldn't anything be better than slavery?

And of course, there was the question of Meri. Would she come with him?

☙❧

Nefertari slumped on the floor, cradling her son's head in her lap, rocking back and forth, sobbing and moaning. Her cries carried throughout the palace. Many of Egypt's sons had died tonight, but in the palace, all that mattered was that Amun-her-khepeshef was dead.

Kamose guarded the doorway of Ramses' private quarters, hands balled into fists at his sides, muscles in his shoulders and neck tensed. He wasn't sure whether he was more heartbroken or angry.

Ramses stood beside Nefertari, head hung to his chest, looking utterly helpless. None of his powers or sorcerers or officials could help him now.

"I begged you to let them go! I begged you—" She pounded on his thigh. "But you could not give up your precious city! Well, now you have it, but you have no son!" She turned back to the still form of her son, wrapped her arms around him, and buried her face in his chest.

The king wheeled to Kamose and pointed. "Bring me that Israelite!" Then he raised his face toward the sky, fists in the air, and howled.

Kamose marched down the hall and found an idle soldier. "Go to the village and come back with their leader, Moses. Be quick!" He returned to the room where Nefertari still wept. He watched her cry and then hung his head. A weight hunched his shoulders. Whether he believed Ramses to be a god or not, no matter how many warnings Ramses had ignored, it distressed him that he could do nothing to alleviate her suffering. It was his job to protect the family, and he had failed. Miserably.

Not that there was anything he could have done to prevent what had happened. Bezalel was right; El Shaddai was in control. This must be His doing, like all the other terrible things that had happened to Egypt. He had to be a very powerful God, more powerful than any of Egypt's gods. Isis could not keep the crops safe from the hail. The greatest god, the sun-god Ra did not show his face for three days. But was a mightier God necessarily a better God?

෨෯

When the Israelites arrived, guards led them to Ramses's rooms. Kamose stepped aside to let them pass. The brothers said nothing, but Moses bowed his head.

"Up! Leave Egypt, all of you! Go, worship your God as you have requested. Take your women, your flocks, your herds, anything you want, and go." Ramses screamed, but there were tears on his cheeks.

"As you wish." Moses backed away and walked down the hall.

"No! Bring him back!" Ramses yelled at Kamose.

Kamose chased down Moses and Aaron and brought them back to the devastated ruler.

When Moses returned, the king said, "First, bless me."

෨෯

"But I have to get in there!" At the edge of the village Bezalel tried to get around Moses, but the older man side-stepped and stuck out his staff.

"If you go in there, you will be killed. Ramses has every guard alive stationed around the perimeter, and he has ordered that any Israelite nearing the palace be instantly killed."

"But Meri! I have to get Meri!"

Moses grabbed him by the shoulders. "You will never get to her." He spoke softly. "I'm really very sorry, but it's too late."

"I have to try!" Bezalel started to go around Moses to the right, then when Moses tried to block him, jumped around him to the left and bolted for the palace.

He ran full-speed until he could see the courtyard, then stopped like he had slammed into a hippopotamus. Moses was right. In the shimmering moonlight he could see armed soldiers posted an arm's length apart all around the edge of the palace.

His chest tightened as if the air had been sucked out of his lungs. All the energy left his body and he collapsed to his knees.

There was no getting past the soldiers. There wasn't an unguarded space around the garden, the courtyard, anywhere. He couldn't get in. She couldn't get out. His heart was ripped from his chest. He dropped his head to the sand and hot tears ran down his face.

He couldn't breathe.

Now what? He promised he'd take care of her. If he stayed, would he even be alive beyond tomorrow? He wouldn't be able to work in the palace anymore. There was no food. The village would be empty. He couldn't possibly support her.

But leave without her? After he promised he would always be there for her? In the palace he was sure she would at least eat. They would get food from somewhere, maybe bring it in from Nubia. She would be safe. Kamose would watch out for her.

And she would hate him for deserting her.

Either way, he would fail her.

Thirteen

Goshen, Egypt
15 Abib

Bezalel concentrated on putting one foot in front of the other. They had been walking since long before dawn and Goshen was now far behind them. The desolate land around him echoed the empty feeling in his soul. Meri consumed his every thought. His stomach was in knots worrying and wondering about her. Had she eaten yet? Was she safe? Did she know how hard he tried to get to her? Did she care?

How could Shaddai do this to him? He finally found the missing piece in his life; then Shaddai ripped it away.

Bezalel, and all Israel, had freedom, but the price was steep. For Bezalel, maybe too steep.

જ્જ

Long shadows fell eastward over the sand as the Israelites reached Succoth. Bezalel's calves and thighs were on fire, his shoulders ached, and he longed to rid himself of his pack—and that of Ahmose, who had early on abandoned any effort to carry his. Bezalel had always thought he was strong, but walking all day and carrying two weighty bags was almost more than his body could bear.

He tossed the bundles on the ground and collapsed on them. He closed his eyes until his muscles no longer burned.

Rising up on his elbows, he surveyed the area. Terrain that was again lush and green had replaced the empty, barren land. A bubbling *wadi* meandered in from the Nile and ran toward the sea, bringing fresh water to this area and leaving it fertile and abundant. Beside the wadi, tents were stacked in neat piles everywhere. He sucked in a lungful of air and the scent of the river washed away his fatigue. A little, anyway.

Sycamore trees and date palms draped shade over him. He stood and grabbed a fig and peeled it, biting into the sweet fruit. The juice filled his mouth and ran down his chin and he wiped it off with the back of his hand. He grabbed several more. When would they have fresh fruit again?

Sabba joined him, with Imma and Ahmose close behind.

Bezalel moved toward his grandfather and took his pack from him. "It was a long day. Are you well?"

"I'm fine, habibi. The pace has been set nicely for all of us. Moses knows how to move a mass of people. I think Ahmose is the worst off. It's more a matter of the mind than the legs, I believe." Sabba chuckled, but Bezalel noticed him rubbing his back.

"Well, at least we have shade again," Imma said. "I'll get some food together."

At least the sand would be soft to sleep on. Bezalel plodded over to a pile of tents and reached for two. He groaned as he bent over, and pain shot up and down his legs. He dragged the tents, along with the willow poles, back to his family, and set them up while Imma retrieved some mat sot from her pack.

Moses had told them tents would be waiting for them. The army tents were made to be put up and taken down easily. *Thank you, Shaddai.* When he finished, Bezalel dropped to the ground and stuffed a piece of mat sot into his mouth.

"Ahmose, you have to eat something." Bezalel offered him a piece of bread. "You've walked half the night and all day and you need food to give you energy for tomorrow."

Ahmose shook his head.

"A fig?"

"I don't want to eat. And I *don't* want to walk tomorrow." Ahmose sat with his knees up, his elbows on his knees and his jaw in his hands.

It was a useless battle.

"Then will you drink some goat milk?" He gave the boy a cup.

Ahmose drank until Bezalel was satisfied he had enough in his belly to sleep through the night.

As the light of day disappeared into the dark of night, Bezalel crawled into the small tent with Ahmose close behind him.

Ahmose slid over next to him and fell asleep, and Sabba joined them later. The tent was big enough for the three of them, with Imma in her own.

Bezalel lay on his back and tucked his arm under his head, listening to the kip-kip of African skimmers flying over the wadi searching for fish. He gazed at the red stripe around the top edge of the tent. The colors indicated which of the four army divisions each tent belonged to. Each division was named for one of the Egyptian gods—Seth, Amun, Ptah, or Ra, but at the moment he could not remember which was red. It didn't really matter. Any day now, all four divisions would come to claim their tents—and their slaves—but he knew they had at least two or three days while the Egyptians carried out the beginnings of their elaborate funeral traditions, especially if the prince was one of the dead.

A jackal howled in the distance. Bezalel kissed Ahmose's head then rolled over and went to sleep.

∂∞✑

The eastern sun streamed between the flaps of the tent and filled it with warm light. Bezalel squinted and rolled over on his stomach and elbows. He looked around at the tent. *Where am I?* He ran his hand over his face and through his hair. The fog in his brain slowly dissipated and everything came back to him. The lamb, the meal, the screams, the gold...

And Meri.

He tried to sit up but his legs protested, reminded him of the long walk.

Then he remembered Kamose, and a realization stabbed his brain like heron attacking a perch. His breath caught in his throat and then escaped as a soft groan. If Ramses's son had died, as Shaddai promised, Kamose would likely be executed for allowing such a catastrophe. Bezalel dropped his head onto his arms.

"Why are you moaning, habibi?" Sabba's voice caused Bezalel to lift his head. He opened his eyes and looked over to his grandfather and Ahmose, who was curled up in a little ball next to him.

"Kamose." Bezalel sighed deeply and rubbed his hand across his face.

Sabba looked down at Ahmose and stroked his cheek with the backs of his fingers. He pushed the boy's hair away from his face. "There is nothing we can do to change that now. Be glad you never told Ahmose."

Bezalel crawled out of the tent. He stood and raised his arms above his head and grunted as his back and leg muscles stretched after tightening overnight.

Sabba followed him out, just as Moses came by. Moses said to them, "We'll be staying at Succoth another night. I don't think the people can take another day of walking yet. We'll go slowly for a while."

Ahmose emerged as Moses was talking. "You mean we can stay?" He clapped his hands and laughed.

"Yes, you can stay." Moses chuckled as Ahmose ran off. "Hur, can you help spread the message? Also ask all the elders to meet me tomorrow morning for instructions."

Sabba gestured to the spacious area around them. "This is a wonderful place to stop for a while. Why are all these tents here?"

"This is a staging area for training and battle. Its one great asset is open, flat space. Ramses's army boasts twenty thousand armed men. I knew there would be tents and other supplies here, and I hoped we could stay long enough to get organized."

Moses stroked his chin. "I see now why Yahweh compelled me to endure the constant military training I so despised in my youth as a prince. I pray I can remember all I learned: evacuation, communication, strategy, safety, supplies, routes, enemies, weapons, protection … it all spins in my head."

Sabba touched his shoulder. "For the present, it is only necessary to get everyone out of the village and safely away from Ramses." He shrugged and spread his arms. "The rest will come later."

Moses shook his head. "That is where you are mistaken, Hur. You must always be several steps ahead. For if you are not, your enemy surely will be."

17 Abib

A day in the shadow of the wadi's sycamores was a welcome rest. Imma milked the sheep, and Bezalel took the skin bags of milk and put them in the river. He made sure all the bags were thoroughly soaked before he took them out and hung them in the trees to cool.

The water cooled his skin as well, and he lay down to nap in the shade by the river while Ahmose chased other boys. Bezalel stared up at the clouds through the leaves of the date palms. Ibises and herons searched for fish in the wadi, and a desert hare bounded by.

Two nights and two days. That's all it had been since they had left, but it felt like an eternity without Meri. It wasn't as if they had even seen each other every day before, but just knowing she was nearby, knowing he might see her at any moment had been enough. Now, knowing he would never see her again was aguish. Wondering if she hated him for it, if she thought he hadn't even tried to find her—or worse, was glad he was gone—was torture. There was a hole in his gut he didn't think would ever heal.

Every time he closed his eyes he saw her face, remembered how it felt to touch her, to hold her, to kiss her. Now she was gone forever.

He didn't see how he would endure it.

☙ ❧

Sabba returned late in the morning from the meeting with Moses and the elders. "We have a long day ahead of us. Yahweh has commanded we take the southern route—"

"But isn't that the long way?" Imma pointed north over her shoulder. "Why are we heading south if the land we are promised is north? Shouldn't we take the northern route, the one that goes directly there?"

"That road has eleven Egyptian fortresses along it. We are not ready for war. Yes, this is a longer route, but safer."

The urgency of the escape had worn off and now the only goal Bezalel had was getting as far away from Pharaoh's army as quickly as possible. The reality of walking and carrying bags and food for many weeks hit him, and he tried to push the thought that he would never see Goshen—or Meri—again far back into his mind.

"We have to carry the tents now. I'll do that." Bezalel tossed Ahmose's small bag to his mother. "Ahmose couldn't carry what he had the other day. What does he have in there?"

Imma rummaged through the bag. "A couple tunics, some jewelry—did you give him that to carry?"

"Yes, but it's not very heav—"

"Wait. Here's the problem. It's a toy. Looks like a crocodile made of stone. Look—its mouth moves!" She pulled a string coming from the animal's head and the jaw moved up and down.

Bezalel reached for the toy. "I don't think he's ever had any toys of his own." His voice was soft. "I wonder where he got this one?"

"There's another one here, too." She handed him a similar figurine, this one a hippo. "No wonder his pack was too much for him."

"All right, if you make the packs as even as you can between the rest of us, I'll go talk to Ahmose. He'll have to leave these here."

"What will you tell him?"

"I'm not sure yet." Bezalel shrugged as he exited the tent. "I'll be back to strike the tents."

Bezalel ambled over to where Ahmose was splashing in the water and beckoned him.

The boy skipped over. "Yes?"

Bezalel knelt before him in the sand and held out the stone figures. "Where did you get these?"

Ahmose's lip quivered. "I didn't steal them! He gave them to me!"

Bezalel reached for the child's face. "You're not in trouble. I'm just asking, habibi."

Ahmose rubbed his eyes and took a shuddering breath. "Samuel gave them to me."

"Samuel? The one who took care of my head?"

Ahmose nodded. "I went to see him one day, and he showed them to me. I really liked them. A lot. So he gave them to me. His boys are grown, so he said I could play with them." The words spilled out almost more quickly than he could pronounce them. "Are you sure I'm not in trouble?"

"Of course not." Bezalel wrapped one arm around the child's waist and pulled him closer. "But you can't take these with you. They're much too heavy. You couldn't carry your pack and I can't help you now, because I have to carry the tents."

Ahmose rubbed his eyes again.

A slight breeze blew through the leaves of the date palms over-head as Bezalel thought for a moment. "You've never had a toy of your own, have you, Ahmose?"

"I've never had anything of my own, except my shenti." Tears filled his eyes.

Bezalel squeezed the child. Ahmose was all he had now, other than Imma and Sabba. He would do whatever it took to keep the little boy happy. He pulled away and looked him in the eye. "What if I make you a special toy, all your own, when we get to our new land?"

Ahmose's eyes sparkled like moonlight on the Nile. "Really? You would do that for me?"

"Ahmose, I would do anything for you."

20 Abib

Ramses II slouched on his throne, and stared with glassy eyes. His elbow rested on the arm of the throne and his head lay against his fist. His legs splayed out, and a cat purred as it wandered between them and under the throne. The double crown lay tossed aside on the dais.

Attendants lined the walls, waiting for orders that did not come. Trays of fruit sat untouched.

Kamose stood at the end of the platform, guarding the miserable man. Stuffy air filled the room—winter was over but spring had not yet taken a firm hold.

For days the pharaoh had not left his quarters. Today was the first time he had entered the throne room. His shenti was badly in need of a wash, and for that matter, so was he. Grime covered his feet and he could do with a shave. He wore none of his jewelry.

"My son is dead." The king addressed no one in particular. "My son is dead." He shifted his weight to the other side of the throne.

A few moments later, Ramses rose. "My son is dead! How can he be dead? I want justice! I want vengeance!" He raised his fists in the air and his voice grew louder.

He strode from one end of the dais to the other, his arms flailing. "My magicians are dead; my officers are dead; my counselors are dead! Who will advise me now?"

Kamose knew better than to answer. He crossed his arms and stared straight ahead.

Ramses descended. His face softened, and his walk slowed. Concentration knitted his brow.

"What have I done?" He put his fists on his hips and walked in circles. "It has been five days. All my workers are gone! They are not coming back. I will never finish my city. I want them back." He halted and raised his face to Kamose. "Get them back! I want every man in Egypt after them!" Ramses screamed, eyes blazing from behind smudged kohl. The muscles on his bare back and neck tightened. "Every horse, every chariot, every rider will follow them! And bring back my slaves!"

৵৽৹

It was late in the afternoon when Kamose arrived at Pi-Hahiroth. He gulped great breaths of air and felt like his lungs might explode. Foamy lather covered his horse.

He reined in his horse at the edge of the camp. Just a little bit longer, then he could stop. Neither he nor the horse could go much farther.

"I am looking for Bezalel, the artisan. Can you tell me where he is?"

People backed away without answering, ducking into tents. They saw him only as an Egyptian—and a soldier at that—not as one who had come to be their friend.

"I need to see Bezalel, son of Uri, son of Hur. I have important information for him. I am here to help." Kamose stared at those still outside. "Please." How could he get through to them that he meant no harm?

A young boy studied him carefully and apparently found him trustworthy. "They are camped at the front."

Moments later Kamose's horse stumbled to a stop once again.

"Kamose! What are you doing here?" Hur motioned to a young man nearby to take the reins.

Bezalel joined them. "Kamose! I was sure you were dead!"

Kamose held up his hand until he could slow his breathing. Then he swung his leg over his horse's head and jumped down. Hidden behind him on the animal, sat Meri.

Bezalel gasped.

"Brought you a present." Kamose chuckled and lifted Meri from his mount.

Meri ran to Bezalel and threw her arms around him. He stumbled back to keep from falling then lifted her off the ground in a strong embrace.

Kamose smiled as he watched the couple walk away, took a few more deep breaths, and then addressed the boy holding the reins. "Please rub down my horse. Wait for him to cool, and then water him and find something for him to eat." Turning toward Hur, he said, "Ramses has sent his army. They are probably half a day behind me, but no more."

"How did you find us so quickly?" Hur spread his hands, his eyes wide. "There are any number of directions we could have gone."

"When you left Etham to come here, you passed the first of several fortresses that make up the northern route. Your position was reported back to the palace."

Another boy approached with a skin of water and held it up. Kamose nodded to the child then upended the bag and gulped the cool liquid. Some spilled onto his bare chest. It felt good after his long ride. He was drenched in sweat and would have loved to jump in the Nile. Too late for that now.

Hur continued. "But we turned back south after we passed that fortress."

Hur apparently did not understand the expansive reach of Egypt's throne. "Yes, but there are traders, Bedouins who pass information to us in return for being left alone. And there are goat and camel herders—"

"All right, all right." Hur waved his hand. "Moses will need to know. We'll have to decide what to do. Do you want to come with us to tell him?"

Kamose shook his head. "I leave that to you." He was too tired to face a conversation like that, and felt he had no place in that decision.

"All right. For now." Hur turned and went to find Moses.

As Kamose paced and tried to figure out what "for now" meant, Bezalel and Meri returned, hands entwined.

Bezalel grabbed him and hugged him.

Kamose slapped him on the back. Bezalel was the closest thing to a friend he had known since he left the field and came to the palace. How many years ago?

Bezalel led Kamose and Meri to some rocks on which they could sit and rest, and handed them figs and mat sot. "I was sure you had been killed for allowing Amun-her to die. What happened, exactly?"

Kamose fingered a fig as he spoke. "I don't believe Ramses could think clearly. And I think he wanted protection more than vengeance. The funerals took three days—the beginnings of them at least. Of course, it will be months until they are all properly buried." He finished eating then stood and stretched. His body ached from the ride. It had been a long time since he had ridden a horse this far. Horses were usually reserved for chariots. His back ached, his thighs burned, and his knees screamed in pain.

"Ramses thought of nothing but Amun-her. Nefertari was still not speaking or eating when I left. After the ceremonies, Ramses looked at Egypt for maybe the first time since Moses arrived. The country is destroyed. There is no food to eat now; no crops will come in. We've lost a good portion of our livestock, and so many men. He blames all of you for that."

Kamose looked toward Egypt. "He *will* do whatever it takes to bring you back. He ordered me to assemble the armies. I decided I could no longer serve him. Ramses is not a god."

He paced again. His right hand rested on his dagger. "So instead, I grabbed a horse and rode here as fast as possible to warn you. I don't know what can be done. His army has horses, chariots, weapons, and trained soldiers. You have some men, but also women, children, old men, and no weapons."

Kamose finally stopped moving and stood before Bezalel. He drew his arm across his brow. Sweat mixed with the dust to form mud. All his training could not help him now. The energy produced by the excitement and danger of the ride was wearing off and fatigue was setting in fast. He feared his legs would collapse under him and returned to the rock.

"I don't know what I thought I could accomplish coming here." He sighed. "But when Ramses sent me to inform the division leaders, I realized I would rather fail here with all of you than be successful for him. I can ride much faster alone than an army, and it will take a while for him to realize the message never got to the leaders, and then more time to assemble the men and chariots, but the first division could be here by nightfall. Three more divisions besides that. His six hundred best chariots." He sat down next to Bezalel. "I can see no other end but slaughter."

Kamose studied his filthy feet, his dirty sandals laced up to his knees. "You know I can't go back now." He looked up Bezalel. "Once you told me Shaddai would welcome me as His. Do you still say so?"

Bezalel touched his arm. "You will be more than welcomed here. Not just by Shaddai, but by me, my family, and the people here."

Moses approached with Hur.

Kamose searched their calm faces. Would Moses remember the last time they were in the same room, when he had warned the Egyptians of the boils? Kamose had stepped between him and Ramses. Would Moses hold it against him?

"Yahweh has told me He will fight for us."

Kamose marveled at the authority in Moses's voice. It was utterly calm. He did not speak loudly—in fact, Kamose couldn't remember ever hearing him raise his voice, even when Ramses screamed at him. Moses kept one arm at his side, the other on his staff. Again, a total contrast to Ramses, who couldn't seem to speak without flailing his arms.

"We must assemble at the sea's edge. I passed the word down through the elders." Moses turned to Hur. "If you would gather your things, get there first, please, and help keep people calm. Wait for me. I'll be there shortly." He nodded to Kamose and left.

Kamose watched him leave then let out a long breath he didn't realize he'd been holding. He turned to Bezalel. "I'll wait there for you." He ambled toward the sea behind Hur. Would these people truly welcome him? Many Egyptians had come with the Israelites, he knew, but none were soldiers. None from the palace. Except Ahmose, of course, but he was a child. And even if the people accepted him, would El Shaddai? Bezalel said to trust Shaddai. But how could Kamose trust in a God he had never seen? Even the gods in Egypt, which were useless, he could see.

As a warrior, all he knew were facts, numbers, and strategies. He could only work with what he could see. And he saw no way out of this.

Fourteen

Relief flooded Bezalel. Away from Kamose, Sabba, and everyone else, he embraced Meri, her quivering arms around him. Her hot tears slid down his neck under his tunic. His body trembled and he couldn't control his breathing. Nothing mattered, other than Meri in his arms.

His fingers explored her face, moving over her cheeks, her eyes, her mouth, trying to decide if she was really there. He lowered his head to kiss her. That familiar shock—the one he thought he'd never feel again—pulsed through him. He breathed in her scent. "You don't smell of jasmine anymore."

"I know. We stopped making the perfume after the locusts. We ran out last week. I'm sorry."

He chuckled. "I wasn't complaining. Just noticing." He was afraid to let go, fearing she was just an illusion and would disappear. "What happened? How did you get here?"

She caressed his face. "It's a very long story. But I had no idea how difficult and painful a ride that would be. I've never ridden a horse before."

His breath caught in his throat. "Would you have changed your mind if you knew?"

"Of course not. I'm just saying I'm glad it's over. For many reasons." She brushed his lips with hers. "And I'll tell you all of them later."

After hearing about the advancing forces from Kamose, Bezalel laced his fingers with hers as they jogged toward the tents. "I have to take you to Imma now. She'll take care of you while I go with Sabba and Moses."

She planted her feet. "You're leaving me alone?"

"You heard Kamose. The army is chasing us!" He tugged her arm, but she remained fixed.

"Exactly!"

Bezalel growled to himself, and considered his next words carefully. He didn't want to anger her—again. "And you'll be safer with Imma. I'm going to the shore to see what happens. I want you back here, away from any danger."

"Danger?" She pointed at him. "Will *you* be safe, then?" Her voice wavered between anger and fear.

He'd said the wrong thing. He put two fingers to the side of his head and rubbed his temple. "I think so. But I don't want to take any chances with you." He stepped toward her and cupped her face in his hands. "I just got you back. I thought I'd never see you again, and it was agony. I would rather stay with you, but first we have to get across the water and away from Pharaoh's army. Then we'll have all the time we want. All right?"

She hugged her midsection tightly. Her gaze seemed to drill holes through him.

"I know you're afraid, but Yahweh said He'll fight for us. Nothing will happen. To either of us. I promise."

She said nothing.

"He said He'd get us out of Egypt, and He did. Right?"

She nodded.

"Then let's go." He arched an eyebrow. "All right?" He jerked his head in the direction of the tent.

She followed, but continued hugging herself.

They walked the short distance to his tent. Sabba had already been there and told Imma what was happening. She had packed the food and Egyptian gold.

"Imma, this is Meri. Kamose brought her."

Imma laughed and rushed to hug Meri. "Meri! It is good to finally meet the one who has taught my son to smile!" Meri stared at Bezalel with wide eyes and an open mouth over Imma's shoulder.

Bezalel hurriedly began to strike the tents while Imma continued to dazzle Meri with unexpected affection. Meri kept glancing his way. He ached to be alone with her, to reassure her. But he wanted to know—needed to know—what was happening. They were trapped between the Egyptians and the sea. He couldn't imagine what Shaddai had planned, but then he couldn't have imagined anything that had happened so far.

He grabbed his pack and the tents. "Imma, I'm taking the tents and my bag and going with Sabba. You and Ahmose and Meri can come with the rest of the group. Will that be all right?"

Imma smiled. "Go, go! We'll be fine. I'll take good care of her, don't worry." She stepped toward him and held him close for a moment. She had always given him such comfort, such strength. He needed that now. He knew Shaddai was in control, but beyond that…He took a deep breath and shoved his fears away. "I know you will."

He drew Meri to him and embraced her. "Remember I love you. I told you I would keep you safe. And I will." He wasn't at all sure how he would do that, but he needed her to believe he could.

She pulled back and looked him in the eyes. Her body trembled, but she nodded.

He kissed her, entrusted her to Imma, and left.

Before he could take two steps, Ahmose ran toward him from a group of children. He bounced on his feet, peeked in Bezalel's bag, and played with the tent strings. "What are you doing? Where are you going? Can I go with you?"

"One question at a time! Grab your bag, and *if* you can keep up and follow directions, you can come." He looked over his shoulder. "Imma, Ahmose is coming with me."

"Why does he get to go?" Meri pouted and pointed at Ahmose.

Bezalel raised one hand, palm up. He opened his mouth, but closed it again without speaking. Nothing he said would make her feel any better.

Imma laughed and put her arm around Meri. "You'll be better off here, habibti. Come with me."

Ahmose grabbed his pack and caught up with him quickly. At the shore, as the pair approached Kamose, Ahmose ran and leaped into his arms. "Kamose! I didn't know you were here, too!"

Kamose responded with an affectionate embrace.

"What's happening, Kamose?"

Kamose gazed at the crowd gathering at the water's edge. "Habibi, I wish I knew."

෧෩

Word rushed like a harsh eastern wind through the camp. The Egyptians were coming!

Bezalel and the others hiked to the shore. Every eye looked westward, waiting. Tension and fear settled on the crowd like a fog on the Nile. The last bits of sunlight shot from one horizon to the other. The sound intensified by the moment as six hundred war chariots thundered east.

"We've got to get to the shore, Ahmose. No matter what, don't let go of my hand!" Bezalel grabbed Ahmose and squirmed through the panicking throng. Jostled by the crowed, he fought to get to Sabba and Moses. His heart beat faster and his face flushed. Worried cries rose around him and, for a moment at least, it was difficult not to agree with the mistrust and hopelessness of the crowd. Slavery was worse than almost anything except death. But he had to believe Shaddai was in control.

Just as they reached Sabba, Moses clambered atop a rock near the shore.

"The Egyptians are coming, but Yahweh will protect us. We need to be patient—and trust." Moses's voice carried well across the flat land on the banks of the *Yam Suph*.

The crowd moaned and wailed. "Why did you bring us here to die?"

"Shouldn't you have just left us in Egypt?"

A man rushed toward Moses. "It would have been better to serve the Egyptians than to die here!" He swung a fist at Moses, but Kamose stepped in and restrained him with one arm. The man spat at Kamose's feet but retreated. The captain stayed in front of Moses from then on, arms crossed, feet spread, daring anyone to test him.

The sun withdrew, and the noise grew deafening. The army would reach them in only moments.

Bezalel had told Kamose to "just trust." Could Bezalel do that now? It seemed easier before he could hear the chariots.

He caught his breath as Moses walked into the water. Surely, he did not expect them to swim! They had to fight! That was the only way out. People whined and moaned so loudly—how could Moses think?

As the people groaned, a tower of cloud formed and twisted in front of them. It expanded, exploded, growing until they could see nothing else. Then it climbed into the air, floated over Israel, and alighted behind them. Raging fire within, surrounded by white smoke, it hovered, pulsating between Israel and Pharaoh's army, blocking any contact. The colossal, flaming cloud showered light on the Israelites, though the sun had set. Beyond it, Bezalel could see only darkness. In the safety of the pillar, the camp began to calm as it settled on the shore. It was as if the cloud poured out peace as well as light.

"Sabba! What is he doing?" Bezalel stepped closer to his grandfather.

"Hush!"

Bezalel winced. It was the first time in his life his grandfather had ever addressed him so abruptly.

When the water reached his knees, Moses lifted his staff and stretched it out over the sea. Nothing happened.

Is he praying?

Then slowly, the water began to churn, bubble, swirl. The movement became more violent and the noise grew louder. A dry, burning wind gusted.

Bezalel had to remind himself to breathe. He bent and picked up Ahmose, who was grabbing at his arm, without taking his eyes off Moses. He could feel Kamose standing behind him, breathing rapidly.

The water separated at Moses' feet.

Was it like this when El Shaddai brought forth the land from the sea at the world's creation?

࿓ ♦ ࿓

For hours after sunset, the water divided. The crowd sat on the ground and relaxed, knowing that now escape was imminent. Some even slept.

The fiery cloud behind them blocked the enemy's advance. The sound of the arid wind was strange, reminding Bezalel of the thunderous noise the swirling, often dangerous khamsin winds make rushing through the desert late at night each spring. The tempest whipped through his hair and nearly pulled off his robe. He couldn't tear away from the sight of what was happening. He tired of holding Ahmose, who had fallen asleep on his shoulder. When Kamose offered to take the sleeping child, he let him slip into his uncle's arms.

Kamose stood transfixed by the water. "I have never dreamed anything like this."

They wandered until they found a less windy spot to sit, away from the shore. Kamose held the boy as easily as he held a piece of papyrus. As Kamose lay the boy down on the sand, Bezalel noticed how much Ahmose looked like a miniature Kamose. They shared the same nose, turned up a bit at the end. And though Kamose rarely smiled, when he did, the corners of his mouth raised up just like Ahmose's, one side first and then the other.

Bezalel looked up to see a young man his age standing before him. He was tall but slight, and a half-moon scar peeked out above his right eyebrow. Dark, curly hair fell onto his shoulders. His full beard covered quite a bit of his face, and Bezalel rubbed his own sparse beard. He asked to sit down near Bezalel. "You're Hur's grandson, right?" His voice was deeper than Bezalel expected from his wiry build.

"Yes." Bezalel wondered how he knew his kin.

"I'm Amminadab's son, Nahshon." His dark eyes sparkled when he spoke.

"Amminadab? Elder of Judah? But how is that possible? Your father is the same age as my grandfather."

"My father remarried late in life. I have half-brothers and sisters your father's age." Nahshon reached into a bag and took out a sycamore fig.

"Well, if my sabba has become Moses's top advisor, along with Aaron, and your abba is the chief elder of Judah, we shouldn't have any problems finding out what's going on." Bezalel chuckled and reached for the bag. He took a fig and handed one to Kamose then grabbed another for himself.

"That's not all. Aaron and Moses are my brothers-in-law. Aaron married my sister."

Bezalel chuckled again and shook his head.

A stout man with coarse, sand-brown curls approached. His face was square and his beard and eyebrows were quite bushy. He sat down without being asked.

Nahshon shoved his thumb in the man's direction. "This is Michael, my neighbor."

"Who are they?" Michael pointed at Kamose and then Ahmose, asleep at Bezalel's feet.

Bezalel bristled at Michael's bluntness. "This is Kamose, and this is Ahmose." He pointed at the sleeping child. "He's … my little brother."

"Kamose. Ahmose. Those are Egyptian names."

Nahshon stared at Michael. "And?"

Michael glowered back. "I thought they were who we were trying to get away from."

"We're trying to get away from Ramses. There were many Egyptians in the village in Pi-Ramses." Bezalel glanced at Kamose, whose face, as always, remained blank. "They weren't enslaving us. Many of them came with us."

"Well, they shouldn't have."

"Michael!" Nahshon frowned.

Michael turned to Bezalel. "Why haven't I ever seen you before? Where did you work?"

Bezalel swallowed the last of his pulpy fig. "I worked in the palace."

"Oh. I heard about you."

Bezalel clenched his jaw. "Heard what?"

Michael leaned back on his hands. "Heard about the traitor who thought he was Egyptian, stayed in the palace."

Bezalel closed his eyes against the anger rising inside him.

"He was a slave. He had no choice." Kamose spoke slowly.

"Does he always fight your battles for you?" Michael sneered at Bezalel.

Bezalel ignored the question. "I was a slave. I would have preferred to live in the village, but they forbade me. They beat me often for disobedience. Do you need to see the scars?"

Nahshon leaned forward. "Come on, Michael. None of us were in chains, but we were all slaves. We all know what happened if we didn't do what was required. You have no right to question him."

"I still say they shouldn't be here." Michael narrowed his eyes at Kamose and Ahmose.

"That's enough." Nahshon glared at Michael.

"Fine. I'll leave. I don't like it here anyway." Michael stood and sauntered off.

Nahshon watched him leave then turned back to Kamose. "I'm sorry. That was unnecessary."

"But not completely unexpected." Kamose tossed the peel of his fig aside.

"No, not everyone thinks like that. Most of us don't, please believe me. Michael is … Michael hates everyone." Nahshon shook his head. "Don't judge us all by him."

᷾᷾

A soggy path through the Yam Suph widened and pushed its way east. Water piled on itself until the sides began to tower noisily over Moses.

Bezalel craned his neck to find the top, but the walls grew higher.

"Bezalel, look at the water. It reaches the sky!" Ahmose raised his sleepy head and pointed at the liquid walls.

Bezalel smiled at him. "Kamose, do you know this area? Do you know how far it is to the other side?"

"I do. I have never crossed here, of course, but I would guess about three hours of marching for an army. For this group, with women and children and animals, I'd at least triple that."

"Nine hours. We've done more than that. The first day, we left long before dawn and walked until almost nightfall. If we do it slowly enough, everyone can manage."

∂∾∾

Back at the water's edge, or rather, where the water used to end, Bezalel and Kamose stood near Sabba and Moses. The path had finally reached across to the far shore. A narrow land bridge connected the two shores under the water, leaving a gentle slope down, now exposed and totally dry.

Moses turned to Amminadab, elder of the tribe of Judah. "Cross over now, tribe by tribe, each with its leaders." Amminadab and his assistant elders went first, and the people of Judah followed. Their sandals stepped on dried mud.

Bezalel turned to Imma. "I'm staying here until the end with Moses and Sabba. You go with Meri and Ahmose now." He kissed Meri on the cheek and she and Imma followed the others of Judah.

Bezalel watched each tribe take its place behind the one before it and begin the walk down the hallway between the watery walls. Hours later, the last of the final tribe, Benjamin, had trudged about halfway when the sun shot fingers of light into the distant darkness. Men from Judah and Issachar returned to help those who needed it, carrying children and embracing the shoulders of the elderly.

Bezalel and Kamose were among the last to cross, following Benjamin. Moses and Sabba had gone over about halfway through. The wet, salt air surrounded them, yet the dry ground beneath felt strange. The world had turned upside down. Despite all Bezalel had seen in the past year, this was extraordinary. The air rushed between the walls and created a wind tunnel. Salty droplets sprinkled their faces.

Almost to the end, Bezalel looked back. The cloud now waited in front of them, a beacon. The sun peered above the mountains. Surely the Egyptians could see them. A bit of fear snuck back into his head and he fought to push it out. He knew the army would be readying itself for war. Two soldiers would step onto each chariot—one to drive the horse and another to send as many arrows as possible toward his people. Foot soldiers would follow to pick off any stragglers the charioteers didn't slay.

The remaining Benjamites picked up the pace. Pounding hooves told Bezalel the army had begun the chase, horses riding hard. His breath came faster and he willed the Israelites around him to run. *Hurry, hurry, hurry!*

From the other direction, frenzied shouts rose from those on the shore. They had to look like easy targets, standing there unarmed, counting on an invisible God for protection. Fearing that the break of day would bring the soldiers upon them before the rest of Benjamin arrived, they called for Moses to close the sea.

"Release the water! Better to lose one tribe than all twelve!"

How could they think that? What if they were last instead?

Moses waited with Sabba and Aaron, framed against the rising sun.

As he neared the shore, Bezalel looked over his shoulder. The army of Ramses was closing the distance. The pummeling of hooves and the spinning of chariot wheels were deafening. He gasped and started to run. Men all around him sprinted for the shore.

He reached the beach and climbed a rock, panting. His heart pounded in his chest and echoed in his ears. The screaming stabbed his head and the crowd was close to rioting. Some ran toward the desert as fast as they could.

How far do they think they could get?

Kamose again shielded Moses from the people as some rushed at him, demanding that he act.

Just a moment from shore, the Egyptians halted as if slamming into an invisible wall. Chariot wheels came off and carriages stopped short and tipped over. Horses dragged wheel-less coaches behind them. Charioteers tumbled forward and were trampled by hooves and wheels. Men and animals piled upon one another.

Israelites fell silent as the shrieks of soldiers and the neighs of horses filled the air.

The walls of water quivered. The tempest still raged across the path from west to east.

Kamose clambered up to join Bezalel on the rock. "Everyone is across. Moses is safe for the moment." He shouted to be heard over the wind and the noise from the collapsing army.

Moses raised his staff over the sea.

The water trembled. The wind stilled. The only sounds were those from the chariots and horses of the Egyptian army. Soldiers scurried about. They checked their animals and themselves for injury. They tried to right carriages and reattach wheels. Some wandered aimlessly among the dead.

A low roar began, as if from a great distance. It grew louder and stronger. The ground rumbled. Bezalel grabbed Kamose to keep from falling. The wet walls quaked, then torrents of water collapsed onto the army. Salt water splashed Bezalel's face. He held his breath and his body tensed. He heard the shrieks only for an instant, but he would never forget them. Some of the soldiers were close enough for Bezalel to see their faces. Their wide eyes, pale skin, open mouths, flailing limbs, bodies tumbling like rocks in the river—they were indelibly burned into his memory.

Bezalel saw Kamose's face as he stared speechless at the churning sea.

Not a single Egyptian survived.

☙❧

Bezalel stood on the rock and gaped at the sea. The morning sun beat on his shoulders as it climbed in the sky behind him. The water lapped on the shore, as calm as before it parted last night. Seagulls cawed and searched for breakfast as if it were any other morning.

He looked out over the quieting sea. The water had collapsed in the west first, and forced everything toward the Israelites. Spears and knives washed up on shore, a few at first, then hundreds. Shattered pieces of cedar from the chariots floated among bows made of horn and sinew.

What just happened? El Shaddai had said He would rescue them, but Bezalel never envisioned the entire Egyptian army destroyed. He saw their faces, heard their screams again. Thousands of people, just like him—and his family—gone. They too had families, loved ones who would never see them again.

Then he thought of the slavery his people had endured for over four hundred years. He thought of women taken from their husbands because an Egyptian wanted one of them, of men—like his father—dying much too young because their bodies had given out, of children who never had the opportunity to go to school, or sometimes even to grow up.

And he thought of Ahmose. Sweet Ahmose, who never had an ugly thought about anyone. Bezalel remembered the angry, bloody stripes on the child's back. His breathing became rapid and his body stiffened. His hands fisted.

They deserved it. They had all had a chance. Many chances. They chose to follow a man—a brutal, insane man—instead of Shaddai, and now they were paying the price.

The Egyptians could never come for them now. Their freedom was secured.

Men grabbed weapons and piled them up on the sand. Younger

men ventured into the water and removed daggers from the belts of the soldiers, and shields from their arms. Children searched for arrows.

As the men scrambled for weapons, Bezalel heard a song wafting on the breeze and he strained to hear it. At first only a few women sang. Then the music grew stronger, as more and more joined in.

It was a song of praise.

ಾ⚭

Kamose stepped into the sea towards the slain soldiers. Weapons bounced against his shins. Children darted around him.

He knew many of these men. The twelve hundred charioteers were the best of the best and he had served with them as a young man. And now the entire army was gone—wiped from the land.

He dropped to his knees in the water and his chest tightened. It was too much. He could not make sense of this.

He sat back on his heels. He had seen more death than he cared to remember. He had often been the cause of it. He'd even seen senseless death, just because the king was displeased. And Ramses had been warned. Many times. But still... this was more than he expected, more than he could have possibly conceived. He hung his head and wept.

Had he made the wrong choice?

Fifteen

21 Abib

East of the Yam Suph

Bezalel trudged toward camp with leaden feet. The sun's blazing light pierced his eyes and the sand under his lids rubbed them raw. He just wanted to find Meri and then his tent. The long night had stolen all the energy from both his body and his mind.

Around him Benjamites staggered. The last tribe to cross, they were exhausted. More Judahites arrived to help. They pointed them toward camp, carried sleepy children and packs. The sounds of rustling tents and crying babies assaulted his ears, and the smell of burning wood from thousands of campfires stung his nose.

Wells dotted the area and reached deep into underground springs. They supported vibrant, colorful blooms that kept the region from being completely barren. Hares and foxes darted back to their holes in the rocks. Mourning doves cooed. He shaded his eyes and craned his neck to study the cloud that had protected them from the Egyptian army. It had spread wide and now hovered over them, alleviating the sun's deadly intensity. How long would it stay there?

Stirring music swirled around Bezalel's head. Young girls grasped hands and formed large circles, dancing and laughing. Their hair swung to one side while their feet kicked to the other. Older women slapped tambourines or clicked bone castanets carried from Egypt. Men beat drums or huffed into reed flutes and double pipes while stringed lyres filled the air with worshipful melody.

I will sing to Yahweh, for He is highly exalted.
The horse and its rider He has hurled into the sea.
Yahweh is my strength and my song; He has become my salvation.
He is my God, and I will praise Him;
My father's God, and I will exalt Him.
Yahweh is a warrior; Yahweh is His name.
Pharaoh's chariots and his army He has hurled into the sea.
The best of Pharaoh's officers are drowned in the Red Sea.

When Bezalel lumbered into camp, Sabba, Imma, and Meri sat around a welcoming fire. Imma was warming some mat sot. Bezalel caught Meri's tired gaze as she sat huddled next to Sabba.

Her face brightened and she ran to him. She slammed into him then hammered his chest with her fists. "Why did you take so long? Why didn't you cross with us? I was terrified! All night I have been so frightened!" She collapsed against him. Her tears drenched the shoulder of his seawater-splashed tunic.

"We're safe now. Everyone's safe. It's over."

She looped her arms around his neck and clung to him.

"I'm sorry. Am I forgiven?" he whispered in her ear, his voice rough.

Her hair tickled his neck as she nodded, but she still clutched his tunic. He held her until she calmed then led her to the fire. With one hand he grabbed a mat sot and stuffed it nearly whole into his mouth, then grabbed another, realizing he'd eaten nothing except a fig since the afternoon before. His other arm wrapped around Meri, who had her head on his shoulder, arms securely around his waist as if he might leave her again. Not that there was any chance of that happening. Not that there was any chance of her believing that right now either.

"Where's Ahmose?" Bezalel spoke around the food in his mouth.

"Poor thing is exhausted." Sabba chuckled. "He's still asleep. He waited up for you, too, as long as he could."

Bezalel shook his head. "I'm sorry you waited. I thought you understood we would be a while. That's why we sent Ahmose and Meri ahead."

"I understood, habibi, and we tried to get them to sleep, but Ahmose was too excited, and I think Meri was too worried." Imma leaned forward. "I think she's asleep now, though."

Bezalel tucked a finger under her chin and lifted her face. "Yes, she is. I'm sure she needs it. I know I do." He kissed the top of her head.

"I think she loves you very much." Imma handed him one more mat sot. "Let me take her to the tent."

Bezalel held the flat bread with his mouth while he stood and helped Meri up then shifted her onto Imma's shoulder. "Well, that's good, because I love her very much, too."

24 Abib

The gravelly floor of the Desert of Shur crunched under Bezalel's feet. They had found no source of water all day.

His throat scratched and his parched skin resembled the animal hides stretched over the tambourines the girls played three nights ago. His legs throbbed, and his shoulders ached from the pack and tent. Thank Shaddai it would be only a few weeks' journey.

There was little wildlife and even less vegetation. In the honeycombed rocks, a few blue-headed Agama lizards and golden mice darted about. Nubian vultures circled ominously, searching for carcasses.

Bezalel raised his eyes to the sky. *Go away. You won't find any food here. I hope.*

Chalky limestone mountains created an unbreachable wall. Layers upon layers of cemented sand, in unending colors of white, gray, and black, stood like sentries and filled the air with an invisible dust that invaded his eyes and made him cough.

Walls north and east. A sea to the west. They were completely protected.

From the Egyptians at least. If the desert didn't kill them.

❧❧

The path between the sea and the wall of rock became more rolling and Bezalel's legs burned hotter with each knoll. The air turned drier as they slowly moved southeast and away from the sea.

Ahmose rushed off. Bezalel peered ahead to try to figure what the child had seen. He sucked in a breath. A spring! He sprinted after the boy, who dropped to his knees in the gravel. Bezalel fell beside him and they scooped up some of the precious liquid. They slurped noisily. He smiled and closed his eyes as it trickled down his throat—for only a moment. He coughed and spat it back out, water dribbling down his chin. The water was so bitter that even in his misery he could not drink it.

Around them everyone else gagged on the water as well. Ahmose fell backward on the sand and stared up at the cloud that glowed above them. Bezalel grasped his wrist and pulled him up. The boy probably would have cried had there been enough moisture in his little body.

Bezalel cringed as the crowd once again revolted. Unrecognizable sounds turned into words and then formed into sentences. The people wailed and cried against Moses as they swarmed around the spring. Fists waved in the air and some pushed. Bezalel grabbed Ahmose's tunic as they were jostled and nearly separated.

"What can we drink?"

"We'll die! Where can we find water?"

Moses approached the spring as the crowd yelled and shoved, looking for someone to blame. Bezalel pulled Ahmose close.

Kamose stood tensed nearby, ready to act should anyone threaten Moses.

"Israelites! Listen to me!" Moses raised his staff to draw the mob's attention.

The crowd quieted some, but not much.

"Yahweh will provide for us. You cannot think He saved us from the Egyptians to let us die of thirst, can you?"

"I have no idea what He intended," a man shouted from back in the crowd. "But if we don't get water today, we'll die!"

"Who's talking? Show yourself."

Bezalel searched the crowd.

No one came forward.

Sabba drew near Moses. "All the water we brought with us is gone. And without more water the animals will no longer produce milk. Many are dry already."

Moses took a deep breath and looked at the cloud above. "This is the worst spring on this entire route. It always has been. I know there are sweeter ones less than a half day away."

"I don't think the people will last that long—at least they don't think they will."

"Let me talk to Yahweh."

When Moses returned, he carried a branch from a tall shrub. He snapped it into several pieces and tossed them into the spring. He pointed toward the nearby stand of brush. "We need more wood to make the bitter water sweet. Bezalel, could you get some more branches?"

Bezalel shifted uncomfortably at being singled out.

Moses motioned to someone behind Bezalel. "You help him."

"No."

Bezalel snapped his head around. Michael stood defiantly, hands on his hips, jaw jutted out.

Moses pointed to someone else. "You?"

Nahshon made his way out of the crowd. At least it was someone Bezalel already knew. Two more young men came forward as well. Snaps and pops filled the air as they pulled and broke branches and produced an armful of wood to carry back to the spring.

Bezalel started to toss in a branch but Moses stopped him. "You must break it first. The sap inside is what sweetens the water."

The crowd murmured and glared as the young men snapped the branches into smaller chunks. Vultures circled and shrieked. Soon a large pile of broken pieces lay at Moses's feet. He moved his lips but no sound came. Then Moses nodded to them, and they threw the wood, piece by piece, into the bitter water.

Moses waited for a moment, watching the cloud. "Hur, will you taste it?"

"I will!" Ahmose shouted from behind Sabba.

"Shh!" Bezalel frowned at Ahmose and rushed toward him.

Moses moved toward Sabba and peeked behind him.

"And who are you?"

Ahmose looked up. "I'm Ahmose."

"I know you. You are Egyptian?"

"Yes. They said I could come!" Ahmose shrank behind Sabba.

"Of course. It's all right." Moses crooked his finger and beckoned the child. "Do you believe the water is sweet now?"

Ahmose emerged. "You said it is. Shaddai healed Bezalel. He can make the water sweet."

"You have greater faith than my people. Go ahead; test the water."

Ahmose ran to the spring and plunged his hands in. He brought them up to his mouth and slurped. Then he looked back and smiled.

Cheers erupted from the crowd, and those closest drank and then filled their skins before backing away to allow others access.

They found a place to camp, and Imma passed around the few remaining mat sot they had. "We are almost out of food as well as water. I hope Moses's oasis has something to eat."

"I guess we'll find out in the morning." Sabba yawned and stretched.

Bezalel began setting up tents—one for Imma and Meri, then one for himself, Sabba and Ahmose.

Ahmose plopped on the ground and moaned.

"Come here, habibi." Meri pulled Ahmose into her lap and pulled off his sandal. "Where does it hurt?"

"Here." Ahmose pointed to a spot on the sole of his foot.

"I think you had a tiny rock in your sandal. Didn't you feel it?"

Ahmose shrugged.

Meri turned to Imma. "Do we have any honey or oil?"

Imma rummaged in the bag. She found the precious liquid and handed it to Meri.

Meri put a few drops on her fingers and gently rubbed it onto Ahmose's dirty foot.

Ahmose sighed and snuggled into her chest.

"Don't fall asleep yet. You have to eat." Meri reached for the plate of flat bread.

Ahmose grabbed the last two pieces and began gobbling them.

"Wait—" Bezalel leaned toward the empty plate.

Meri shot him a warning look. When Ahmose had finished, she shooed him into his tent.

"Did you get anything to eat?"

"He needs it more than I do. I'll eat tomorrow."

Bezalel chuckled and shook his head. "I'd have saved you some if I knew you were going to do that."

"One missed meal won't hurt me. I missed more than that when Jannes locked me up. I'll be fine." She kissed his cheek. "I'm going to bed. I'll see you in the morning."

Before he crawled into his tent, Bezalel lay on the warm sand. The heat crept into his muscles and soothed them. Meri was here. Sabba and Imma. Sweet Ahmose. An oasis tomorrow. And freedom. They should be in Canaan in a few weeks. A whole new life. Everything he never even dared hope for.

His body relaxed as his mind shut down. The sun dropped in the west, and the cloud above them metamorphosed from fluffy white, to transparent, to glowing.

25 Abib
Elim

As soon as the sun rose over the mountains, Bezalel and his family began walking south. Other groups were ahead of them on the path, having started in the gray hours before dawn. Everyone knew that just a few hours away waited a beautiful oasis called Elim, with palm trees and water. Abundant, sweet water—Elim had twelve massive springs, with succulent dates and figs. And luscious shade.

They reached Elim before midday. As Imma set out lunch under a tree, Bezalel took all of the water skins and found a spring. He quickly filled each bag and brought them back to the others. The little group gulped the cool water and enjoyed fresh fruit.

"I don't think I can walk another step!" Meri rubbed her shoulders.

"I hope we can stay here a day or two." Bezalel knelt behind Meri and massaged her neck.

"I think I'd like to lie down a while."

"I'll set up the tent for you." He placed a kiss on the top of her head.

"Moses says we'll be here for quite a while. We only move when the cloud moves." Sabba pointed at the sky above him and then stretched his arms above his head.

Bezalel set up the tent for Imma and Meri, and they disappeared inside.

"Sabba, take a walk with me?"

"A short one. I was hoping for a nap under one of these trees." Sabba chuckled.

"Sure, a short one."

They wandered toward one of the springs surrounded by palm trees. "I told you I asked Meri to be my wife."

"Yes, you did. You still want to marry her?"

Bezalel stopped and faced his grandfather. "Without a doubt."

"She is how old?"

"Old enough. Fifteen."

"She has no family to ask. I don't see why not, if she agrees." Sabba ambled on, his hands behind his back. "Are you ready for the disapproval you will receive from some here?"

"I've already gotten a taste, just for being with Kamose."

They reached the spring. "You know it will be much worse with Meri. She is a wonderful girl, and we have already fallen in love with her as well, but others will only see her as a concu—"

"But nothing happened that night!" Bezalel pounded his fist into a palm trunk as rage whipped through him like a desert wind. "And you know what? I wouldn't care if it did! She was a slave to him as much as the rest of us. She wasn't in control of what happened to her body any more than I was."

Sabba put his hands on his shoulders. "Habibi, if you cannot control your anger with me, how will you control it with anyone else?"

Bezalel expelled a long breath. He obviously couldn't control his anger at all. But if he wanted a life with Meri, he had better learn. And quickly.

⮜⮞

Bezalel sat leaning against a date palm tree as Meri giggled and splashed around in one of Elim's many glistening pools.

"This feels so good on my feet."

He enjoyed watching her face light up whenever she experienced something new. At this particular moment, he also enjoyed watching the way the silky fabric of her tunic hugged her curves.

She snuggled down next to him, facing him, and then caressed his cheek. "You look so different with a beard."

He laughed. "I'd hardly call it that. It's been less than two weeks."

She reached behind his neck and touched his hair. "Why do you still wear it tied up? You're not in the palace anymore."

He shrugged. "It's habit, now. I'm not used to wearing it down yet."

She tilted her head and looked at him. "You've never told me what your name means."

"What?"

"In your language. What does your name mean?"

"In the shadow of God." He blew out a harsh breath. "It's appropriate. I've always felt like I'm in the shadows—cold, dark, forgotten."

"Hmmm. That's not what comes to mind when I think of shadows at all."

"What do you mean?"

"When I was a little girl, before my imma died, we all worked in our field together. When we weeded, or planted, or picked the crops, I always tried to stay in her shadow. I thought it was a little cooler, but mostly I always knew that she was nearby, without even having to see her. I knew I was safe, and loved."

She stared into the distance, as if seeing a memory. "Later, in the evening, as she made dinner outside, I would lie down in her long shadow. I would try to lay my head on her shadow-head, and see where my feet ended up." She laughed. "She always scolded me for lying in the dirt, but I never listened."

She looked into his eyes. "Maybe that's how you should think of it. You don't seem to be forgotten now."

"Maybe." He played with a lock of her hair.

She grinned. "Do you know what my name means?"

He laughed. "Of course, *beloved*." He kissed her cheek. Then he paused for a moment. "You do know I tried to come for you. Soldiers surrounded the palace. I couldn't get near you."

"I know. I couldn't get out."

He took her hand and held it, drawing circles on the back of it with his thumb. "Tell me what happened the day you left."

"Ramses finally realized Amun-her was dead and his slaves were gone. I guess he knew he couldn't bring back his son, but he could try to bring you all back, so he sent Kamose to ready the army. He was screaming from the throne room. I could hear him in the harem." She shuddered.

"The rest of the harem was upriver, so I was alone. Kamose burst into the room, told me if I wanted to go with him to find you I had to leave right then, not to pack anything, just to follow him. He grabbed my hand, and I went with him to the stables. He helped me on a huge horse, the biggest one I have ever seen, and we rode for what seemed like forever."

"The ride was hard?"

She laughed. "Kamose rode so fast, I thought I'd fall off many times. My legs hurt. My back ached. I was hotter than I've ever been. But I just kept thinking that at the end of it all … would be you."

He ran the backs of his fingers down her cheek. "I thought I'd never see you again. Those first days without you were … agonizing." He closed his eyes a moment. "I don't ever want to feel like that again."

She smiled. "I'm here now. You won't."

"I want to marry you."

She scoffed. "Out here? In the desert?"

"Why not? I thought Egyptian weddings were simple."

"They are. But yours aren't."

"Sabba can do the blessing; the rest we can do without."

"Are you sure?"

"I've asked you twice now. You're the one who needs to be sure."

She giggled. "I think I proved that by riding a horse for hours to get here." She wrapped a hand behind his neck and pulled his head to her. She touched her lips to his forehead, his temple, his cheek.

He slipped his arms around her and drew her closer. Her mouth moved to his jaw, kissing him from his ear to his chin. Heat coursed through his body. A moan rumbled low in his throat as her lips hovered over his, her tantalizing mouth just out of reach. He leaned forward and claimed his kiss, and she returned it with such intensity it left him breathless.

"Need more proof?"

"Need or want?" His voice was raspy.

She giggled. "Marry me and you can have all the proof you want."

❧❦

Bezalel woke with the sun and stretched. He stared up at the stripe around his tent—why was it blue instead of red? Then he remembered he was in a new tent, one he now shared with Meri. He rolled over on his side and draped his arm over her sleeping form, pulling her closer and breathing deeply. Even without the jasmine, her scent was intoxicating. Her black hair spilled onto her bare shoulders. He never would have believed skin could be so soft. Raising himself up on his elbow and resting his head on one hand, he traced his finger over her eyes, her cheeks, her jaw. He left his hand on her neck and drew his thumb over her full lips.

She stirred. Her eyes fluttered open and rested on his face. A look came over her he could not name, but which caused his entire body to shiver with delight.

The wedding had been far more Egyptian than Hebrew. After a

blessing by Sabba, Meri had simply moved from Imma's tent to his. There was no procession to her house to ask her father for permission. There were no attendants for either of them. There was no dancing or feasting long into the night after the bride and groom retired to their new home.

For Meri's sake, they had wanted as little attention as possible. He didn't care. He didn't want attention. He only wanted her.

And now he had her.

15 Ziv
Wilderness of Sin

Bezalel gulped water from a skin as Imma set out the last dates and figs brought from Elim. The white-hot desert sun, high in the sky, poured out more heat than ever. The hot and dry season of Egypt had arrived early and in full force. The unbroken expanse of sand and rock reflected the heat and kept the air much hotter and drier than the delta ever was. Only the cloud kept the heat from turning them into the dry bones they saw scattered along the way.

They left the large pools of Elim and found only pockets of water hidden in the rocks, and several small pools. Clearly, there was water underground to supply the acacias and tamarisk trees, but so deep as to be useless to travelers. The winter had apparently been an especially dry one.

They had camped at Elim for most of a month, to allow everyone to rest, gather energy, and fatten the animals for the weeks-long journey, and at this moment Bezalel wished they had never left. They had eaten most of the food from the oasis on the last few days' journey into the desert. The gnawing in Bezalel's stomach demanded his attention. Would he ever be full again?

Around him, the grumbling of the people grew louder. Again. True, in Egypt there was always food and drink, but they had also been beaten, controlled, and harassed. Slaves died for no other reason than the taskmaster of the day disliked them. Surely they could see this was a vast improvement. And they would be in their new land in no more than a month, even at the slow pace they kept. Never again would they be hungry. Never again would they be slaves. It was almost over. Apparently, Shaddai really did have a plan after all.

Bezalel reached for a date and ripped it in two. He offered half to his grandfather.

Sabba held out his hand, but a breathless young man—a tanned, tall, muscled, and filthy intruder several years older than Bezalel—raced up to Sabba and fell at his feet.

"Sir, are you Hur, son of Caleb?" Gasping for breath, he looked up from where he had fallen on his hands and knees.

"I am." Sabba knelt and faced the young man. "What can I do for you?"

"I am Joshua, son of Nun, of the tribe of Ephraim. I have been searching for you all morning." He sat up and gulped more air before continuing. "I cannot get to Moses. He is talking to Aaron, and guards stand outside their tents. They sent me to you instead. They said you could help."

Sabba placed a hand on the young man's shoulder. "What is it that is so important? And what happened to you?"

Bezalel marveled at Sabba's compassion, one of the things he loved most about his grandfather. Well known by now as one of Moses's most trusted advisors, Sabba was bombarded all day with silly questions. Yet with each person he acted as if he had all the time in the world.

"We were attacked early, just as the sun rose. I fought them, all morning. I killed some of them, but we still lost many...."

"Who attacked you? Where, exactly, and how?" Sabba raised his eyebrows, and the tone of his voice lowered.

Joshua breathed deeply and sat up straighter. His ebony hair hung straight and coarse and was pulled back with a leather tie, though some of it had escaped and fallen around his neck. The battle he had been through was obvious from his tunic, bloody and ripped in several places, and from his feet, caked with dried blood.

He took a deep, ragged breath. "I don't know who they were. We are always at the back of camp. My grandfather is old and slow, so we are among the last to make camp, on the edges. They came before we awakened. They attacked with astonishing force, slaughtered many, and left as quickly. We tried to fight back, but we were severely outnumbered, and of course unarmed. They took what little food we had left and looted some of the tents."

Joshua paused and stared, his eyes glassed over, shaking his head. "I tried. I tried so hard … they just wouldn't stop killing…."

Bezalel had to strain to hear Joshua's whispers.

"And your father?"

Joshua turned his attention back to Sabba. "He, my mother, my sister … all were killed. I have no one left."

"And you've been fighting since dawn?"

"No. The attack didn't last very long. I tried to calm those who survived. Then I looked for Moses."

"Bezalel." Sabba spoke so only he could hear. "Take Joshua inside my tent. Give him some food and water and let him lie down. Then we'll go talk to Moses."

"Yes, Sabba." Bezalel went to Joshua and helped him up.

"I'll tell your mother and Meri where we are."

Bezalel put his arm around Joshua's waist and helped the silent and exhausted man to their tent. Joshua's weight felt heavy on Bezalel's shoulder. Inside the tent, he pulled out a mat and helped Joshua lie down.

Joshua mumbled, "Thank you. I'll just rest for a while."

Bezalel stepped outside and got some dates and water from Imma. When he returned, Joshua had drifted off to sleep.

So, obviously it was not almost over. Things had taken a dramatic turn for the worse. He should have known better.

Bezalel looked at the bloody and wounded young man who had collapsed in the tent. He could not imagine how he would feel if his family were all killed. Then he did the only thing he knew to do to help Joshua—he found a pitcher and basin and washed his bleeding feet.

Sixteen

Bezalel rubbed at the dried blood smeared on his hands as he sat on a cushion across from Moses in the leader's tent. Perhaps if he avoided looking at Moses and his grandfather, he could pretend this conversation wasn't happening. But that would be disrespectful.

"He was far too fatigued and distraught to give me many details." Sabba waved his hand. "He only said they attacked at dawn and looted their tents."

Moses stroked his chin as he listened. "I have lived in this desert for forty years. Only the Amalekites fight in such a cowardly manner." He sighed and shook his head. "They do not fight with honor. They attack the very young and very old, the slowest, those who remain behind. They are a most violent people. They kill and maraud, steal and destroy. They live by death." The old man started to pull himself up with his staff.

Bezalel stood and offered his arm. He grunted as Moses yanked on his forearm and shoulder.

Moses circled the tent and rubbed his hip. "When they return, we will have to fight." He held the flap of the tent open.

Outside, Aaron tried to calm a growing crowd held back by ten men acting as guards. Bezalel's heart sank as yet again the mob shouted with fists raised.

A tall, bald man shoved his way forward. "If only we had stayed in Egypt! There we ate all the food we wanted!"

Another joined him. "We had meat! You have brought us out into this desert to starve us to death. Take us back!"

Back? To a wasteland? To slavery?

Moses stepped out of the tent and raised both hands for silence. "I have spoken to Yahweh. He has promised meat and bread by tomorrow morning."

As Bezalel slipped around Moses, he noticed Michael standing amidst the leaders of the impromptu rebellion.

He left Moses and Sabba explaining and quieting the crowd. Again.

∂◦⟨

As the sun slithered westward, Bezalel sat by the glowing fire.

Meri joined him. "What did Moses say?"

Bezalel picked at the hem of his tunic. "He said there would be meat and bread by morning." He did not mention the rest.

"Good. I'm hungry."

He put his arm around her and she placed her head on his shoulder. Pink and orange fingers of light reached above the mountains in all directions to color the sky. It was breathtakingly beautiful and calm at first glance—but in reality there was nothing calm or beautiful at all about this evening. Images of warriors attacking sleeping children invaded his thoughts.

Chirps and the squeal of children's laughter floated in from the edges of camp. When the sounds grew louder, he stood to see who—or what—could be the source of the noise. He and Meri wandered toward the excitement.

Quail glided just above the sand. Exhausted from their migration north to escape the heat of the deadly desert summer, they lay scattered on the sand like stones along the Nile. Moses said quail always flew through this part of the Sinai at this time of year, but Yahweh had promised there would be more than usual, enough for everyone.

Children from all over the camp chased the birds. Actually, there was more chasing than catching. Bezalel and Meri chuckled as Ahmose ran after one lying motionless on the ground, but it flew away as soon as he neared. Ahmose fell down in its place in a spasm of glee.

Bezalel decided he'd better help or there would be no meat for dinner. Meri giggled as he dove for bird after bird, missing every one.

Finally he caught one of the little fowl and managed to hold onto it. "Think it's funny?"

Meri squealed and stepped back when he shoved the squirming quail toward her.

He laughed and snapped its neck then handed her the dead bird.

She scrunched her face and took it by the feet, holding it at arm's length.

He chuckled again, grabbing her by the waist and nuzzling her neck. "Maybe next time you shouldn't laugh at me so hard."

"Maybe." She giggled. "Maybe it's worth it."

He caught several more, enough for the evening meal, which everyone had postponed until the promised meat arrived. He twisted their necks, and Meri took them to Imma to begin roasting. He stayed to catch more birds so they could smoke and dry the meat to last for several weeks.

Kamose strolled toward him.

"Here to help?"

Kamose's face was more stolid than usual, and Bezalel searched for a clue to his thoughts.

"Sure." Kamose snatched a quail in each hand, in one swift motion. He broke their necks, twisted off the heads, and draped them on a nearby young acacia tree to drain the blood.

He turned back to Bezalel and stopped short. "What?"

Only then did Bezalel realize his mouth was hanging open. "You just did that so quickly, and so well. All the rest of us have to scramble to catch one, and you caught two at once."

"You forget I have spent weeks at a time in the desert. I could do this in my sleep." He grabbed another bird. "Which I haven't been getting much of lately."

Ahmose raced toward them, a quail clutched in his hands but struggling to escape. "Kamose, Kamose! Take it, take it! It's trying to fly away!"

Kamose took the squirming bird from the boy, and Ahmose scampered away.

"You're not sleeping?" Bezalel tried not to probe too far.

Kamose gazed at Bezalel as if trying to make a decision. "I don't know my place here. I'm just wandering around looking for something to do." He rubbed a hand over his face.

"It must have been hard, walking away from everything."

"I'm not always sure ... that I am welcome here."

Bezalel shrugged. "I suppose there are those who don't like Egyptians being here. But then, they are likely the same ones who don't like Moses or anything else that's happening, and beg to go back to Egypt. I wouldn't worry too much about them."

Kamose snagged several more quail then hung them with the others. "What if I said I wanted to tell Ahmose who I am?"

Bezalel crossed his arms and dug at the ground with his sandal for a moment. "I don't see any harm in it now. There's no one here who can hurt either of you."

"Perhaps. What if he becomes angry because I didn't tell him all these years?"

Bezalel tried to think how he would want to hear such news, especially as a child. "Tell him what you told me: You were keeping a promise to Tia and trying to protect him. If you had claimed him, would you have been able to care for him? And keep him safe?"

"No." Kamose paced back and forth. "As it was, he was part of the harem, even though a servant. He was still one of Ramses's sons, no matter how lowly. He would have lost that protection had I taken him as my nephew."

"I'm sure Ahmose will understand that. Anyway, you're here now. That's all that matters." Bezalel headed toward the acacia tree and collected half of the tiny carcasses. "You know, there are plenty of tents. You don't have to sleep outside."

Kamose retrieved the rest of the birds, now drained of their blood. "I'm used to it. Maybe when it turns colder. For now, I enjoy seeing the stars."

☙❧

Bezalel stirred until a few embers glowed, then he ripped some branches from a dead tree and added them to the fire. Even in dried wadi beds vegetation always grew, meager as it was.

Kamose appeared soon after the flames had roared to life again.

Ahmose tagged along behind, rubbing his eyes. "Look! On the ground! What is it? It's all over!"

"What are you talking about?" Bezalel continued tending the fire.

Soon people from the tents around them were also staring at the sand beneath their feet.

Ahmose brought Bezalel a handful of white flakes. "Perhaps it is the bread Shaddai promised."

Joshua emerged from his tent. "That's not bread. But I don't know what it is."

"Well, Shaddai promised bread, and this is the only thing that's different this morning." Sabba looked at the families milling around. "The entire camp is mumbling. All I hear is '*Manna? Manna?* What is it?' Perhaps we should go see Moses. Ahmose, want to come with me?"

They hiked toward their leader.

Joshua slumped down beside Bezalel and followed them with his eyes. "I don't understand why that man is so happy so early in the morning. It's annoying."

"Sabba? He's always happy." Bezalel chuckled, and added a few more twigs.

"I'll bet nothing bad has ever happened to him."

Bezalel cast a sideways glance at Joshua. On the surface, it was an absurd statement, coming from one escaped slave to another. But practically speaking, their lives in Egypt could have been much worse. They weren't shackled, and as long as they obeyed, they lived fairly normal lives—making bricks. Children didn't work until about age six. They could marry whom they wanted and have families and live where they wanted within the villages. Most of them, anyway.

"You'd lose that bet." He stirred the fire, rearranged the wood, and added a larger log.

"What?" Joshua looked over at him.

"You'd lose the bet. That nothing ever happened to Sabba."

Joshua drew circles in the sand with his finger. "Well, what happened?"

"My grandmother was taken from him by one of the Egyptian guards when my abba was but a small boy. I was taken to the palace when I was young, and then Abba died in the brickfields. So it's been just he and my mother for most of my life.

"Sabba says we have to believe that El Shaddai knows what He is doing, and that He will keep His promises. He said He would free us and make us His people. To do that, He has to take care of us. You have to trust Him to do that."

Joshua stared into the fire for several long moments. "I'm not sure I can."

ॐ◌ॐ

Ahmose volunteered to try it first.

Bezalel and the others watched as Imma handed him a small, cooled manna cake.

He nibbled it at first. He took a bigger bite. Then he stuffed the rest in his mouth. "It's good!"

Bezalel laughed and Imma handed a plate full of cakes to him. He took a few, gave one to Meri, and passed the plate around.

Golden brown biscuits lay in his hands. Imma had made dough from the flaky substance and cooked it in a pan over the open campfire flame. He broke one in two and examined it then bit into it. A honey flavor spread over his tongue and filled his mouth. He swallowed. "That *is* good."

Words of agreement followed from everyone around the circle, except Ahmose. His mouth was too full.

ॐ◌ॐ

After breakfast Kamose found Bezalel. "I think I'd like to tell Ahmose today about Tia."

Bezalel searched Kamose's face. "Are you worried?"

"A little. I worry... he doesn't need me."

"Kamose, I've seen him with you. He loves you a great deal. And in my opinion, a child can never have too many people who love him."

Kamose only nodded, but the affirmation soothed his wearied soul.

Bezalel pointed. "Here he comes now."

Ahmose skipped up with Meri. "We found a little water, but there's not much left."

"He's right. The water is running out. We'll have to leave soon, or find another source."

"Let's go look some more." Kamose put out his hand to the boy.

Ahmose looked skeptical but took Kamose's hand. "All right, but unless you know a secret place, we won't find any."

Kamose's stomach tensed as he led Ahmose to a shady place. It had been years since he had felt fear. Fear was useless in battle. It interfered with thinking clearly and making strategic decisions. He patted the ground beside him. "Sit by me."

Ahmose plopped down next to him.

Kamose rubbed his hand over his face. "I have a story to tell you."

"I love stories." He bounced on his heels.

"It's about a secret I was asked to keep."

"A big secret?"

"Very big." Kamose told him about Tia and the baby she bore.

"She had a baby and then she died?"

Kamose nodded. "She did. She was too sick to live."

"That's so sad. Did you know her?"

"Yes. She was my sister."

Ahmose reached up to touch his cheek. "I'm sorry."

"There's one more big part to the secret. And I hope you don't get mad at me for keeping it." Kamose massaged his neck and took a deep breath. "You were the baby."

Ahmose's eyes grew wide and his jaw dropped. "You knew my mother? Why didn't you tell me?"

Kamose cringed at the hurt in the child's eyes. "Because she made me promise not to. And I'm very sorry. But the only thing I knew to do then was to keep the promise I made to her. I was a soldier, and I didn't know how to take care of a baby." He shrugged. "And I didn't know Jannes would hurt you, and I didn't know…a lot of things. And I might have made the wrong decision. I don't even know if I am making the right choice now. But I thought now that we are here, and safe, I could maybe be your uncle. If you can forgive me." He reached toward the child but pulled back.

Tears streamed down Ahmose's face.

Kamose's heart collapsed as if a hippo had stomped on it. Maybe he never should have said anything. He searched the boy's face. He had no idea what to do next. "Do you want me to take you back to Bezalel and Meri?"

Ahmose took a long, ragged breath. "I think it's like Sabba said. Sometimes when bad things happen, El Shaddai makes better things happen. It wasn't your fault my mother died. Or that Jannes beat me. And we are all here now." He met Kamose's gaze. "So yes, I want you to be my uncle." His smile widened. "Then I can have you and Bezalel. And Aunt Rebekah, and Sabba, and Meri." He leaned over and gave Kamose a soggy hug. "Do you know what?"

"What, habibi?"

"I didn't used to have anyone. Now I have lots!"

22 Ziv

Sitting by the fire, Bezalel opened the pottery jar that Imma had filled with manna the day before.

"Did it last?" Meri leaned over his shoulder.

He sniffed the white substance, and the sweet fragrance rose from the pot and danced around his head. He looked at his mother and smiled. Imma scooped out a handful of the flaky substance and patted it into cakes for breakfast.

Around him, a few others emerged from their tents and searched for the manna. When they found none, they went from tent to tent asking for some from their neighbors.

"I am sorry, but I have only enough for my family." Imma repeated the sentence yet again.

"The manna was there for the last six days. I thought it would be there again. What are we supposed to do now?" A young woman held out her hands, palms up. Her whiny voice grated his ears.

"I don't know. I'm sorry." Imma reached for the girl's shoulder, but she wrenched away. "There will be more tomorrow. Next time do as Moses says."

Bezalel watched as the girl stumbled away, seeking food.

He lay back against a rock and closed his eyes, enjoying the honeyed aroma as he waited for the cakes to cook. Soaring walls of rock both north and south flanked the dry wadi in which they camped. Pockets of shade, hidden amongst the roots and stones, offered safe havens to birds and small desert mammals.

The murmur began so slowly that he hardly noticed it at first. A pair of owls roosted nearby and their hoots masked the human voices. As the grumbling gained strength and volume, he realized that the noise came not from the wind or desert animals, or even from their own herds, but from the people.

"What's the matter? Where's Sabba?" Bezalel stood, glanced around, and peered inside Sabba's tent.

"I'm not sure." Imma shrugged.

Kamose approached with Ahmose on his shoulders. "They can't find enough water. That's why everyone is so angry." He lifted Ahmose over his head and placed him on the ground near the fire. "There is quite a lot of water around, but you have to dig for it. And it's hard to find. It's been an especially dry spring, and this is obviously a much larger army—uh, crowd, than the desert is used to supplying."

Bezalel suppressed a chuckle at Kamose's slip. "That can't be the only reason. The people are angry constantly. They don't like the manna, the sun is hot, the nights are cold—you name it, they complain about it. I think they expect Moses to be El Shaddai Himself, and not His servant. I wouldn't be surprised if the lack of water has them ready to stone him."

"There's already a crowd gathering at his tent." Kamose jerked his thumb over his shoulder toward their leader's campsite.

Bezalel stood. "Let's go see what's happening. There's no sense sitting here guessing."

～～

As Bezalel and Kamose neared Moses's tent, the crowd erupted. Voices grew louder, and several men lunged at Moses.

"Water from a rock! He really is crazy!"

"We should have stayed in Egypt! There we had water!"

A line of ten or twelve men tried to hold the line of angry Israelites at bay. One young man broke through, and Kamose darted toward the group and stopped in front of the challenger.

The attacker was Michael.

Michael tried to skirt around Kamose, but the captain calmly sidestepped, and the younger man bumped up against Kamose's substantial chest. The former officer stood feet apart, fists on his hips. His armbands glistened in the sunlight. He bent his head and glared down at Michael.

Michael's eyes traveled down from Kamose's face, over his flexed biceps, and then stopped on the dagger that rested in front of his fist.

Bezalel sucked in a breath as he watched Michael drop the rocks he carried in both hands.

Kamose looked behind Michael at the rest of the agitators, who wilted under his stare. Chucks of granite fell from their grasps and they slithered away.

Bezalel's heart was as heavy as the rocks Michael had dropped. He knew there had been resistance to Moses, but until now he didn't know any of the opponents personally. He didn't really like Michael, but even so....

He tried to concentrate, but Moses's words faded as he focused on Michael.

"Yahweh promised water would flow from the rock." Moses pointed to a mountain north of the campsite.

The people left to follow Moses to where Yahweh promised He would supply the precious water.

Bezalel sprinted in the direction Michael had headed after his confrontation with Kamose. He saw him up ahead and doubled his pace. When he was close enough he grabbed Michael's shoulder.

Michael spun around, fist raised as if to strike, until he saw who had taken hold of him.

"What was that?" Bezalel jerked his thumb back toward Moses.

"What?"

"The rocks? Would you really—"

"Really have thrown them? Absolutely, if your bodyguard hadn't been in the way."

"But why?" Bezalel spread his hands. "I don't understand. What did he do to you? He got us out of there. We're *free*."

"Free to do what? Starve? Die of thirst? How long do you think he can keep up these tricks of his? We have to go back. Or we'll die. It's as simple as that."

Bezalel poked his finger at Michael's chest. "If we go back, they'll kill us."

"No, they won't. They want their slaves." Michael started to walk away but stopped and turned around. "We have to go back. And I'm going to take us there."

Seventeen

23 Ziv
Rephidim

The sun slipped behind the mountains, marking the end of another day. The sound of flowing water in the north was sweet and reassuring to Bezalel, and helped soothe his joyless, weary heart. He sat in the sunbaked sand on the western edge of camp and watched crimson and gold paint the evening sky, Meri's head on his shoulder. He slipped into the rhythms of the desert, hearing hoots answer howls as the predators of the plains emerged from their haunts while their prey scurried for cover.

Even basking in the sunset was better when someone you loved was beside you. In fact, everything was better with Meri. The simplest things: gathering manna, sitting by a fire, taking a walk, just waking up in the morning. The joy she brought to his life was immeasurable.

Meri lifted her head and stared at him. "What are you thinking about?"

"How different everything is."

"From what?"

"From the way it was in Egypt. Now that I have you, and Sabba and Imma."

"You always had them."

Bezalel shook his head. "Not really. I rarely saw them. Until the last several months."

"But they were always there. They loved you. You told me yourself. They cared about you, thought about you every day, trusted that El Shaddai would take care of you. You always had them, whether you saw them every day or not."

Meri always found the best in every situation. And she was teaching him to do the same. Or at least trying to.

Meri stood and glanced toward camp. "I'm heading back to help with the evening meal. Are you coming?"

"Not yet. I'll be back in a little while." He stood and kissed her cheek.

A sizable herd of antelope grazed in the distance, attacking any plant growth still remaining after the dry spring. Their long, dark horns contrasted with their white coats.

More movement drew his attention, perhaps one of the many groups of wandering drovers who called the desert home. He'd grown used to seeing them roam with their herds of goats, sheep, or even cattle, depending on the terrain. But this crowd seemed much larger than those nomadic tribal groups. And he saw no animals.

His hands began to sweat. Searching for something to climb for a better view, he noticed the rocky foot of a mountain trailing into the sand. He scrambled up as high as he could and stood on his toes, hand to his forehead. As he watched, their numbers grew. Worse, they came straight toward the Israelites' camp, although still a distance away. Bezalel hopped down and ran to find Joshua.

He burst into Joshua's tent. "Joshua! We have to go see Moses. Hurry!"

"Why? What's the matter?" Joshua jumped up and followed Bezalel out of the tent.

Sabba sat by the fire. "What's going on?"

"There's an enormous group of people just beyond the edge of camp." He paused and watched for Joshua's reaction as he delivered the next bit of information. "They are not nomads ... and they are headed straight for us."

Joshua's face lost its color. "What do they look like? Very tall? Dark? With long spears?"

"I don't know; they were too far off. Come on. We have to tell Moses." Bezalel took off for Moses's tent and Joshua followed. Good thing they always camped near Moses.

Moses sat cross-legged on a cushion in front of his tent, his shepherd's staff at his side. Although he had not tended sheep for over a year now, ever since he first returned to Egypt, Bezalel had never seen the old man without it.

Bezalel relayed what he had seen.

Moses's eyes swept over Joshua, head to toe. "You are Joshua, son of Nun?" He wasted no time with pleasantries or formalities.

Joshua nodded.

Sabba arrived and Moses gestured to a cushion beside him.

"Hur speaks highly of you. Sit with me, both of you."

They lowered themselves onto the sand. Moses's calmness annoyed Bezalel. Didn't he understand they were almost here?

Moses studied Joshua for a few moments. "You fought the Amalekites?"

"I don't know who they were. They attacked a week ago. They were tall, dark, and carried long spears as their only weapons."

"Yes, those are the cursed Amalekites." Moses spat. "They have terrorized this desert for generations." Moses offered Joshua a skin of water, but the young man shook his head.

"Yes sir. They killed my mother, father ... little sister ... my whole family. I have no one left."

"You have Yahweh. You will always have Him. Never forget that." Moses set the skin aside. "I want you to gather men to fight the

Amalekites. You have tonight to gather and prepare. When the sun rises, be ready, for they always attack as soon as the sun is fully up. For tonight, we have nothing to fear. They will not fight without the sun. It is their 'protector.' But we have Yahweh.

"Tomorrow, I will be on the top of the hill, watching, with the staff of Yahweh in my hands, raised toward His throne. Aaron and Hur will accompany me."

Moses pulled himself up with his staff, and without a word disappeared inside his tent.

Bezalel snorted. *Well, that was just strange.* Go gather an army. Made of former slaves. Who have never fought. Should be easy.

Sabba put a hand on Joshua's shoulder. "Joshua, you have much to do tonight."

"Why should he choose me? There are others.… " Joshua shook his head.

Sabba chuckled. "Moses makes no decisions lightly, or without consulting Yahweh, be assured of that. The choice was a good one, or it would not have been made."

"How do I begin?" Joshua looked at Sabba then at Bezalel.

Bezalel lifted one shoulder. "Start with Kamose."

❧ ❦

Bezalel, Joshua, and Kamose sat around a fire outside their tents. The sun would be up in a few hours, but no one could sleep.

Bezalel stared into the fire. The carefree flickering of the flames mocked his mood. "What do you think our chances are, Kamose?"

Kamose took a deep breath. "I don't know. None of you have ever fought before, probably never even handled a weapon. The Amalekites know this area much better than you, and obviously they have far more experience. And once the battle begins, we cannot retreat. They can. They have a myriad of hiding places in these rocks.

"However, they have lost the element of surprise, and they know we will be waiting for them. That's a huge disadvantage for them. We have more men. We have more motivation to win. They fight only to loot and steal, but we will be fighting for our lives, and those of our families. And of course, we have Shaddai, who has promised to fight with us. If He can defeat the Egyptian army, He can handle this sorry group of raiders."

Bezalel blew out a sharp breath. "Kamose, I didn't know you had such faith in Him."

"I admit, at first I wondered if I had made a mistake following you, abandoning my king." Kamose recrossed his feet at the ankles. "But I have seen too much to doubt El Shaddai's superiority. Crossing the Yam Suph was, of course, beyond amazing. But every day there is a new reason to believe. Manna, quail, water made sweet, water from a rock. I can make no other choice." He pronounced the decision as if it were a logical military strategy.

Bezalel looked up and watched the twinkling stars. Joshua and Kamose both had experience in battle, even if Joshua's was just one morning's worth. Bezalel had no idea what to expect once the sun rose.

What would it be like? Soldiers were in and out of the palace all the time, but they were always polished and shined, never bloodied. Could he do it? Could he actually kill someone? Or would he run? Would he come back tomorrow—or would he leave Meri a widow before she had a chance to be a wife?

He shoved those thoughts deep inside his mind. "Joshua, do you remember the one who killed your family?"

"I will never forget his face." Joshua's eyes glazed over. Bezalel leaned forward to hear his soft voice. "I was helping my cousins. They were camped next to us. We managed to fight off their attackers, but when I turned around, my parents…"

Joshua was silent a moment. "They were all dead except my baby sister, Annah. He raised his spear and drove it through her. As he ran off, he looked back at me and laughed. I went to Annah and held her. Blood poured out from her little body all over me. She died in my arms. I should have gone after him....."

"Joshua!" Bezalel grabbed Joshua by the arm and shook him. It was like waking him from a dream.

Kamose touched Joshua's shoulder. "You did what was needed. You can't always control everything. In battle you often have no control at all."

"But if—"

"No." Kamose's voice was low, but firm.

Joshua looked at Kamose, then Bezalel, but said nothing. He twisted his arm free and lay back.

But no one slept.

28 Ziv

Bezalel jumped up and brushed the sand from his cloak. As he watched Joshua stride through camp, wordlessly jerking tent flaps open, he removed his thawb and tunic and tossed them inside his tent.

Meri crept out of their tent and stumbled over to Bezalel. She wrapped her arms around his waist and rested her head on his chest.

His chest constricted. He embraced her and kissed her head.

Her eyes were moist as she looked up to him. "Promise me you'll come back."

Her request sliced through his heart. He didn't want to lie, but he had already learned the hard way not to make promises he could not keep. It was not up to him. He stroked her hair and gave her a gentle kiss while he tried to decide what he could say.

The tear on her cheek told him she knew what he was thinking.

He gave her a squeeze and closed his eyes tightly. When he opened them he saw Imma standing outside her tent.

He laid his hands on Meri's face and kissed her, savoring the taste of her lips, excruciatingly aware it might be the last time he ever touched her or even saw her. "I have to go now," he whispered.

Imma stepped behind Meri and grasped her shoulders. She smiled at Bezalel and nodded, telling him with one gesture everything he needed to hear from her, then led Meri away. Tears rolled down Meri's cheeks as she slipped from him.

He was left standing by the fire, alone.

The sun was barely up, casting a rosy glow over the camp as he made his way toward Joshua where the men gathered. Most carried weapons they had scavenged from the Egyptians. They milled around, munched on manna cakes, sharpened daggers, gathered arrows for bows. Five men brought a large, open, tarred basket full of water. He joined the crowd filling skins and tied two onto his belt. Hundreds of low-voiced conversations melded into one constant hum around him.

Fear and excitement mingled in Bezalel's gut. Part of him wanted to start, to get on with it. The waiting only heightened his anxiety. The rest of him was happy to wait. He paced like a palace cat, headed nowhere in particular, wandering in between and around clumps of men standing in groups of twos and threes.

As the sun finally climbed over the mountaintops, the Amalekites attacked. Spears held high, the enemy raced toward the camp, screaming. This time, the Israelites waited for them.

Raiders and Israelites blended in a sea of flesh and metal. Pounding footsteps and clanging blades competed with shrieks and shouted orders.

Armed with only a dagger, Bezalel fended off spear thrusts from every direction. Raiders surrounded him. A giant Amalekite smirked as he separated Bezalel from the group. Blows rocked his shoulders even when he blocked them.

Fury fueled unfamiliar strength. He dodged a jab and aimed for his enemy's heart. He thrust his dagger deep but missed by a hand's breadth. Bright red blood pumped out over his hand and the metallic smell filled his nostrils. The wound slowed down the enemy, but the attack continued. The Amalekite's spear sliced a gash from the top of Bezalel's left shoulder to just above his elbow. Pain screamed throughout his left side. The blood was warm as it streamed down his arm and chest.

Bezalel's vision narrowed to only the Amalekite standing before him. He tightened his grip on the dagger and again sought the raider's heart. The blade plunged into his chest. Blood spewed onto Bezalel's face. The Amalekite looked at him with horror-filled eyes, grabbed at Bezalel's tunic, and collapsed.

Bezalel stared at the fallen warrior. He had taken a life. He had killed someone. That person had been trying to kill him, and had been enjoying it, but still he had killed. What kind of person did that make him?

He realized standing there thinking made him an easy target when another Amalekite rushed at him. He fell backwards. A raider stood over him with a spear aimed at his heart. Bezalel's chest heaved and his heart raced. Was this it? Was this the end? He should have paid more attention.

Behind his attacker, Joshua rushed at the enemy's back and wrapped his left arm around him. With his right he dragged his blade from one ear to the other, slicing his throat.

The Amalekite slumped to the ground, blood pouring from his neck. Bezalel scrambled up and out of the way before the crimson liquid covered his feet. As Joshua reached for the spear the dead Amalekite still grasped, he was gripped from behind. Dagger dripping blood, Joshua slashed his attacker's forearm. Muscle and bone were revealed as more blood drained over Joshua's tunic. The arm released its choking grip.

Bezalel rushed to help, but Joshua shoved him aside.

Joshua turned to face his attacker. His scream echoed as he lunged at the Amalekite. He drove his dagger into his enemy's shoulder, his hands, his calves. Anywhere but the most effective targets.

The Amalekite responded by jabbing his spear straight into Joshua's left thigh, and blood spurted. The enemy yanked out the spear, twisting it, ripping flesh as he did.

Joshua never slowed. He thrust his blade into the Amalekite's throwing arm. He sawed the blade in a long, deep gash.

The enemy's spear fell to the blood-drenched ground, and he grabbed his wound.

Joshua drove the dagger into his belly. When the man finally collapsed, Joshua picked up the spear. He stood over him for a moment and scowled. Then he cried out as he drove it straight into his heart.

Bezalel rushed to Joshua. He pointed to the fallen Amalekite. "Was that ...?"

Joshua looked to Bezalel, chest heaving. "Yes. That was the man who killed my family. And this"—he held up the spear—"is the weapon he used to do it. I have made sure he will never kill again."

❧ ❧

Partway up the hillside, Bezalel and Kamose studied the battle under the bright, noon sun.

Joshua limped near and stared at the mass of frenzied people below.

Suddenly Kamose spoke. "Look down there."

Bezalel strained to see but saw no order or planning in it at all.

Kamose leaned in toward Joshua, pointing toward the battle raging beneath them. "See what they're doing? The enemies go to our weakest point. Then we send reinforcements. Then they send their men to the other side. And it starts all over again. We end up constantly defending ourselves."

"So somehow, we have to make them the defenders. But how?" Joshua paced. Red-spotted lambskin wrapped around his thigh.

Bezalel rubbed his arm, where his own tightly wound bandage stopped the bleeding but not the pain.

"I know. We divide them." Joshua pointed his spear to a point in the fracas. "We send a column of men down the middle of the largest group, and divide it into two pieces." He drew his spear from the bottom to the top of the fray. "That way they can't reinforce each other. Then we'll keep dividing until they are defeated."

"Excellent. You learn quickly." Kamose slapped Joshua on the shoulder. "But make a wedge. A point will allow you to break the fighting. But then expand it as you go, further separating the army into two pieces. Then they will not be able to break your line."

Joshua turned to Bezalel. "I want you to lead the first column."

"Me?" Bezalel gulped. "Why me?"

"Because I trust you, and you will do as I ask. All you need to do is lead. Later, as I find more good leaders, I'll send them to cut the army yet again."

He pointed toward a group of men nearby. "Take them with you. Have them spread out as you go, until you get a line of men all along the length of the army. You don't need to be able to fight, so your arm won't matter. Just keep the Amalekites from crossing that line."

Joshua called to a group of men and told them to follow Bezalel. The group clambered down the hillock.

At the bottom of the hill, Bezalel faced his warriors. "I'm going to make a way straight through the battle. You follow me. Leave men behind as we go, until we make a wedge. The last ones will stay here at the beginning. Spread out all along the line. They may attack at first, but they'll leave for weaker areas. Hold the line until you receive other instructions."

The makeshift soldiers nodded, and Bezalel headed into the mob.

He snaked between the hand-to-hand battles. His only goal was to stretch out the line as quickly as he could.

When he reached the far end, opposite the hill, he looked back at the battlefield. As hoped, they had split the battle wide open.

He left instructions with those behind him, leaving two in charge. He swung wide around the battle to rejoin Joshua. About halfway around the field he noticed another man who appeared to have just finished doing the same, perpendicular to his line. He stopped to see who the captain was. "Nahshon?"

The man jogged over to him. "Bezalel! It's hard to tell who anyone is. We all look alike—bloody, hot, and dirty."

Bezalel grabbed the skin from his belt, took a long drink of hot water then passed it to Nahshon. "I wonder if this is doing as much good as Joshua expected."

"It kept them from sending two or three men after only one of us. I lost several men that way this morning. They never had a chance."

"Have you seen Michael?"

"No, but I doubt he would risk his own safety for anyone else. As long as he stays in camp he'll be safe. And I'm sure that's exactly what he will do."

☙❧

Joshua fidgeted with his spear. "We're capturing weapons from them; we have almost as many as they do now. We have killed more of them than they have killed Israelites. The men don't seem to be too exhausted. I fill in all the weakened areas with new fighters. What more can we do?"

As the commanders studied the field, Bezalel looked up toward his grandfather and Moses. Moses's arms were drooping. They were now almost at his side after the long morning of holding them heavenward. Aaron and Sabba knelt beside him, praying to El Shaddai for victory and protection.

Moses began walking from side to side. The resultant surge of energy enabled him to raise his arms higher for a while. Bezalel turned back to the battle. He was shocked to see the Israelites advance on the Amalekites. But after just a short while the Amalekites regained control, and when Bezalel looked toward Moses, he was not surprised to find Moses's arms had again fallen.

Bezalel ran to the young commander. "Joshua, I know the answer."

Clearly irritated, Joshua spun on his heels. "What are you talking about?"

Bezalel stepped back. "I-I know why we're losing."

"Well, show me. Come on, hurry!" Joshua scanned the field.

"But that's it. It's not the men. It's Shaddai."

Twin furrows appeared on Joshua's brow.

"Moses can't keep his arms raised to Shaddai." Bezalel pointed to the hilltop. "He's too tired. When they fall, we lose. When he raises them again, we win. It's that simple. It's not your strategy or assignments or the men's strength. It's all Him."

Joshua frowned and shook his head. "No. Can't be." He walked away, sputtering.

Bezalel fisted his hands on his hips and looked skyward.

After a few moments, Joshua returned. He took a deep breath. "So what do we do? Moses has to raise his hands; he was very clear about that. We can't do it."

"I know, I know." Bezalel paced. An idea popped into his head. "But we can help him."

Bezalel raced off to the top of the hill before Joshua could question him. He reached Moses and Sabba in just a few moments. "Sabba. Sabba!" He put his hands on his knees, breathing hard, trying to catch his breath.

"Bezalel! What are you doing up here?" Sabba glanced furtively at Moses. "You should not be here."

"But I know what's wrong." He took several more deep breaths.

"What's wrong? What do you mean?"

"I know why we're losing."

Sabba narrowed his eyes. "You do? Why?"

"Whenever Moses raises his hands, we win. When he drops them, we lose. If he walks, he gains more energy, and raises them, and we win again, but then he gets tired, and they fall, and we lose. It's a big circle."

Sabba shrugged. "Well, I don't see how we can do any—"

Bezalel spread his hands. "You can raise his hands for him. Get him something to sit on. Anything to keep his arms up."

Sabba and Bezalel found a rock large enough for Moses to sit on, and Bezalel recruited a couple of men to move it. Aaron and Sabba lifted Moses's arms for him, and occasionally Moses took breaks to walk back and forth.

Within moments, the tide of the battle turned and Israel began to win. Amalekites staggered back in bloody waves, retreating before lines of invigorated Israelites. Groups of raiders gave up and bolted for their camps. Bezalel kept turning to check on Moses, to see if he had his arms raised. He smiled as he saw time and again they were, and watched the Israelites dispatch Amalekites one after another.

It was nothing short of amazing.

࿇࿇

As the light retreated from the western sky, Bezalel bit into his last dry manna cake. He drained his water skin and wiped the drops from his beard with the back of his hand. He leaned onto his right hand and pushed himself up. Pain shot through his chest whenever he moved his left arm. He started down the hill, placing his feet carefully so as not to jar his body. Halfway down he stopped, looking across the sandy battlefield stained with dark, red blood.

Younger boys gathered weapons, cloaks, and sandals from fallen combatants. Closer to camp, girls ripped clothing for bandages while women tended to wounds and handed out bowls of hot manna. Older men repaired broken spears and arrows and lashed new handles to dagger blades.

The ordinariness was unsettling. People talked and moved about, but compared to the clamor and chaos of battle, the quiet echoed in his chest. The metallic smell of blood was overpowering and his stomach rebelled.

Bodies, both Amalekite and Hebrew, littered the field. Crumpled in the positions in which they had fallen, they lay silent and horribly disfigured. The Israelite bodies would remain until survivors could bury them, or find or create enough tombs in the walls of rock that surrounded them.

Bezalel continued his painful trek down the hill. The blood on his shenti, his skin, his hair, was a sticky, foul reminder of every gruesome action he had taken that day. Every muscle and joint resisted moving and demanded rest. The memories of what he had seen and done flooded his mind and refused to give him peace.

As he neared camp, the sounds of mourning reached his ears. Widows wept over husbands who would never again come home; children cried for fathers who would never again kiss them good night.

He had taken many lives today. The first time it appalled him. Horrified him so much it had almost gotten him killed. Each time after was a little easier. He didn't see them so much as people, fathers, husbands. They were only the enemy. Just like the soldiers who died in the Yam Suph.

Now he didn't feel anything. He was numb.

El Shaddai, what have I become?

Eighteen

1 Sivan

Mount Sinai

Fading sunlight sparkled on the high, narrow granite walls that led the Israelites through the dry wadi from Rephidim. Their arduous trek into the mountains had finally leveled out. As Bezalel emerged from between the stone alley onto a narrow but long plain, he dropped his packs and gawked at the land before him.

Three imposing peaks lay directly in front of them to the east, and far lower mountains surrounded them on all other sides. Rivers wandered in from cracks in the mountains and fell into pools that looked deep enough to swim in, and at least four streams crossed the hanging valley floor before trickling out again.

Two long gardens stood tucked along the south wall. Tamarisk, lotus, acacia, and sycamore trees spilled out of the gardens and up onto the mountainsides. Date palms stood guard over an abundance of fruit trees and vibrant flowers.

A bump from behind told him to get out of the way. He picked up his packs and made his way down the path from the mountain's mouth to the valley floor. The soft green grass reached over his sandals and tickled his feet. There would be plenty of food for the animals.

The next morning, Bezalel found Meri gazing at the mountain as the honeyed aroma of manna cakes cooking over a flame filled the air. He wrapped his arms around her waist. "Feeling better today? I know the climbing was difficult for you. Are you comfortable up this high?"

She put her hands over his and leaned her head against his chest. "I'm fine as long as I can't tell I'm up high. With the mountains surrounding us it's easy to forget. These mountains are incredible. I've never seen anything like them. Back home it's all just flat, flat, and more flat. Here, we've slept by them, walked around them, we even walked through them yesterday. And now, this field, or whatever you call it, this area, it's tucked away up here, and no one would ever find it unless they knew it was here."

"Moses lived out here a long time. He knew about it."

Kamose strolled up, catching the end of their conversation. "I have fought in this desert in many battles, but I never knew about this valley. I know of several oases, but nothing as large as this."

Bezalel pulled away from Meri. "I think the shepherds keep these to themselves. Moses says there are a few more. This is the largest, where he often summered."

Ahmose skipped up to them. "Bezalel, will you take me to the water over there? I want to swim."

Bezalel chuckled. "Do you know how to swim?"

Ahmose made a face. "No. But it is not all too deep, is it? Can you teach me?"

Joshua approached them carrying the spear he'd taken from the Amalekite who had murdered his family. He had not been without it since the battle. "Moses said we are to put a barrier around the mountain, so no one can touch it."

Bezalel gestured in a circle. "Which mountain?"

Joshua pointed east with his spear, over his shoulder. "That one. Mount Sinai. Moses says that's where Yahweh appeared to him in the burning bush. I need some more men and a great deal of rope."

"You go get the rope. I'll gather some more men. I'll be back later, habibti." Bezalel placed a kiss on Meri's cheek.

"But what about the pool?" Ahmose tugged on Bezalel's sleeve.

"Come on, I'll take you." Kamose extended his hand, and they wandered toward one of the many watering holes.

ॐ∽ঔ

The recruits all gathered near Joshua's tent, and he led the group toward the base of Mount Sinai as he spoke. "We'll work together to make sure no one touches the mountain. Remember Moses's words: 'Anyone who touches the mountain must be put to death.'" He pointed to two of the group. "You and you, what are your names?"

"I'm Isaac. He's Asher."

"Start cutting some support poles from the trees growing around here. Do you have a knife?"

Asher held up a dagger.

"We'll dig holes, set the poles, tie the rope, and move to the next spot to begin again. Everyone understand?"

They all nodded.

"Let's go, then."

Isaac and Asher disappeared, and the rest started digging. Bezalel started on a hole, but being only days away from the battle, his wound ripped open and blood trickled down his arm. He dropped the shovel.

Joshua came over and grasped Bezalel's forearm. "Go back and wrap it up again before it rips any further."

"Digging puts too much pressure on the wound. Perhaps I can tie the rope."

"Get it wrapped first. If you can tie rope without pulling on it, go ahead. But I'm not answering to Meri if you come back worse than when you left."

༃∾ఀ

Kamose held his nephew in his arms as they made their way down the sloped ground toward the center of the pool and stopped when the water reached his chest. Warmed by the sun, it was refreshing, and reminded him of the Nile.

Ahmose squealed when the water touched his chin. Kamose moved his hands to the child's waist and pushed him away until he was at arm's length.

Ahmose gasped softly.

"You're fine. I've got you. Kick your feet."

Ahmose kicked and giggled. He started splashing.

"Don't get me all wet!"

"You're in the water. How will you not get all wet?" Ahmose laughed.

"Very true." Kamose laughed with him.

"Uncle Kamose?"

"Yes."

"Tell me about my mother."

Kamose studied the boy's face. "She looked a lot like you. You have her eyes. And her cheeks."

Ahmose smiled.

"Yes, her cheeks looked just like that when she smiled. And she loved to run and play when she was little. She liked to laugh a lot. She never became sick." He chuckled. "She didn't like to help at home very much, though."

Ahmose laughed.

"You remind me of her when you laugh."

Ahmose splashed and kicked some more. Then his face clouded a moment. "Did she ever tell you who my father was?"

Kamose took a deep breath. "No, habibi. She never said his name." She hadn't, since it was obvious, so Kamose didn't actually lie.

Ahmose looked toward the edge and smiled when he saw some boys his age. "I want to play now."

"Let's get to a shallower part then, where you can stand up." Kamose pulled him closer and swam toward the edge. He set him down and Ahmose scampered off.

Kamose stood and watched him run and splash and giggle. Ahmose loved to laugh. He saw the best in everyone he met. Kamose saw no reason to spoil that by telling him his father was the creator of all that was horrible and awful in his life. He would eventually figure it out, and by then, hopefully, he would be old enough to forgive his mother, his father, and maybe even Kamose.

❧ ❦

Joshua looked at the sun shining through the cloud blanketing the valley. It was well past its zenith. "We've still got quite a way to go. This is going more slowly than I thought."

Bezalel took a long drink from a goatskin and handed it to Nahshon. "Can't we finish tomorrow?"

"Moses wanted it done today, but we might have to."

"I can go find some more men." Nahshon offered Joshua the skin.

"All right. At least four more." Joshua drew the back of his hand across his brow.

Nahshon returned with five more men and some manna, along with some dried quail. He gave food to the others who had been there all day and brought the rest to Bezalel and Joshua.

Saul, one of those Bezalel had drafted, called to Joshua. "I need to get on the other side of the rope. I can't set this pole from here."

"No!" Joshua strode over to Saul. "The boundary has been put up and it must be observed. We can't risk you touching the mountain."

"Well, then, I won't touch it. But let me get on the other side, or the rope will never be put up."

"I said no."

Saul grumbled and went back to trying to set the pole. At that moment, Isaac and Asher came up with some more cut branches, and Joshua walked over to meet them.

"Here are twelve more. How many more to finish?"

"I'm not sure," Joshua said. He looked from where the group was working down to where the rope would need to end. When his gaze returned to the group, he saw Saul climb over the rope. They were trying to get the branch to stand up straight enough to hold the rope at the right level, but were having trouble. Saul looked around, as if searching for something. Joshua yelled to get his attention, but Saul ignored him.

Saul pointed at something as if he had found what he was looking for, and walked over toward the mountain. He walked to its base, picked up a large rock, and turned back toward the rope fence.

In an instant, Joshua grabbed the knife from Isaac's hand and expertly launched it at Saul. Saul dropped to the ground, the knife in his heart.

The others digging with him backed away. Bright red blood gushed from Saul's chest and colored his tunic.

Bezalel struggled for breath and his legs went weak. He couldn't take his eyes off Saul's lifeless form lying among the rocks. He'd seen Joshua kill in battle. He'd seen him kill brutally when he encountered the Amalekite that had murdered his family. But this was different. This was an Israelite. Without anger. Without vengeance. Without any hostility. Without thought, apparently.

How could he do that?

Although he knew El Shaddai had commanded death for anyone who touched His mountain, and although he knew Saul had deliberately and knowingly violated the order, he still could not believe Joshua had killed him.

He looked to Joshua, who stood staring at the fallen man. The color had drained from his face. His voice shaking, he mumbled to Nahshon to take over, and stumbled away.

Bezalel and the others finished the rope line in near silence. When they reached the end, Nahshon dismissed the workers.

"What about Saul's body?" asked Bezalel.

"We can't get it without touching the mountain ourselves."

Bezalel shuddered. "I guess not. Still, it seems wrong to just leave it there." He stared in the direction of the body.

Nahshon shrugged. "I know. But what can we do?"

The pair walked back toward the body. In that place where Joshua had pierced Saul's heart, a pile of rocks from Mount Sinai itself now covered the body.

Around the fire late that night, when everyone else had gone to sleep, Bezalel told Sabba about the incident at the foot of the mountain.

"I don't understand." Bezalel poked at the fire.

"Don't understand what, habibi?"

"Any of it. Why Joshua killed Saul, why we had to put the ropes up in the first place, none of it."

"The ropes were put up to set Mount Sinai apart as a holy place. Yahweh resides there now. He wishes to dwell among us, in a way we can see and be aware of. So He has chosen to live there for the present. But He is not man. He is El Shaddai, God Almighty. He is perfect and holy, and He must be set apart from us."

"So the ropes are to keep us away?"

"Yes. Moses ordered the boundaries be placed to remind us. We can approach Yahweh, but only as Yahweh proscribes. Saul chose to disobey. Joshua, on the other hand, chose to obey. I am sure it was a difficult thing for him to choose obedience when the consequences were so great. He will carry the memory of today with him forever."

"Where is he? He didn't eat."

"He's been with Moses. He hasn't come out of Moses's tent since he came back. When he does come home, I am sure he will need your understanding, not your judgment."

6 Sivan

The Israelites spent three days preparing themselves to meet with Yahweh, washing their clothes, cleansing themselves. On the third morning, exploding thunder and crackling lightning shook the camp awake. A cloud, heavier and duskier than the one above them, sat atop Mount Sinai.

Bezalel slipped from his tent and quickly built a fire and set some water to boil.

Imma returned from gathering manna and poured some into the bubbling water then scooped it into bowls. The meal was without conversation, but was far from quiet. The mountain's noises had everyone on edge. They had no sooner put the last bites into their mouths than a single trumpet blast echoed down the mountain. A shudder went through Bezalel, and Meri shook next to him.

Clan by clan, the Israelites filed toward the bottom of Mount Sinai, shoulders stiff, steps slow, mouths set in grim lines. Apprehension grew along with the crowd, and the trumpet continued to blare. The people faced the craggy peak, the portentous cloud floating atop it.

Waiting, waiting, waiting....

The thunder silenced. The people stilled. Then the deep, strong voice of Yahweh rumbled from the mountain.

"I am Yahweh, who freed you from slavery, and rescued you from Egypt."

If thunder could form words, it would sound very much like Yahweh. The earth under Bezalel's feet quaked. The shiver ran all the way up through his body. His heart beat rapidly.

"You must have no other gods but Me.

"You must not make any idols.

"You must not misuse My name.

"Remember the Sabbath day and keep it holy.

"Honor your father and your mother, so that you will have a long and happy life in the land I am giving you."

Bezalel's upper arm stung. When he glanced down, he saw Meri's fingernails digging into his skin. Her eyes squeezed shut so tightly her nose wrinkled up. Her body shook violently.

On the other side of Meri, Ahmose grasped Kamose's hand, and the soldier picked him up and held him close. Ahmose wrapped his small arms around Kamose's neck and hid his face. Kamose pulled at his tiny fingers to loosen the grip.

The voice continued. *"You must not murder.*

"You must not commit adultery.

"You must not steal.

"You must not give false testimony against your neighbor.

"You must not covet anything that belongs to your neighbor."

The voice stopped as suddenly as it began, and the mountain rumbled.

One by one, the people dropped to their knees. Some fell on their faces. They raised their hands and cried out to Moses. "Let Yahweh talk to you, not to us! You can tell us what He says. We shall not live if we hear the voice of Yahweh. He must speak through you!"

The cries continued, and Moses relented. "The word of Yahweh to you then, is finished." The lower peaks acted like an auditorium, and his voice was heard as clearly as Yahweh's. "I shall receive the rest of Yahweh's word to you and I will bring it to you in the morning."

The people dispersed.

At their tents, Bezalel looked to Sabba. "I don't understand. What happened? We all spend three days getting ready for this, and it lasts only a few moments. What was the point?"

"The point was we aren't ready." Sabba shrugged. "Yahweh was ready for us, but we aren't ready for Him. Not yet."

"But they didn't even seem to want to try."

Sabba walked toward the gardens that reached into the foothills of the lower peaks, his hands clasped behind his back. "Some did. Not all. For four hundred years, El Shaddai has been silent. He was there, He was watching, waiting, but we did not hear Him, even in our hearts. Most of us lost faith He even existed."

"You never did, did you? You always believed."

"No. I always knew He was there, waiting."

Bezalel huffed and spread his hands. "Why? In the midst of all the suffering, the pain, the questions, you never gave up. When *Savta* was taken, whom I never even got to know; when Abba died; when I was sent to the palace—why not?"

"I don't know. Maybe Shaddai gave me a gift as well, a gift of faith. But I was not the only one. There always had to be some of us who believed, until He was ready to come back for us. This is a new thing, to all of us but Moses. It will take some getting used to. We always had El Shaddai, God Almighty. He is the God who promised to give Abraham descendants like the sands on the ocean, and the land for them to live in."

Sabba stopped and faced Bezalel. "But now He wants to have a deeper relationship with us, to make us His people, to be the God that lives with us, among us. He has revealed to us a new name, Yahweh. We've heard of His name before, of course, but now He has given it to us to use, has told us what it means. It means He is here now, will be among us forever now. He will never leave us again."

"Then why does everyone want to run away?"

"Again, not everyone. It's a little like falling in love. It can be scary. Sometimes you back off."

"I didn't."

Sabba smiled. "Ah, but you were ready. You were lonely. We are not all so lucky. You were also trying to protect her. That gives one courage. When I met your savta, she scared me senseless."

"Really?"

"Yes. I avoided her for weeks after I first met her. But I got over it. And then I married her."

Bezalel laughed.

Sabba put his arm around Bezalel and headed for the gardens again. "And we'll get past this too. We'll all be fine. It will just take time."

Nineteen

10 Tammuz

Bezalel and Kamose stood next to Sabba in front of Moses's tent as Michael continued his angry tirade. Five brawny friends stood in a circle behind him. "What's he doing up there, anyway? When's he coming down? He's been gone for over a month now!"

"He is talking to Yahweh." Sabba's body stiffened as he enunciated each word.

"You know what I think?" Michael shoved his finger in Sabba's chest. "I think he left. I think he went down the other side and is never coming back."

"A man eighty years old could find an easier way to leave than by climbing up and down a mountain." Bezalel reached over and removed Michael's finger from Sabba's chest. "Besides, why would he leave?"

"Because he brought us out here and now he doesn't know what to do with us. He's scared."

"So what are you suggesting?" Sabba asked. "That we go back to Egypt?"

Michael smirked. "Why not? We had food and houses, and ways of getting out of slavery there if you really wanted to."

Bezalel scoffed. "Only by becoming one of them! Is that what you would do?" He couldn't accept the idea of voluntarily selling out to the Egyptians. Some Israelites had done it, but at the expense of losing all friends and family.

"You should know." Michael's voice was cold. His friends snickered.

"I've told you before, I had no choice."

Michael raised his eyebrows. "I don't know. You seem surrounded by them even now. There's your bodyguard here, that little imp running around, and I heard you even married one."

Bezalel closed the space between Michael and himself. "Do not bring my wife into this."

Michael rolled his eyes. "Right, right, I'm sure you love her."

Bezalel clenched his jaw.

"And I hear—" Michael laughed as he looked back at his friends "—she is very good at loving you back."

Blood and heat rushed to Bezalel's head. A rage not known since the soldier had thrown Ahmose against the wall took over and he drew back his right arm and rammed his fist into Michael's face. He attempted to follow with his left but found it restrained.

Breathing hard, he turned around to see Kamose grasping his upper arm in a solid grip. "What are you doing?" Bezalel tried to wrench his arm free.

Kamose stared him down. "Protecting you."

Bezalel glanced at Michael, who had stumbled back a few steps and stood rubbing his bruised and bleeding nose. His cohorts stood around him, faces red and hands fisted, but apparently unwilling to take on Kamose to get to Bezalel.

"From him?" Bezalel, his brow furrowed and mouth hanging open, jerked his thumb toward Michael.

"No." Kamose freed Bezalel's arm. "From yourself."

Bezalel huffed and turned to face Michael again.

Michael stepped back toward the group, and again jabbed his

finger at Sabba. "What you don't want to admit is that this crowd is stranded out in the middle of this desert, that we are going to die out here, and that a bunch of crazy old men—including you—is leading us nowhere. And I for one am going to do something about it!"

Sabba leaned toward Michael. "And you don't want to admit that you are a little boy trying to be a big man, with no idea about how to do that other than to make others look small. I haven't heard of anyone, except you and your friends here, who wants to return to Egypt. You stir up trouble because it is the only way you can get attention. We are not going back. Stop acting like a child and grow up."

Heat flared in Michael's eyes. His hands clenched into fists as he backed up a few steps. Then he stormed off without looking back.

৵৽৽

Aaron paced as Sabba, Bezalel, and Nahshon waited for him to speak. "What am I supposed to do with this information? If Moses were here, he could calm them. But I don't think they will listen to us. They're a mob, ready to stone us. Moses is the only one who can handle them, and he is still on the mountain. He's been there five Sabbaths."

"Did he say when he would be back?" Bezalel looked to Aaron.

Aaron stopped pacing. "No. He just took Joshua and left, said we should wait for him."

"Just let them complain." Sabba waved a hand. "There will always be those who complain and grumble. They complained in Egypt and they complain here. And my guess is they will complain in Canaan as well. Nothing will come of it if we ignore it."

"But I can't stand to hear them moaning and groaning all the time. Isn't there something we can do?" Aaron said.

"Not until Moses comes back." Sabba shook his head.

Aaron settled his fists on his hips. "Moses is not the only leader.

Yahweh sent me to Egypt as well. I did most of the talking to Pharaoh, as a matter of fact. I always do most of the talking." He stuck out his jaw. "I am the oldest. Everyone forgets that."

Nahshon placed his hand on Aaron's back. "We know, Aaron. That's not what anyone meant."

"It is usually best to let these things run their courses, instead of interfering. You could just make it worse," Sabba said.

"But I could stop it for good, too."

Bezalel rubbed his beard. "You could, but it's doubtful."

"And that's quite a risk. Are you willing to risk so much when you could just wait a few days?" Sabba raised an eybrow.

Aaron shook his head. "I don't know. I just don't know."

16 Tammuz

The sound of tambourines, drums, laughter, and singing floated into Bezalel's tent. He pulled back the flap and rubbed his eyes. The sun barely peeked over Mount Sinai. At the base of the mountain, a growing crowd of people appeared to be celebrating. Had Moses come down?

Bezalel peeked back at Meri, still curled up amongst the cushions, asleep. He crawled out and peered in the next tent.

"Sabba? I think Moses has returned."

Sabba looked out. "Why do you say that?"

"There is rejoicing at the mountain's base."

Kamose stepped out of the tent, fastening his dagger to his hip. He tilted his head toward the noise. "That doesn't sound right. It sounds...drunken."

Sabba crawled out after Kamose. "Go get Aaron." Sabba gestured toward Moses and Aaron's tent.

Bezalel went to the tent and looked inside. He turned back to Sabba. "There is no one in here."

They walked toward the festivity, scanning the area for Aaron. Up on a massive boulder that lay nestled next to the base of the adjoining mountain, Bezalel spotted Nahshon looking down on the gathering, and sprinted toward him. "They're up there!"

They scrambled up smaller rocks to reach Aaron sitting curled up in a ball, his head wrapped in his arms. Nahshon sat next to him, his hand on his brother-in-law's back. "He won't say much. Just keeps saying he did something terrible." He pointed toward Sabba as he stood. "Maybe he'll talk to you."

Bezalel, Nahshon, and Kamose climbed to a lower rock. Below them thousands of younger Israelites danced and caroused around a platform in the middle of the open, grassy area in front of Mount Sinai. A gold sculpture about the size of a man but in the form of a bull, its head lifted to the sky, stood on a raised structure built hastily of acacia wood. Revelers swayed, kissed, banged tambourines, and played flutes. Some held plates of manna in offering to the idol.

The music pulsed in Bezalel's head and his stomach churned. Beside him, Nahshon's lip curled in disgust. Kamose stood, arms crossed, feet apart, his lips in a thin line.

Pebbles skittered behind them. Sabba stumbled but regained his footing. "Aaron did something which is indeed 'terrible.' But he wants you to know why he did it."

"What did he do?" Bezalel tore his gaze from the revelers. "What could be so terrible?"

"Michael came to Aaron and asked him to make a god. Aaron, in his desire to stop the grumbling, gave in. He hoped the people would see that Yahweh is the only true God, and that an idol can do nothing. But he underestimated Michael."

"As did we all." Nahshon sounded bitter.

"Michael told the people that the idol brought them out of Egypt, and they are now celebrating and worshipping it."

Nahshon raised his eyebrows. "They are what?"

Sabba nodded. "You heard me."

Bezalel surveyed the rabble at the bottom of the mountain. "We've got to stop them!"

Sabba shook his head. "I'm afraid it's not that easy. A great number is involved. How do you suggest we stop them?"

Bezalel spread his hands. "I don't know. But we can't just let it continue."

"It is past the point of stopping. There will be retribution for this."

"Retribution? From *whom*?"

"From Yahweh. He gave us His laws, and we broke them. There will be consequences."

"But we didn't do it. They did!" Bezalel pointed toward the revelers. *How could He hold us responsible?*

"There is no difference in a covenant. Yahweh made a covenant with Israel, and Israel broke it. That's all there is to it."

Fear coiled around Bezalel's heart like a serpent. "What will happen to us?"

"I don't know. We'll have to wait and see."

≈⚬≋

The full moon rose over the mountain, but the celebration continued unabated. Bezalel and Nahshon remained with Aaron.

At last Aaron unfolded his limbs. He joined the pair as they contemplated the depraved scene below them. Fires around the idol cast unnatural shadows over the festivities. Men and women danced, ate, and drank. Music competed with laughter and shouting. Aaron watched the debauchery then ran behind the rock and vomited.

Bezalel surveyed the revelry. As his gaze lingered on those dancing around the idol, he recognized Michael's unmistakable form. Both he and the young girl he clutched to him were naked above the waist, as were countless others. If he had not known there was only water to drink, he would have sworn the whole group was drunk.

Young men and women were doing things that should never be seen in public. They didn't seem to care who was watching, or even whom they were with. They changed partners constantly.

Bezalel was astonished at the complete lack of inhibition. After a time, his stomach stopped churning and his eyes grew moist. The revelers continually offered praise and food and drink to the calf, thanking it for its provision. Precious lambs and goats had been slaughtered. They had no real knowledge of Yahweh. The covenant they had made only weeks ago meant nothing to them.

Bezalel glanced back over his shoulder at Aaron. Nahshon knelt near him. Tears flowing freely down Aaron's face glimmered in the moonlight. His heart seemed to break within him, and there was an almost visible weight on his shoulders.

"What have I done? What have I done?" His plaintive cry rang through the star-filled night.

Did Yahweh even hear it? Or had He already abandoned them?

17 Tammuz

In the cool, gray morning light, Bezalel stepped outside his tent, where Nahshon waited for him. "Any more news?"

Nahshon shook his head. "Someone said they thought they saw Moses and Joshua coming down last night just before sunset, but they weren't sure. I think we should go get Aaron and Hur, anyway."

"How is he?"

"Aaron? He is nearly destroyed with grief. Everything just happened so fast for him. He doesn't even want to see Moses, doesn't know what to tell him."

"What is there to tell? It happened. Aaron is no match for this crowd. No one is. Except maybe Moses, and he has Yahweh telling him what to do."

They reached Aaron's tent just as he and Sabba came outside. From the base of the mountain, the sounds of the wild festival continued.

"There are too many for us to do anything. How can we stop them?" Aaron moaned, more to himself than to anyone in particular.

"Aaron!"

Bezalel jumped at Moses's voice. He hadn't seen him draw near. Joshua stood behind him, holding two tablets made of stone, writing carved into them.

"What is going on here?" Moses bellowed. "Yahweh stopped giving the Law to send me down here. We were almost done. Why?"

"The people are worshipping an idol. That is the noise you hear. They started yesterday morning and continued through the night." Sabba spoke calmly and without laying blame.

Moses narrowed his eyes. "Where did it come from?"

Aaron finally answered, his voice filled with pain. "They begged me for an idol. They were afraid you were dead. So I asked for all their gold jewelry. I never thought they would go along with it. But they did. So I threw all the gold into the fire, and that calf came out." He raised his arms toward the idol.

"It just came out? All by itself?"

Aaron refused to look at his brother.

"Never mind, it doesn't matter!" Moses dropped to his knees, his head in his hands. "Oh, Yahweh, You were right! Oh, why did I stop You? Why?" He raised his head and fisted his hands. "Now these stiff-necked people, who refuse to lower their heads to You, are bowing to a calf! An idol, which cannot hear them or see them, while they ignore the God Who brought them out of Egypt. They made a covenant they had no intention of keeping. Well, now they shall keep it! One way or another!"

Bezalel looked at Joshua, but Joshua just shrugged his shoulders and returned the same blank stare.

Aaron hung his head as tears welled in his eyes.

Moses marched off toward the mountain's base, yelling for Joshua.

Joshua ran to catch up, with Sabba, Bezalel, and Nahshon close behind him.

Moses strode to the center of the festival and scrambled atop the pedestal on which the calf stood. He placed his foot firmly on the calf's side and kicked it over. The people below, now acting quite sober, scattered.

Moses grabbed the tablets from Joshua's arms and threw them to the ground, where they shattered into thousands of pieces.

Bezalel leaned toward Sabba. "That's not very helpful."

"That is the sign of a broken covenant," Sabba whispered.

Moses addressed the crowd. "Men of Israel, what are you doing? Only forty days ago, you stood here and agreed to obey all the laws of Jehovah, the first of which was, 'You must have no other gods before Me.' Yet here you are, worshipping a calf made from jewelry once worn by the Egyptians who enslaved you! Yahweh will not allow this!"

Michael, however, was not so easily silenced. Bezalel recognized his voice. "And what if we refuse to do what you say?"

"Who speaks?" Moses scanned the crowd. "You must keep your promises. Yahweh will not be made second to any idol!"

"But you don't keep your promises; why should we be made to keep ours?" Michael shouted back but kept his face hidden from Moses.

"What promises have I made that I did not keep?"

"You promised to lead us to a land flowing with milk and honey, and yet you bring us into a desert, where we eat flakes of bread and drink water! We were better off in Egypt! We should have stayed there!"

"Why would you wish to be slaves again? To be beaten, worked from sun up to sun down, in control of no part of your life?"

"We had food there. All we wanted. And meat, vegetables, fresh fruit—not manna. We slept in houses, not tents. It was better there!" More of the rebels shouted out in agreement.

"All who agree with them, all who want to go back to Egypt, to slavery, go join them." Moses called in a clear, loud, and confident voice. "And all who are with Yahweh, come to me now."

All the Levites, Moses's tribe, rushed to him, and many from other tribes, including Bezalel, Joshua, and Nahshon. Kamose joined him as well. The Israelites who had joined neither side backed farther away, retreating to their tents.

"All those with Yahweh shall take up the sword against those who oppose Him, whether against brother or neighbor. Go gather your weapons, and return."

Bezalel raced back to his tent to grab his knife. He stripped off his tunic and tossed it inside.

Meri and Imma sat together outside the tents. When Meri saw him step outside with a dagger, she stood and opened her mouth.

Bezalel shook his head. "Don't say a word."

Back by the calf, Bezalel again found himself with blade in hand, but this time it was much different. It would be harder to kill another Israelite rather than an Amalekite. He remembered back to a few weeks ago when he had judged Joshua for doing what he now prepared to do.

He surveyed the group of rebels. Most of them were quite young, many younger than he was. The rising sun reflected off their sweaty and half-naked bodies. Their bleary eyes showed the effects of their all-day, all-night revelry.

One rebel rushed toward Bezalel with a short sword much too heavy for him. Michael had obviously raided the weapons cache. The boy didn't know how to handle it. He waggled it in Bezalel's direction.

Bezalel tried to avoid hurting the boy and at first made only defensive moves, blocking the clumsy advances.

The young attacker, apparently frustrated, swung even more wildly. The blade slashed Bezalel's arm, the same one the Amalekite had cut in the first battle. *Not again.* The slice was deep, and blood flowed from shoulder to elbow again. A familiar pain flooded the left side of his body.

The youth stopped flailing and his eyes grew wide. He laughed at the sight of the blood he had drawn—it seemed to energize him.

Even at that, Bezalel could not bring himself to kill him. He backed away, holding his knife in front of him.

His attacker laughed again and charged. He held his sword straight out. Not a particularly smart move, as it left the rest of his body unprotected, but at the moment it was effective.

Bezalel jumped aside, barely missing the blade. He turned to see the attacker coming at him again. He stepped aside, just enough to miss the charge, but placed his foot in the youth's path, tripping him. The boy fell on the hilt of his sword and toppled to the side. He grasped his belly as he rolled side to side; the blade remained upright in the ground next to him.

Bezalel tossed his knife to his left hand then pulled the sword free with his good arm and walked away. He left the boy writhing on the ground.

He had barely taken a few steps when the youth jumped on his back, reaching for his sword over Bezalel's shoulder. Bezalel leaned to his left and shook off the boy.

Bezalel breathed heavily. Blood from his arm streamed onto the boy's tunic. He still resisted killing him while he lay there, even after the youth had attacked him twice. But he couldn't walk away again, either.

The boy grabbed for the knife. Bezalel's wounded arm was too weak to lift the weapon out of the way; he could barely carry it. Instead, when the youth extended his arm, Bezalel slashed with the sword.

The youth screamed at the sight of the blood. He rolled into Bezalel's legs, knocking him down. Bezalel landed on top of the boy, and they scuffled for the weapons. The boy was younger, but tired and undisciplined. Bezalel was bigger and stronger, and possessed both blades, but the pain in his arm grew more intense with every move. Rather than let the boy have a weapon, he pushed himself up on his knees and shoved the short sword into the rebel's chest.

The youth slumped underneath him. Bezalel pulled himself away and stood. He looked down at the body. His stomach was a stone in his belly, and movement around him ceased to exist.

He had killed again.

બ∞≪

The fighting continued with casualties on both sides. With the rebels so severely outnumbered, the battle wound down quickly. Kamose stationed himself near Moses and Sabba, helping where he could, while making sure they were never in danger. There were only a few rebels left—Michael and his staunchest supporters. Most of the fighting was concentrated around the calf.

In all his years, in all his battles, Kamose had never fought his own people. Many of the rebels he recognized. As opponents, they were easy prey. Physically. Mentally, it was far harder to attack them than the Amalekites.

Michael slunk toward Moses, brandishing a long knife.

Kamose rushed to Moses's side and grasped his arm, pulling him away to the other end of the pedestal. He glanced around for Joshua and beckoned to him. He turned back toward Hur, just in time to see Michael thrust his knife into Hur's gut. Bright, crimson blood gushed from the slice in his body, and he doubled over then collapsed.

Michael laughed.

For the first time in his life as a soldier, Kamose froze.

"Still say I'm just a little boy?" Michael glared down at Hur, glanced at Kamose, and dashed off.

Kamose bolted for Hur. He had crumpled in a heap, the front of his tunic saturated with blood.

Joshua reached Hur just after Kamose.

Kamose raised his eyes to his young commander. "Get Bezalel."

ᘐ∞ᘺ

The battle all but over, Bezalel was helping to gather the wounded for medical help when Joshua reached him. "Bezalel, come quickly. It's your grandfather."

The breath rushed from Bezalel's chest. He was unable to think. The words didn't make sense.

"Bezalel! Now!"

Bezalel sprinted after Joshua then stopped dead, unable to move as he saw his grandfather lying on the ground in Kamose's arms.

"Sabba," he whispered.

Joshua gently pulled him forward.

Bezalel looked to Kamose for an explanation as he dropped to his knees. "What happened?"

"Talk to him first. I'll explain later." Kamose transferred Sabba's head onto Bezalel's lap then stood by Joshua. Kamose's hands and lap were covered in blood. The ground under Sabba was stained red.

Sabba groaned.

Bezalel pulled his gaze from Sabba to Kamose. "But what was he doing fighting?"

"Later!" Kamose said then added softly, "You have no time to argue with me."

Bezalel stroked his grandfather's face, willing him to open his eyes. He hovered his hand over the soggy wound, fingered the slashed tunic.

"Oh, Sabba, I'm so sorry." Tears flowed down his cheeks. "Please, talk to me—don't leave me yet. I need you. Don't go."

Sabba's eyes fluttered.

Bezalel's heart jumped, but his grandfather's eyes fell closed again. *Please look at me. Just once more.*

Sabba moaned and opened his eyes. But the look Bezalel so desperately hoped for was only a glassy stare. Was his grandfather already gone? He looked at Bezalel as if he had never seen him before. He tried to raise his head but it fell back. He opened his mouth, but no words rose above the sound of his rasping, rapid breath.

The memories of the last year, of everything Sabba had taught him about Yahweh, about life, about love, whirled in Bezalel's head. He couldn't lose him now, not when everything they had waited for, when all that Bezalel had thought was impossible had finally come true.

Sabba closed his eyes. Blood poured from the gash in his abdomen. His tunic was now completely drenched with blood.

Bezalel reached for a lifeless hand lying on the ground. It was cold and moist. He clutched it to his chest and leaned toward Sabba's face.

"Sabba, what will I do without you? Who will answer my questions now? I can't do it alone. I can't." He slipped his arm under Sabba's head and rested his forehead against Sabba's.

He let go of his grandfather's hand and embraced him, pulling him close. Wet, sticky blood was warm against his chest. The rapid, shallow breathing slowed then finally stopped.

Sabba was gone.

☙ ❧

They buried Sabba at sunset. The graves were lined up in rows at the western end of the field near the entrance from the mountains.

Bezalel's family surrounded him. Ahmose wrapped his little body around Kamose, his sobs drowning out all other sound. For once Imma's quiet strength, usually a bastion, did not help. Meri's arms encircled his waist, but he found no comfort in her nearness. He glanced at Joshua and Nahshon on the other side of the grave, focusing on the grass beneath their sandaled feet.

Bezalel saw Moses's lips move, but the words seemed to evaporate before they reached his ears. Time crept as slowly as a Nile turtle. He knew his grandfather lay beneath the long pile of dirt in front of him, but he wanted to turn and ask him why he felt this way. Sabba always had an explanation.

The ceremony ended and Bezalel began the walk across the field back to the tents. Facing him was Mount Sinai. It mocked him, standing there, pretending to be majestic, the last of the sun's golden rays illuminating it.

It's all Yahweh's fault.

Bezalel continued the march to Sinai, to the dwelling place of Yahweh.

Yahweh, who demanded absolute loyalty and promised to always be there with them, but then left them with no sign of His presence. Again. Took the only person who understood how this new relationship was supposed to work and left them to try to figure it out on their own.

How could He have expected them to react any differently?

Twenty

18 Tammuz

The retiring sun threw shades of pink and orange over the mountains. Blue agama lizards skittered across the ground. An ibex scaled the mountain to bed down for the night. Bezalel stared at the fire in front of his tent, vaguely aware of Meri sitting next to him. She'd been trying to talk to him all day, offer some comfort, but he'd ignored her. There was simply nothing to say, nothing left in his heart.

Moses approached the dying campfire near Bezalel's tent. "May I speak with you?"

Bezalel jerked his chin at a space near him and pushed a cushion toward Moses with his bare foot.

The fire sizzled as the old man lowered himself to the cushion. "Yahweh has told me He wants you to build a dwelling for Him. An enormous tent, with gold furnishings: an altar, a lamp stand, a laver—it all requires someone with incomparable skill in working with gold, silver, and bronze, in cutting and setting stones, working with wood. You were a craftsman for Ramses. I am told you would have been chief craftsman if you were not an Israelite."

Bezalel's mouth dropped open. His lungs froze in mid-breath. He could not believe Moses would ask him to do such a thing. He'd buried Sabba only last night. He released a loud breath. "What makes you think I would do anything for Yahweh? Or for you?" He stared at Moses.

Moses raised his shoulders. "Why not?"

Bezalel stood. He fisted his hands. "He took Sabba!" He felt Meri's hand on his shoulder but shook it off.

Moses grabbed his shepherd's crook and pulled himself up. "Your grandfather worshipped Yahweh in a way few Hebrews did. He was one of those who kept the faith during these long dark years. He—"

Bezalel threw his hands in the air. "And a lot of good it did him! All it did was get him killed! It got me a life in the palace away from my family, and it got him killed. I owe Yahweh nothing!" Bezalel sprinted for the low mountains to the right of Sinai, at the edge of the gardens. At the base, he scrambled hand over foot until his breath was gone and then searched for a flat place to rest. He found a spot tucked away under the umbrella shade of an acacia tree.

He collapsed on the ground. Tears fell that he had not released since he had first seen Sabba's motionless body. Sobs came faster and louder, and his whole body convulsed. Groans he could not control escaped from his throat. He was no longer connected to anything; he was falling with nothing to hold him. Leaning back against the tree, he sobbed until he had no more tears left.

He sat for a while, his knees up, forearms resting on his knees, his sorrow spent. He gazed over the darkening grassy field before him. Sabba was the only one who had ever had any answers for him, who had ever helped him make sense of anything.

What will I do without him?

Even when he thought Meri was gone, when he thought he would never survive the pain, he knew deep down he could eventually endure, because Sabba was there.

And now he was gone. Forever. It wasn't fair. Sabba hadn't done anything wrong.

He stood and started to pace in his spot above the camp. Sabba had been faithful all these years, his entire life, during every painful loss, and now he would never see the land Yahweh promised. He would never see his grandchildren. In fact, he hadn't even seen Bezalel grow up.

It wasn't supposed to happen this way. Sabba was a good man. This shouldn't have happened.

This was Michael's fault. He had set Sabba up. He had threatened Moses, knowing Kamose would protect him. That left Sabba alone—just what Michael wanted, so he could get his revenge for Sabba calling him a child, humiliating him in front of his followers. Michael had taken Sabba's life deliberately, maliciously, for no other reason than vengeance.

The image of Sabba lying in a pool of his own blood filled Bezalel's mind. Rage replaced grief. Wrath took over for mourning. His breath came faster. He clenched his jaw.

Bezalel slammed his fist into the tree. It felt good. Pieces of bark broke off, crumbled, and fell to the ground. It should have been Michael's face, but it was the closest thing he had at the moment. His knuckles were scratched and bleeding from the rough bark. He smashed the trunk once more anyway.

He pulled his fist away and shook it. He'd tapped into his anger now—it had to be released. He grasped a branch with both hands and ripped it from its trunk. The thorns from the tree dug into his palms, slicing them in several places. Roaring, he slammed it over his knee, cracking it in several places.

He spun around and spotted a young tamarisk, still more of a bush than a tree. Ripping off the small, reddish branches, he stripped them of their pink flowers and flung them to the sandy floor before tearing the stems apart. He tugged on the remaining plant, yanking and pulling until most of its roots lost their hold on the foothills. One deep root snaked its way into the recesses of the mountain.

Bezalel wrapped his hands around the base of the taproot, set his feet, and yanked. Too bad the root wasn't Michael's neck.

The root held its ground.

Bezalel tugged.

It didn't budge.

He jerked and screamed.

The root didn't give way.

Bezalel yanked one last time. His hands slipped along the stem and he fell flat on his back.

He sprang up and returned to the acacia tree. He pulled his foot back and kicked the gnarled trunk as hard as he could. He slammed his sandal against the tree again. And again, screaming until he was out of breath. Sometimes the tree was Michael, sometimes Yahweh, sometimes even Moses.

He stopped and rested his head and forearms against the tree, chest heaving. For the first time since the battle, his head felt clear. Nothing made sense yet, but he could think. Or at least he could if he wasn't so tired. He sat down and leaned back. Then he lay down on the dirt and slipped into an unsettled sleep.

19 Tammuz

Bezalel awoke the next morning as the sun crested the mountain. He turned his head to look down on the camp. No one was stirring yet; the camp still lay deep in the shadow of Sinai.

His left arm throbbed from the young attacker's blade. He could barely lift it. A disgusting mixture of blood and dirt covered his arm. He must have split the wound open again last night without noticing it. He lifted his right hand in front of his face. Dried blood caked his palms and knuckles, and the backs of his fingers were already green and blue. His hands throbbed when he moved them.

He started to sit up, but agonizing pain shot through his left side.

Since he couldn't use his left arm, he rolled onto his right elbow and pushed himself up on the heel of his hand then rolled to his knees.

Sabba always said his temper would get the best of him. *I guess he was right.* He would have a constant reminder of that for at least several days, if not weeks.

The shimmer of a small pool of water caught in a cleft in the rocks drew his eye. Steadily melting snow kept the streams supplied all spring, and some of the water remained in puddles like this throughout the year. It was well-shaded; it looked like it escaped the sun's wrath all day. A hardy yellow flower's root had found its way down into it from above. The pool was just big enough to put his hands into. He crawled over and scooped out enough to drink. The water soothed his abraded knuckles and his parched throat. If only it could heal his battered heart as easily.

He sat down again in the shade and examined his hands.

He had been angry before—but never that angry. His fury usually came and went rather quickly. He listed those he had attacked in his imagination last night. One of the blows had been for Kamose for leaving Sabba to go to Moses. He could blame that one on being very tired and upset.

A few were for Moses for being gone so long and for being the only one who could handle this crowd.

Several were for Aaron because he wouldn't listen to Sabba and wait a few more days.

Most of them were for Michael. *He deserved every blow. He's been causing trouble from the day I met him.* What made him most angry was that Michael got away. He lived. He walked away without a scratch. Talk about unfair.

Which brought him to Yahweh.

He thought back over all the things Sabba had said about Yahweh: You can trust Him or be blown about like a leaf in a khamsin. This is a new relationship. His plan does not always make sense. He wants to have a deeper relationship with us, to be the God that lives with us. And Bezalel's favorite: One step at a time.

Sabba had always said Yahweh had a reason for putting Bezalel in the palace. Was it to build this dwelling place for Him? If that was true, His plan started twenty years ago. He put Bezalel in the palace to learn all the skills he would need to build a house for Yahweh.

Moses had said they needed gold, silver, bronze, jewels. Where were they to come from? He remembered. They asked their Egyptian neighbors for gold and jewelry before they left that night. It was payment for four hundred years of free labor. Yahweh had thought of that, too.

And Moses. That had begun eighty years ago, when He put Moses in the palace as a prince, to learn all he needed to know to lead the Israelites out of Egypt and into Canaan. Then forty more years in the desert to learn how to survive, to learn where places like this hid.

How many other plans were in place Bezalel couldn't even see?

The palace—his prison, which he had despised almost every day he was there—had given him Ahmose and Meri. And even Kamose. And of course, the skill to build a dwelling for Yahweh. Yahweh had given him the gift, but Egypt had developed the skills.

Without the palace, he would have none of them.

He couldn't see how anything good could possibly come from Sabba's death. But if Sabba's life was to mean anything, Bezalel had to keep his grandfather's faith alive.

He reached up to find a rock he could grab with his right hand and pulled himself up. He groaned. Pain radiated throughout his body. Every muscle fought against standing up. The battle, not to mention last night, had taken more out of him than he realized. He leaned against the wall. Climbing down was not going to be easy.

After an excruciating—and exhausting—trek down, he headed for his tent. The sun now fully up, the first gray rays of light filtered over the top of Mount Sinai. He had probably half an hour before it rose high enough to shine on the still-sleeping camp. He stumbled toward his tent, suddenly realizing how little he had slept.

Kamose came near and stopped in front of him, his gaze sweeping from head to foot. "We've got to get you cleaned up before your mother sees you, let alone Meri. She'd never survive it."

Bezalel looked down. He hadn't noticed the left side of his tunic was soaked with blood. He laughed to himself. Meri had nearly fainted when he came home that day at Rephidim, and he wasn't nearly as bloody then as he was now. A lot dirtier, but less bloody. Kamose was right. Meri would not take it well.

Kamose pointed to Bezalel's arm. "What happened to the lambskin?"

"I took it off to change it, but the new one was still a little wet from washing, so I let it dry a little longer. Then Moses came to talk to me, and that's when I … left."

"The wound is full of dirt now." He pulled at Bezalel's crimson-stained tunic. "I don't think this can be saved. You have another?"

Bezalel nodded.

Kamose grabbed his dagger, cut the garment at the right shoulder and then down the side. He slipped it over the mangled arm and held up the tunic. "I think you should burn this." He put his hand on the slice in Bezalel's flesh. "It feels hot. Disease may be setting in. Come." He walked toward the stream.

Bezalel followed and waded into the water. He bent over and splashed water onto his arm.

"No. You need more force to get the dirt out. Get under the water." Kamose pointed to where the water was dropping into the stream from the gap in the rocks above them. He stood there with his arms crossed as if he were instructing a new recruit.

Bezalel grimaced. He moved toward the falling water and slid his arm under it, groaning as the liquid pounded into the raw flesh for a few moments. He pulled it out and checked it, rubbing off the caked-on blood from his side and chest before he emerged from the water.

Kamose used a relatively clean part of Bezalel's tunic to stop the bleeding the running water had prompted and looked at the wound. "At least it's clean now. But if you open it again, it will need to be sewn up. Use linen to wrap it. You can wrap it more tightly, keep it closed until it heals. There's some by my tent."

He squinted and lowered his head to get a better look. "It looks red, though. We need some honey. Or copper salts. I know someone had some after Rephidim. I'll see if I can find something. For now, let's get back. Sun's coming up."

They headed across the field toward camp. Kamose stirred the fire when they reached the tents and tossed the ruined tunic in it.

Bezalel watched Kamose out of the corner of his eye. Kamose would never ask him where he had been all night, although it was probably easy for him to guess what had happened.

Meri wouldn't be so easy.

He stared into the fire and thought over what he had learned—had he really learned anything last night? Only time would bear that out. It was easy now, in the bright morning sun, to say he could trust Yahweh and honor Sabba's life, but if—when—things went bad again, would he really do it? Or would he just let his anger take over?

Bare feet appeared by the fire. Bezalel raised his head to see Meri standing over him with her hands on her hips.

"All night? You're gone all night and I have no idea where you are!" Her eyes shot daggers at him.

Bezalel dragged himself up and reached for her. "Habibti—"

She backed up. "Don't do that. You left and didn't even—oh, look at your arm!" She reached for him. "You ripped it open again." Spreading her fingers, she drew them down the sides of the wound as tears filled her eyes. She walked over to Kamose's tent and grabbed the linen from it. She gestured to Bezalel's seat and sat down next to him, gently winding the strip of cloth around his arm.

She tucked the end of the linen under. "What were you *doing* all night long?" Her eyes pleaded with him.

He tried to explain what happened on the mountainside, what he had thought about.

She took his hands in hers and turned them over, examined the cuts. "So have you decided it's all right to be in the shadow?"

"What?"

"Remember? When you told me what your name meant? You thought being in the shadow of Yahweh meant being forgotten, cold. I told you about being in my imma's shadow."

"Ah, yes." He stared at the fire. "Maybe. Maybe that's how I need to look at it."

Meri took a deep breath. "Well, the way you're looking at it now is not helping you much."

❧≪

The noon sun brightened the camp without its wilting heat, and children scampered through the streams and chased each other around the tents. Sheep grazed lazily where the day before Israelites had killed one another. Moses stood at the edge of the flock, his head resting on his hands, his hands on his staff.

Bezalel drew near Moses. "I came to apologize for last night. My anger was … inexcusable. I'm very sorry. I apologize to you, and I'd apologize to Yahweh, if I knew how. I shouldn't have raised my voice and I shouldn't have said what I said."

"I accept your apology for raising your voice. But you needn't be sorry for what you said. You didn't say anything offensive to me. And Yahweh is great enough to hear whatever you have to say to Him."

"You think so?"

"I know so. Do you know that when He sent me to Egypt I argued with Him?"

Bezalel opened his mouth, but no words came out.

Moses handed his staff to Bezalel and picked up a lamb. "Yes, I argued. I told Him I wasn't important enough. I told Him they would never believe me. I told Him I needed proof."

"Did He give you proof?"

"Enough. I went, didn't I?" Moses chuckled, and stroked the lamb's head.

Bezalel was silent for a while. "Why was He absent for so long?"

"Not absent. Just still. But I don't know. Until we were numerous enough to inhabit the land? It's hard to say. He does not give us all the answers." Moses looked into the lamb's ears, at his eyes. "Tell me, are you still angry?"

"No, I don't think so." He raised his hand to show Moses his palms. "I... thought... about it a lot last night."

Moses laughed. "I know a little about anger. I left Egypt forty years ago because of anger."

"What happened?"

"I saw one of the taskmasters beating an Israelite for no reason. I became angry. I hit him; he hit me. I hit back harder—too hard. I killed him." Moses set the lamb down and picked up another.

Bezalel nearly choked. "You killed an Egyptian?"

Moses strolled toward the center of the flock. "Then I buried him and tried to hide it. But someone saw me, and I had to run. Anger, my boy, will destroy you, if you do not learn to control it."

Bezalel followed. "That's what Sabba always said."

"Your sabba was right." Moses inspected this lamb as he did the first.

"Well, I had all night to think about that, and I'll have several days'—or weeks'—worth of pain to remind me.... Just what are you doing?" He pointed to the lambs.

"Sorry. I was a shepherd for forty years. Now, what about Yahweh's request?"

Bezalel shook his head. "How can I possibly build a dwelling for God? I wouldn't know where to begin. I don't build houses; I make jewelry."

Moses stopped and faced Bezalel. "He will give you all the wisdom you need. And you will not be alone. He has chosen another man, Oholiab, of the tribe of Dan. He is skilled in embroidery and working with cloth. He will build the outside—the tent—and you will build the furnishings. And you will have many helpers."

Bezalel paced and thought for several moments.

Moses continued to examine sheep, wandering away from Bezalel.

"I will do it. But I am in no shape at the moment. I can't even lift my arm."

"I agree. And I think you need time to grieve." He set a lamb down, and patted it on the head. "I have to return to the mountaintop for another forty days to receive another copy of the law, as well as the instructions for the dwelling. Also, the entire camp needs to be rearranged. Aaron has the plans for that. The tabernacle will be in the center; the camp will be around it by tribe. Make sure you are near my tent, at the front, so you are close to the center." Moses placed his hand on Bezalel's chest. "By the time all that is done, I should be back, and your arm should be healed, as well as your heart. At least enough to begin work."

11 Ethanim

Bezalel faced the people, assembled once more before Moses and the mountain.

"Yahweh brought you out of Egypt. Now each of you shall pay a ransom for your deliverance—one-half silver shekel per person.

"Yahweh has promised He will dwell among us, so we are to provide for Him a dwelling place. To build this, He asks you for offerings of gold, silver, and bronze; linen; gold thread; ram, badger and goatskins; acacia wood, and spices. Your ransom price also will go toward building the tabernacle. You may begin to present your offerings to Yahweh in a few days."

Moses pointed to Bezalel. "To build his dwelling place, Yahweh has appointed these two men. Bezalel, son of Uri, son of Hur—that same Hur who gave his life for Yahweh—of the tribe of Judah. Bezalel is an artist of the highest order, once artisan to the king of Egypt, now artisan to the Creator of all. Bezalel is skilled with gold, silver, bronze, precious stones, and the carving of wood."

Bezalel stepped back and Oholiab stepped forward.

"Also I present to you Oholiab, son of Ahisamach, of the tribe of Dan. Oholiab is excellent at making all kinds of cloth, at putting designs in cloth, creating tapestry and the like.

"Both have also been blessed to teach and lead others. They will need many assistants, so when you bring your offerings, if your heart is stirred, you may also talk to them about helping.

"And now, we are here to dedicate them."

Bezalel and Oholiab knelt.

Moses raised his arms. "You have a great work ahead of you. It will take many months, and much talent, patience, and skill at supervising and teaching others as well."

Bezalel groaned as all the air escaped his lungs. Talent and skill he had; patience, no. He had never worked with or taught anyone.

"You cannot possibly do this on your own. You will need skills far greater than you could ever develop."

Then why did Yahweh ask?

"Yahweh, we come before You this day at the beginning of a great undertaking. You promised me on Mount Sinai that You would fill these young men with wisdom and understanding, knowledge and craftsmanship, to complete that which You have asked of them. I believe You have already done so. But they themselves need to know this, too. So I ask today that You give them one more gift: anoint them with confidence. Fill them with the knowledge that You have equipped them with all they need for this task. Give them the gentle authority they will need to manage the hundreds of workers You will call forth. Give them wisdom to know who should do what, the willingness to share their great knowledge with others, and discretion to know which tasks to keep to themselves. Remind them daily that You are with them and to ask You for help when they need it."

Bezalel opened his eyes and took a deep breath. He didn't *feel* any different. Could he do this?

Twenty-one

18 Ethanim

Bezalel stood in the acacia-wood fenced enclosure surrounded by gold and silver, skins and linen. He laughed at the incongruity. Most of his life he'd spent in the midst of opulence, but in the palace it was revered—jewelry adorned necks and ears and fingers, gilded furniture stood on polished stone floors, artwork hung on frescoed walls—none of it was tossed in raw heaps on a grassy field.

A Levite brought him a skin and held it up. The priest poked at it with a reed dipped in ink made from soot. "So far we have forty-three talents of silver, fifteen talents of gold, and thirty-two of bronze." He pointed at a pile in a corner. "And over there is the linen, and behind that—"

A scuffle at the fence drew Bezalel's attention. A guard restrained Ahmose by the back of his tunic. "No children allowed!"

Ahmose's face was red, and he put his hands to his throat. "But he's my brother! I have to see him!"

Bezalel dashed for the gate.

"He said he was your brother." The guard sneered. "With a name like Ahmose! No Israelite would name a son Ahmose."

Ahmose fought to hold back tears. "I was trying to come see you, but he won't let me."

Bezalel glowered at the guard. "He *is* my brother. Now let him go."

The man snorted and released Ahmose, who rushed to Bezalel's side, grasping him around the waist.

Bezalel pulled him away and dropped to one knee. He grasped the boy's shoulders. "What's wrong?"

"My heart is stirred."

"Your heart is what?"

"My heart is stirred. Moses said anyone whose heart is stirred to help should come and see you. Well, I want to help."

Bezalel swallowed. What could a child possibly do to help? *If I tell him he's too young, I'll break his heart. And who am I to say Yahweh has not called him?*

"All right, for now, you can be my special assistant. And then, when we find the perfect job for you, we'll know, and the job will be yours."

"Yes! Thank you." Ahmose jumped into Bezalel's arms and hugged him.

Bezalel set the boy back on the ground. "Let me finish counting, and you go play, all right? We won't start building for many days yet, but I promise not to start without you." He winked at Ahmose, and the child ran off.

5 Av

Kamose and Ahmose strolled back from the garden with pomegranates, walking through the neat rows of tents now set up by tribe around the center of the camp.

"He said I could help. We just don't know how yet." Ahmose struggled with his pomegranate.

Kamose stopped and took the fruit from the boy and sliced it open. "That's a very special job. Bezalel must love you very much to let you help make Yahweh's house."

Ahmose beamed up at Kamose. "I love him, too."

The corners of Kamose's mouth tipped up in a smile. He handed Ahmose his pomegranate and headed down the row again.

Ahmose skipped ahead.

Kamose kept his leisurely pace. Ahmose had far too much energy for him to keep up with. He hated to admit it, but he was no longer a young man. He'd enjoyed his time here at Sinai. The area was beautiful, Bezalel and Meri and Rebekah were wonderful people to be around, there was no Ramses screaming at him and becoming more bizarre and malicious by the day. The only problem was that he had time to realize how lonely he was—

Ahmose's cry interrupted his thoughts. He bolted toward the sound.

Michael stood towering over the boy, scowling.

Kamose placed a hand on Ahmose's shoulder, easing him back. He inserted himself between Ahmose and Michael, who came up only to his chest.

Michael took a step back. "The mighty Egyptian soldier, the famous bodyguard. Didn't do such a good job last time." He curled his lips into a sneer.

Ahmose peered out from behind Kamose's legs.

Kamose glared down at Michael. He'd never killed before unless in battle or under orders. But for Michael, he'd make an exception—if Ahmose weren't watching. "You were, and always will be, a coward. You cannot be proud of attacking an unarmed old man. And you accomplished nothing."

Michael stepped closer. "You don't belong here. You should leave."

"There are many Egyptians here. And many of other lands as well."

"And none of you belong here. Watch out. Or you're next." He peeked around Kamose. "Or he is." He spun on his heels and walked away.

Ahmose took Kamose's hand. "I don't like him. He's always saying mean things like that."

Kamose arched his brow. A shudder went through him. "You've seen him before?"

Ahmose shrugged. "He finds me all the time. He says something to scare me and then leaves."

Kamose knelt to face him and placed a hand on his shoulder. "Why didn't you tell me, habibi?"

"I knew you would protect me if he really tried to hurt me. So far all he's done is talk."

Kamose smiled weakly.

If only Ahmose knew what Michael had already done.

20 Av

"It's been three weeks. What do we have now?"

The Levite studied the skin and made some final calculations. "One hundred talents of silver, twenty-nine talents of gold, and seventy talents of bronze."

Bezalel locked his hands behind his neck. "That's more than enough. Tell the people to stop bringing gifts."

"I did. Day before yesterday. They won't." The man pointed toward the gate. "More are coming now."

Bezalel scanned the area for Aaron and spotted him just outside the enclosure. He hurried across the field and hopped the fence. "Aaron, the people are bringing too much for the tabernacle." He waved his hand toward the piles of precious metal. "We are running out of room and spending all our time cataloging and sorting the materials. We have spent the last two days telling people to quit, but they won't listen. You have to tell them."

"If you wish. But you are sure you have enough?"

"We have more than enough. Add the silver from the ransom price and we are full to overflowing."

"We'll stop, then. And I'll put Asher there in charge of all the guards and the inventory. You worry about the building."

❧❧

The sun shone its last rays over the western mountains. "All right, Ahmose, there should be no more offerings. When you are finished sorting these last few pieces, we're done." Bezalel looked over the list one last time to ensure they had enough of all the necessary materials.

"Then what will I do?"

"I'm not sure yet. But we'll find a special job for you. Maybe you can help me melt the gold. We'll need a great deal of that." Bezalel nodded to Asher as the pair stepped through the entrance to the enclosure.

"That sounds like fun!"

"It can be exciting at first, but believe me, it will get boring. And it's a very hot job, too."

"I'll love it as long as you're there."

Bezalel mussed Ahmose's hair.

"Last one." Ahmose took a pitcher to the towering pile of gold.

"Ready to go then?"

"Wait." Ahmose scrambled to the top of a large pile of rams' skins.

Bezalel laughed as he peered up at the child. "What are you doing up there?"

"Just looking."

"At what?"

Ahmose spread his hands. "All the stuff Yahweh provided. We needed it, and He gave it. Just like the ram! Like the ram in the bushes with Father Abraham! What was that name Abraham called him again?"

"Jehovah-Jireh?"

"That's the one! Jehovah-Jireh." Ahmose climbed back down. "Jehovah-Jireh. Yahweh. El Shaddai. He has many names, like the pharaoh. Did you know Ramses had more than twenty different names?"

"No, I didn't." They sat down near the gold that already been counted, and Bezalel grabbed a jug of water.

"Well, he did. I used to know them all, but I forgot. It's been a long time."

"Yes, it has been. And we are very far from the palace, aren't we?"

Ahmose sighed. "What now? We have all we need. What do we do next?"

"Now we wait for Moses to come down from the mountaintop. He has the instructions." He handed Ahmose the jug. "For now, let's go home."

੶੶ঔ

Meri was nearly asleep when Bezalel crawled in beside her. He kissed her cheek and she rolled on her back.

"Why are you so late tonight?"

"We were almost done. The moon was out so I wanted to finish up. Ahmose was so excited and having so much fun. Everything is counted and ready now, so there is nothing left to do until Moses comes down."

She reached up and stroked his cheek. "You'll be such a good father."

"Some day."

"Sooner than you think." She took his hand and put it on her belly.

He furrowed his brow for a moment. Then he realized what she was saying. "A baby?"

She giggled and nodded.

"A baby!" He leaned over and kissed her again.

"Will we still be here or in Canaan?"

Bezalel shrugged. "I don't know. I have no idea how long this will take. But maybe the baby will be born in the new land."

"New baby, new land."

"That would be great. But I really don't care where he's born."

"Ha! He? What makes you think it will be a he? Maybe it will be a she."

"If she is as beautiful as you, I'll take her."

15 Shebat

Bezalel rolled over in the dark hours of the night and pulled another blanket over himself and Meri. Winter was here and the nights were colder, but the cloud of fire above the camp kept them comfortable. He placed his hand on Meri's swelling belly and drifted back to sleep.

Morning dawned earlier than he wanted. Meri slept with her head on his chest, her hair falling around his shoulder. He'd moved her to his right side after the first battle, and his left arm was still weak. He could move it, but only with a fair amount of pain. Even seven months after the battle he still didn't have anywhere near the flexibility he used to have, and it worried him. Would it compromise the quality of his work? He was about to begin the most delicate pieces. Thank Yahweh it wasn't his right arm.

He waited until Meri woke up and ate with her, then went to the tabernacle, Ahmose tagging along behind. He checked on the work of his helpers then went to his own work area, away from the noise and bustle.

He'd kept for himself the job of creating the Ark of the Covenant, the only piece of furniture that would go in the Holy of Holies, the innermost room of the tent. The Ark was made of two pieces: a large rectangular box made of wood and covered inside and outside with gold, and the lid, or mercy seat, made of solid gold.

"What do we do first?" Ahmose looked up expectantly.

"I have to estimate how much gold we'll need, then we melt it." They picked through the best pieces of gold that Bezalel had saved for the ark, and dropped them into a large clay pot. "Now we build a very hot fire." He lit the fire under the pot. "You need to stand back so you don't get burned."

Ahmose obeyed.

Bezalel stirred the gold as it melted. When he was done he had an almost pure batch of gold, easily malleable. He poured it into a long, shallow clay form to let it cool.

"This is about the size the lid is supposed to be. When it's cooled, I have to hammer it out thinner, and pull out enough from the ends to make two angels, one at each end." Bezalel gestured with his hands to show Ahmose where the angels would be. "They will face downward to the top of the ark, bowing before the presence of Yahweh, and their wings will spread forward and touch at the tips."

Ahmose frowned. "That sounds like a lot of work."

Bezalel chuckled. "It will take many days, and much patience. I'll start with a big hammer then keep using smaller and smaller ones."

"Where did you get hammers?"

"I made them from some bronze, then I covered the smallest ones with lambskin so they won't leave marks. Would you like to help me make it?"

Ahmose drew in a long breath. "I don't know how."

"I'll show you. You can hold the hammers and make sure I use the right size, getting smaller as we go to the end. Sometimes I don't pay attention and I make the feathers too big."

"You want me to make sure you're doing it right?"

"Absolutely. You can watch over me."

Ahmose laughed. "That's funny. I didn't know you needed watching over."

Bezalel tousled the boy's hair. "Everyone needs to be watched over sometimes."

1 Adar

Bezalel tapped the hammer against the gold, his other hand behind the upright sheet of metal for support. "Chisel."

Ahmose held out a lambskin-covered chisel.

Bezalel took the tool and defined the edges of yet another feather.

"Bezalel, I think you should change hammers now." Ahmose offered a smaller mallet.

Bezalel stepped back and surveyed the wing. "You're right, habibi. You've got a good eye." He winked at Ahmose. "Is this the smallest one?"

"No. Two more." He looked toward the west. "Sun's almost down. Maybe we should stop for today."

"Whatever you say. You're in charge." Bezalel draped a large piece of linen over the angels.

Ahmose laughed and carefully packed the hammers and chisel away in a basket. "Meri sent some manna." He pointed to a plate with a cloth over it, and a skin bag next to it.

They sat on the lush grass facing the sunset.

Bezalel grabbed a manna cake. "The sky is pretty tonight."

"The baby is almost here, isn't he?"

"Almost. About another month. We should be finished with everything by then."

"And then we'll go to Canaan?" Ahmose stuffed the rest of a cake in his mouth.

Bezalel swallowed some milk and handed Ahmose the skin. "I don't know. We leave when the cloud leaves."

"I hope it's soon."

"Why? Don't you like it here? We're away from Egypt."

"I know. But…"

"What?"

"It would be nice to live in a house all together again, like a family. Like we did before we left. I liked that."

Bezalel wrapped his arm around Ahmose's shoulder and pulled him close. "It won't be long, habibi. Soon we'll be in Canaan. And it will be even better than before."

9 Adar

Bezalel ran his hands over the enormous wings of the angels. He had spent almost two weeks hammering out each individual feather on the wings. And they were beautiful. Lifelike. He remembered how just before the darkness, it had taken him hours to fashion a handful of bronze cornflower petals for a necklace, trying to get each one right. It took him six or seven times for each petal at first. He finally became quite good at making them. Now he knew why Yahweh had given him that task.

He inspected the robe of each cherub as it touched the lid, searching for imperfections. He bent down to see their faces, their eyes closed, lips slightly apart, praising Yahweh. It was finished.

"What do you think, Ahmose?"

"It's beautiful," he whispered. "Can I touch it?"

"Yes, go ahead. Soon we won't be able to."

"Why not?" Ahmose fingered the feathers.

"Once it's dedicated, no one can touch it. They'll carry it by poles slipped through the rings on the corners of the bottom part." Bezalel called an assistant to help him lift it from the wooden table he had used as a work place and moved toward the gold-covered box. As he attached the lid, the Ark of the Covenant—already holding a jar of manna, Aaron's staff, and the new stone tablets Moses had brought from the mountain—was closed for the last time.

All that remained was for Oholiab to finish the high priest's clothing. He said he needed about another month.

11 Adar

Bezalel took a hin of fresh olive oil—prepared in the fall by an army of women crushing the fruit and pressing oil from the resulting paste—and poured it into a perfectly round gold basin, just big enough for him to put his arms around, and exactly the right size to hold the oil and spices. *Of course it is, because Yahweh gave the dimensions.* Olive oil was known for carrying fragrances without either diluting them or making them bitter. The oil would keep the fragrance pure for a long time.

Yahweh had said to use a perfumer to make the anointing oil. Bezalel knew of only one.

Meri studied the recipe. She moved slowly now. The baby would come in less than a month.

He liked to watch her walk. He thought it was a little funny, but sweet. Of course, he didn't tell her it was funny. *If I were carrying a baby in my belly, I'd walk funny, too.*

She repeated the recipe. "Five hundred shekels of myrrh, five hundred shekels of cassia, two hundred fifty shekels of sweet cane, two hundred fifty shekels of cinnamon. We also need frankincense, gum resin, cloves, and galbanum for the incense." She looked up at the volunteers surrounding her. "All these plants are in the gardens. Come with me. I can show you." She started for the south side of the camp.

"You can't walk that far!" Bezalel reached after her.

She scoffed. "I can still walk. I'm not an invalid. It's less than a quarter-hour."

"And back."

She narrowed her eyes, and he backed off. The group followed her to the garden and Bezalel trailed behind. She pointed out the shrubs that yielded the myrrh and frankincense. "Take your knife and cut a deep slice into the bark to bleed out the gum resin. Catch it and let it harden." She left several behind to finish that task.

Meri next took them to the cinnamon tree. "You must cut down one of these branches at the ground. Remove the outer bark, beat the branch up and down to loosen the inner bark, then remove it in slices. Cassia is easier. You just remove the outer bark."

"Sweet cane grows in the water. We need the root." Meri showed them where to get the rest of the plants and how to harvest each of them, leaving behind a few to gather what was needed at each location.

After two hours, she looked exhausted, but Bezalel didn't want to say anything.

Meri grinned at him. "Go ahead; say it."

"You look tired."

"I am. Walk me back?"

He smiled and took her arm.

She leaned on him. "Gather everything and weigh it, and clean it. After lunch I'll show you what to do next. I'm going to lie down for a while."

❧

Bezalel swallowed the last of a manna cake at the noon meal. "All I have left is the anointing oil. Oholiab is finishing the high priest's garments. Then we set it all up."

"It's been nearly a year since we left Egypt. It will be good to finally get on our way. Though this has been a nice place to wait." Imma looked around the camp and then back at Meri. She reached over and rubbed her back. "How are you feeling, habibti?"

"Ready for this baby to come. Oh!" She put her hand on her belly. "I think she's ready to come, too. She's really kicking."

"Then let's finish the oil before he decides to get here." Bezalel stood and held out his hand.

Meri took it and he pulled her up.

"You are getting too heavy."

"Hush, or you can make this oil on your own."

"Then please forgive me." He laughed then kissed her.

She giggled.

They walked the few steps to the basin, which was surrounded by the other ingredients. Bezalel removed the linen that covered the basin. "What's next?"

Meri lowered herself onto a wooden stool. "We need to heat the oil. We're going to melt the myrrh and steep the fragrance out of the cinnamon, cane, and cassia. We want a slow fire so nothing burns or scalds or gets bitter. Now, for the others, the recipe said to mix it in equal parts and crush to a powder." She picked up the stacte, onycha, galbanum, and frankincense. "They're all hardened resins, see? So we just need to crush them." She absently rubbed her belly.

Bezalel retrieved the dark yellow myrrh crystals and stirred them into the oil. He scowled. "That smells bitter."

Meri laughed. "Add the rest. They'll sweeten it."

He double-checked the recipe. "Five hundred shekels of myrrh and cassia, and two hundred fifty shekels of sweet cane and cinnamon, mixed into a hin of olive oil." He had nearly doubled the volume of the oil by adding the spices.

She joined him at the fire. "Now let it simmer over a very low heat for a while. When it's finished, we scoop out the solids, and let it cool." She put her hand over his and stirred with him. "Smells better now, doesn't it?" She leaned back against him.

He put his arm around her. Suddenly he gasped. "He's really kicking!"

"I know. *She's* been doing that all day."

"How much longer?"

"About three weeks."

His lips curved into a smile. "I can hardly wait."

She laughed. "You don't have much choice. The baby comes when she wants to, and not before."

Twenty-two

12 Adar

Bezalel studied the tabernacle. The tent was eight or ten times longer than he was tall, and half that wide. Everything was finished—all the furnishings, the tent framework, its coverings, the priests' clothing, the anointing oil.

He walked among the furnishings arranged in front of the dwelling. He ran his fingers over the candlestick and smiled as the sun danced on it. Its base, shaft, and seven arms were fashioned from one piece of gold. Each arm ended in a flower-like cup, so that it held seven candles, enough to light the inner room of the tabernacle.

He turned at the sound of a gasp. Meri stood behind him with her hand to her mouth. "It's beautiful. I've never seen anything like it, not even at the palace." She reached out to touch the candlestick then drew her hand back as though she were afraid it might burn her.

"Thank you. And it's all right to touch it. Nothing's been anointed or dedicated yet." He took her hand in his and guided it toward the gold. "It took weeks. It was the last item to be crafted before the mercy seat."

"Are those almond flowers?" She pointed to the cups at the base of each stem that held the candles.

"I'm glad you can recognize them." He laughed, and gestured to the other pieces around him. "It's all complete. It's been six months of hard work, but it's the best work I've ever done. We're waiting for Moses to tell us when to set it up and put it all together."

Meri strolled among the other pieces of furniture. She ran her hand along the inside of a large basin.

Bezalel joined her. "That's a laver. It's made of bronze, for washing before entering the worship area." He laced his fingers with hers and led her from piece to piece. "And this is the altar. It was carved of acacia wood and then covered with bronze." The altar came to Bezalel's chest, and was wider than he was tall. He pointed to a small table. "This is made of wood and covered in gold, and will go inside along with the lampstand. I'm not sure yet what goes on top of it."

"Bread will sit on it. Twelve loaves." Moses's voice was still quite strong for a man of over eighty years.

"Bread? Why bread?" Meri turned to him and furrowed her brow.

"A symbol of Yahweh's willingness to dwell with us. The bread will be in His presence always. The priests will bake new loaves each Sabbath to replace the old ones. There will be twelve—one for each of the tribes." Moses inspected the pieces around him.

"Aaron has two weeks of training before he and his sons are consecrated. Yahweh said we are to set up the tabernacle on the first day of the first month of the second year – the first of Abib."

He walked around the altar. "These are exquisite, Bezalel. Exceptional. You are truly gifted." He looked at the candlestick. "I think this is my fav—" Moses froze in midsentence.

"What?"

"Hush!" Moses held up his hand.

Bezalel's mind went back to the moment a year ago when Sabba hushed him on the shore of the Yam Suph. His heart panged for more than one reason.

Moses tilted his head. His eyes glistened. "Did you hear that?"

"What?"

He raised one finger. "There! Again."

"I'm sorry. I heard noth—" A crack ripped through the air. Then another, louder. A long rumble shuddered the earth beneath their feet.

"What is that?" Meri grabbed Bezalel's arm.

"That, my child, is the sound of ice cracking. And worse, falling. This time of year there is almost always snow on the mountains, and I've seen the effects of melting snow and ice as we head into spring. And I know that those sounds mean a flood will be loosed. Soon." He looked up at Mount Sinai, and then to the left of the big mount. He tilted his head and listened some more. "It's coming from Sinai. It will flood the east end of the valley, probably to near the center before the water slips through the rocks. We have a little time, but not long."

The old man surveyed the tabernacle and its furnishings. "Warn the Levites. They are to gather the pieces of the tabernacle—they already know who is responsible for what part. And tell the elders to move everyone else either west or to the low mountains. They needn't get too high. The water doesn't rise far but it will be fast, and strong." He glanced at Meri, at her belly, and then back to Bezalel. He pointed toward Sinai. "Get her safe. Tell the elders. I'll go north and send someone south."

The old man rushed off and Bezalel marveled at how fast he could move.

Bezalel grabbed Meri's hand and headed toward his tent, acutely aware of her pregnant body beside him. He was torn between wanting to run to get there faster, and going slower to keep her safe. Would it hurt her if she ran? He had no idea.

He reached his tent and found Nahshon and Amminadab. They started spreading the word and Israelites ran north and south for the low mountains. Bezalel sent Meri south with Kamose for the time being and sprinted back to the center of camp.

Bezalel and the Levites headed in the opposite direction of everyone else. They gathered pieces of the tabernacle that could be carried—mostly the cloth coverings—and ran west. The huge acacia wood poles finished with silver and bronze—sixty of them—were pushed into piles and left together, lying east to west. The gold-plated acacia boards and pillars for the Holy Place were gathered as well. He hoped they could withstand the force of the water. Even if they were pushed along, they were too big to be thrown out of the valley. The altar and laver were set behind the poles. The rest of the pieces were taken by the Levites west or to higher ground.

Bezalel sprinted south to Meri. The sound of falling water grew louder and he shot a glance over his shoulder. Waterfalls popped up one after another, dotting Sinai and the mountains on either side. Pulse pounding, he doubled his speed and checked over the other shoulder. All the Levites were close to the foot of the lower mountains. The tabernacle was safe.

Ahead of him, Kamose helped women and children onto the rocks. Men and youths clambered up around the captain. Where was Meri?

To Bezalel's left the rushing water closed in on him. The roar made it difficult to think. He caught up with Meri at the base of the rocks just before the water reached them. Why wasn't she up higher yet? He found an open space, climbed up ahead of her, and turned to grab her hand.

She was frozen. Terror covered her face. Her eyes were fixed on the rock in front of her, but apparently she couldn't make herself move. Water swirled around her feet.

"Meri! Now!" He reached for her, took her hand, and pulled. The sound of roaring water grew louder. His heart pounded in his ears.

Her eyes met his. Some of the fear melted away and trust replaced it. She put one sandaled foot on a rock and searched for another foothold. Two more steps. She looked to him again for assurance.

He dragged her forward. Almost safe. Just a few more steps. He smiled to calm her.

She placed her left foot and stood. She lifted her right foot again, but a stocky young man rushed by her, shoving her out of the way. She toppled, fell to her left, and bounced down over slippery, wet rocks to the ground.

Terror seized him and for a moment he was unable to move or even think. "Meri!" Bezalel rushed to her as water covered her body. He slid down rocks, banging elbows and knees. He groaned as he tried to pick her up, but between the force of the flow and her lop-sided weight, he couldn't lift her. He cried out as he tried again.

Her belly kept her face under water. She flailed against the lack of air, making it harder for Bezalel to get a grip. She grabbed onto a rock and managed to pull her head out and drew in a gasping, screeching breath. Her face was pale and her eyes were wild.

Kamose stepped in and lifted her and carried her up away from the flood.

Bezalel followed. When Kamose set her safely on higher ground, Bezalel looked for the one who had knocked her down. He was waiting there, wanting to be found. Bezalel recognized his tunic and his build.

Michael smirked. "One less Egyptian. Or should I say, two."

Bezalel clenched his hands into fists as the blood raced to his head. He looked at Michael and then to Meri.

He chose Meri.

She was soaking wet, but safe. She sat up then clutched at her stomach and screamed.

"The baby?" The air left Bezalel's lungs in a rush and he knelt by her.

Meri breathed loudly and rapidly.

Bezalel stood and searched for Imma. He found her and called for her. She pushed her way toward him. Bezalel sat down behind Meri before his mother reached him. He supported her back and wrapped his arms around her.

Meri cried out again.

"What happened?" Imma's eyes grew wide at the sight of her daughter-in-law sitting on the ground looking like a wet cat—and sounding like one.

Bezalel looked to his mother, silently pleading. Meri leaned her head back against him, panting. He had absolutely no idea how to help her. Was the baby still alive or had the fall onto the rocks killed him? Would Meri be all right?

Kamose answered. "Someone pushed her and she fell, and I think the baby is coming now." He gestured toward the valley floor. "The water is already receding. It should be gone very soon."

Bezalel looked down. The flood was indeed nearing its end. The whole thing had lasted less than half an hour. The water was flowing back out of the valley and down into the desert far below them as fast as it had fallen from the mountaintops. People already climbed down.

Meri leaned forward and screamed. Imma knelt beside her and took her hand, whispering instructions in her ear. A couple other women hovered as well. When the pain subsided, Imma brushed back Meri's hair.

Bezalel searched his mother's face. "It's too early, Imma."

"Only three weeks, habibi. Babies often survive coming that early. And three weeks is only a guess to begin with. A good guess—the Egyptians were very skilled at that—but still, it is up to Yahweh. I'll go get things ready."

Bezalel closed his eyes and buried his face in Meri's hair. He fought the tears building up behind his eyelids and tried to remember what he had learned on the mountainside months ago.

Kamose knelt and tapped him on the shoulder. Bezalel couldn't look at him, didn't want Kamose to see him cry. He looked the other way as the big soldier picked Meri up and carried her down the rocks.

Imma had rushed ahead. She found a tent someone was willing to let them use in the dry, western half of camp, then came back to lead them.

As Bezalel followed behind Kamose, his wife cried out once more.

৵৵

Bezalel poked a stick into the fire. It had been hours, and he wasn't allowed anywhere near Meri. He knew she was on the dry side of camp in a tent, with Imma and other experienced women to help her, but he longed to comfort her. Her cries rang in his head.

The sun had dried up much of the water, and though it wasn't quite dry enough to set them up yet, most of the Israelites had were sorting through the tents slammed against the rocks or scattered on the floor of the valley.

He jabbed at the flames. Was Meri all right? Was the baby alive? Why wouldn't someone tell him something?

Michael. Why did it come back to Michael again? How could one person bring so much pain into his life? Was he going to take away someone else now? Would Yahweh let him do that?

Bezalel stood. Nahshon had found his tent and brought it back for him. It lay collapsed on the ground near him. He found the opening and reached inside, fumbling around for a moment until he found what he searched for. He grabbed it and marched off.

৵৵

Kamose watched Bezalel as he left the campfire with a dagger in his hand. What did he plan to do? Surely Michael deserved to be punished for his actions, deserved to die, even. But would Bezalel simply march off and murder him in the camp?

Kamose followed him at a distance. Bezalel was preoccupied enough not to notice. When he left the tent areas, Kamose breathed a sigh of relief. But where could Bezalel be going?

He kept following, although in the open it was harder to stay hidden. Bezalel headed southwest for the gardens and disappeared into the trees.

Kamose entered and sloshed through the trees until he found Bezalel in the still dry western garden. He stood near a tree with dark, twisted bark and pink flowers, head on his arm against the bark.

"What are you doing?"

Bezalel started and turned. "What do you mean?"

"I followed you. You left with a dagger. I thought you might have meant harm to … someone."

"Oh … you mean Michael. I thought about it; I admit it. But that really wouldn't accomplish anything. Meri and the baby will live or die, whether I kill Michael or not." He took a deep breath. "The last time I got angry, I nearly broke both my hands, I couldn't lift my arm for weeks, I terrified my wife, and I spent the night on a mountainside. And after all that, Sabba was still dead."

He fingered the blade of his dagger. "Sabba trusted in Yahweh his whole life. When Savta was taken, when Abba died, when I was taken to the palace—he never wavered. He was not always happy, but he…" Bezalel paused, as if he were searching for the right words. "He had trust, or hope, or peace. I'm not sure what it was, exactly, but … I can't fight my life anymore. I have to trust Yahweh. All I can do is pray." He stared toward the mountain. "I don't want to lose Meri or my baby, but I've learned being in the shadow is warm and safe, not cold and dark."

Kamose frowned. "What?"

Bezalel shook his head. "Nothing. Something Meri taught me."

"Then why are you carrying your dagger?"

Bezalel glanced at a small tree next to him and shrugged. "I just came to see if there were any pomegranates left. Meri loves them. And I needed something to do." He reached over and sliced off some of the deep red fruit. "Going back?"

"Later. I'm going to wait here a bit." Kamose watched Bezalel walk off. He had known who Bezalel was, of course, since he first came to the palace. It was his job to know everyone in the palace. But he had never talked to him until he started searching for Ahmose. In the past eleven months, since they had left Egypt, they had become quite close.

Bezalel seemed different since his night on the mountainside. He'd lost his anger. But his life since then had been rather idyllic, except for the loss of Sabba. A beautiful young wife who adored him, living on this lush, highland plain, freedom from slavery, even the chance to create again. And a baby coming. What was there to be angry about?

But this was different. He had expected a violent outburst. He himself would have gladly killed Michael for Bezalel. Meri had come to mean almost as much to him as Bezalel did.

Kamose paced. How could he explain this?

He had decided even before he left Egypt that Ramses was not a god. And obviously there was something to Yahweh's power—he had seen too much to doubt it. But was there more to Yahweh than raw power?

He thought back to the night Ahmose prayed for Bezalel. Kamose had never understood prayer. It never did any good in Egypt. The gods did what they wanted to, if they were even gods at all. And if Yahweh were really God, and knew everything, and was in control, why did He need someone like Kamose to tell Him what to do?

But Yahweh certainly meant something more than power to Ahmose. He always had to Sabba. And now to Bezalel. Was it worth a try?

Kamose knew only one way to address a superior. So he stood straight and tall and faced Mount Sinai.

"Yahweh, I am a soldier. I understand only orders. And I know that often commanders know things soldiers do not. So if this cannot be done, I understand.

"I have one request: please save Meri and the baby. They have become my family—Bezalel, Meri, Ahmose, and Imma. The only family I have, now that I have left Egypt. We have lost Hur; please don't take anyone else away."

৵৽৶

As Bezalel neared his tent, he noticed Imma returning from the birthing tent. He dropped the pomegranates and sprinted to her.

She grabbed his shoulders. "Habibi, all is well! You have a daughter!"

He threw his arms around her and cried with relief.

"When can I see Meri?"

"You can see her now, but she is exhausted. Come."

He tiptoed into the tent. Meri lay on a pile of blankets, her face pale and wet, her hair falling all around. In her arms was a tiny ... person. His breath caught in his throat. He'd seen babies before, but he had never been so close to one. Her perfect miniature hands, nose, mouth—they were extraordinary. He reached for Meri's face. "Are you well?"

She laughed softly. "I'm fine. Very tired, but well." She lifted the baby to him. "This is your daughter."

He hesitated.

"She won't break."

"Are you sure?" He chuckled. He put out his arms, pulled them back, and then reached again and took the baby.

"Put your arm under her head." Meri adjusted his forearm.

"I've felt more comfortable holding bags of gems and gold dust."

Meri laughed. "What shall we name her?"

Bezalel drew his finger along the baby's face. "She is so beautiful. More beautiful than anything I have ever made, or even seen."

She stared at him.

He looked up at Meri. "What about Adi?"

"Adi?" She repeated the word thoughtfully. "What does that mean?"

He smiled. "Jewel. My precious, faultless jewel."

She reached up and touched his cheek. "It's perfect."

1 Abib

Bezalel rose before dawn and made his way to the tabernacle site. He watched as the Levites placed silver sockets on the ground. Gold-covered wood boards and crossbars were added to form walls.

Meri joined him, carrying baby Adi. "What are they doing?"

"Setting up the tabernacle."

"Why aren't you helping?"

"I'm no longer allowed to touch it."

"Why not?"

"It has been dedicated to Yahweh. Only the Levites can touch it now."

She rubbed his back. "I'm sorry."

He shrugged. "It's all right. My part is over. Now they take care of it. Forever. And they have to carry it." He chuckled and reached for his daughter. "But I get to carry her." He settled Adi on his chest and laid his cheek on her head. "Look, they're putting Oholiab's covering on." He pointed to the center.

Levites pulled a deep purple linen cloth covered with embroidered cherubim over the golden framework. They followed with a goatskin, a ram skin, and finally another leather skin.

One by one, Bezalel's finest creations were carried inside—the ark, the table, the lampstand, the incense altar.

"Why are the others being left outside?" Meri pointed to the laver and the huge bronze altar.

"They stay in the courtyard. Next they'll build a wall around all of this with all of those pillars and cloths stacked over there."

They watched in silence as the Levites continued moving the furnishings.

"What happens now?"

"Tonight Moses will consecrate Aaron and his sons as priests. Each tribe will bring an offering for the tabernacle, one a day for twelve days. Then, sometime soon after that, we leave."

"For the new land?"

"For the new land."

Meri laid her head on his arm. "I can hardly wait."

❧ ☙

Later that day Bezalel met Oholiab and Moses, and Aaron and his sons walked up moments after. Moses led them inside the gate.

Aaron stood before his brother, the brother he had come to know only in the last two years, wearing nothing but his linen, knee-length trousers. Moses plunged a cloth into the laver and gently ran the cool water over Aaron's outstretched arms.

Moses continued to wash his brother and nephews as Bezalel and Oholiab readied the holy garments.

"Which is first?" Bezalel whispered, trying not to interrupt Moses.

"These first." Oholiab handed him a long, linen tunic, and then a sleeveless, knee-length robe of blue, a blue as deep as the sky. Bezalel gave Moses the tunic and then held up the robe to find the neck. Attached to the robe's hem was a row of golden bells and woolen pomegranates. The bells rang softly. He furrowed his brow. "What are these for?"

Oholiab gestured for them to step aside. "They are so the people can hear that he is still alive."

"What?" A lump formed in his throat.

"Once a year, Aaron will approach Yahweh to ask for forgiveness. He will wear the bells to let Israel know that Yahweh has had mercy upon us and has forgiven us and not killed the priest." Oholiab picked up another garment. "The breastplate and your ephod are next."

Bezalel held the thick breastplate that Oholiab had woven of blue, purple, scarlet, and gold threads. He gasped. "Oholiab, never even in the palace did I see any cloth so exquisite as this." He held it while Oholiab attached the ephod Bezalel had made. It had twelve stones on it placed in four rows of three, each different, each representing a tribe of Israel. Bezalel had engraved the names of the tribes on those twelve stones, so Aaron would represent the whole of Israel before Yahweh each time he wore it.

Finally, Moses wrapped a long piece of linen about Aaron's head. Then, with a blue cord he put a gold plate on the turban saying, "Holy to the Lord."

Bezalel held a container of the holy anointing oil for Moses. Moses opened the container and filled a horn with it, then dipped his fingers in the sweetly-scented liquid. He sprinkled some on the tabernacle and everything in it, then sprinkled the altar and everything on it seven times. Then he filled the horn a second time.

Moses stood before Aaron, who sank to his knees and knelt before his brother. Moses poured a single, thin stream of oil from the horn onto Aaron's head. The oil drizzled down his hair, onto his face and beard. Tears escaped Aaron's eyes, and oil and water fought as they made their way down his cheeks.

As he watched, Bezalel understood. He understood it all. The deep and abiding love Yahweh had for His people. A love so great He would lead them out of slavery into freedom. A love so pure He expected holiness and obedience. A love so deep, He offered total forgiveness when they couldn't be holy or obey.

But how could such a powerful and sovereign God love a people so frail and disobedient? Bezalel knew that God loved Israel, but he would never understand why.

20 Ziv

Bezalel sat at the base of the mountain, the same mountain where nine months earlier he had screamed and fought in the dark of the night looking for answers. This time he held his daughter in his arms. Tomorrow they would leave for Canaan, and after a few weeks of travel, arrive in their new home. What would it be like? What would he do? He couldn't make a living being an artist, at least not at first.

But he had created a masterpiece. If he never made anything of gold or silver again, he could be satisfied.

He had Meri. And Adi.

He thought of everything that had happened over the last two years.

Nahshon had married and was now leader of the tribe of Judah. He'd presented Judah's offering at the dedication of the tabernacle two weeks ago, the first of the twelve tribes to do so.

Young as he was, Joshua was recognized as the military leader of the Israelites.

Aaron was settling in to his duties as high priest.

Kamose had finally found his place among the Israelites. He mentored Joshua, but most of all, he was uncle to Ahmose. He was discovering Yahweh and what the Living God could mean in his life.

And little Ahmose. Well, Ahmose was Ahmose. He had lost so much in his short life, but as always, he chose to focus on what he still had. Imma spoiled him, Uncle Kamose doted on him, and Bezalel and Meri both adored him. Ahmose delighted in the new baby, and it was often difficult to get him to leave her alone long enough to let her sleep.

The sun peered over the top of Mount Sinai, but it would be over an hour before the spot on which Bezalel sat was flooded with light.

For now, he was in the shadows. As he pulled his thawb around his shoulders and wrapped a blanket more tightly around Adi, he smiled.

In the shadow.

It was a good place to be.

Acknowledgments

My unending thanks to:

My mother—who never stopped believing in me.

My faithful husband John, and my delightful gifts from God: Emma, Mira, Dara and Johnny—for letting me write for hours on end, for going to movies without me, for sometimes making your own dinner, and for your unconditional love. Success, like life itself, wouldn't mean nearly as much without you.

Sandi Rog—without you this book would never have made it to its present and publishable form, even though you made me rip apart my manuscript and start over. (All right, it wasn't quite that bad.) You're the reason Meri's in the story, who was meant to be only in the first chapter, but refused to go away.

My critique partners from HisFictCrit, Scribes Who Scribble, and She Writes—for your time and knowledge. Because of many of you, Kamose didn't die in Egypt.

My beta readers— Lynn Rose, Carrol Mercurio, and Dr. Sue Pankratz.

Gayle Roper—for teaching me to keep tension all the way through.

Randy Ingermanson—for teaching me to rescue defeat from the jaws of victory.

Kelli Standish—for a gorgeous website. Dazzle where you are planted.

Matt, Tracy and Emily at Jones House Creative—for helping me reach my readers.

Ellen Tarver and Wendy Charot—for polishing my manuscript until it shined.

Dan DeGarmo—for taking a chance on an unknown author.

Nathan Ward—for a fabulous layout.

Reuben Rog—for a cover that was beyond my imagination.

And you, dear reader—for spending some of your precious time with my story. Learn even more about these characters and their world, as well as the stories to come, at **www.caroletowriss.com.**

For a full listing of DeWard Publishing Company books, visit our website:

www.deward.com

CPSIA information can be obtained at www.ICGtesting.com
Printed in the USA
BVOW071835181012

303322BV00002B/2/P